IF I SHOULD
DIE

OTHER BOOKS AND AUDIO BOOKS
BY JENNIE HANSEN:

Abandoned

All I Hold Dear

Beyond Summer Dreams

The Bracelet

The Emerald

The Topaz

The Ruby

Breaking Point

Chance Encounter

Code Red

Coming Home

High Stakes

Macady

Some Sweet Day

Wild Card

High Country

Shudder

IF I SHOULD
DIE

A NOVEL BY

JENNIE HANSEN

Covenant Communications, Inc.

Cover image: *Young Woman Looking Through Window Blinds* © Casarsa, courtesy of iStockphoto.com.

Cover design copyright © 2011 by Covenant Communications, Inc.

Published by Covenant Communications, Inc.
American Fork, Utah

Printed in Canada
First Printing: June 2011

17 16 15 14 13 12 11   10 9 8 7 6 5 4 3 2 1

ISBN-13: 978-1-60861-199-7

In memory of my sister, Vada Little, and her husband, Chuck, who was always there for her.

ACKNOWLEDGMENTS

IN ADDITION TO THE LIST of characters in a book, there's another list of supporters who made this book possible. I want to thank my husband, Boyd, for his constant support and willingness to do whatever needs to be done so I can write; my rough manuscript readers Lezlie Anderson, Mary Jo Rich, and Janice Sperry for their insight and time; and, of course, my editor, Kirk Shaw, for his invaluable input. I also owe a great deal to other writers who have become my friends and have cheered me on.

CHAPTER ONE

"I made a mistake."

"A mistake? What do you mean?" Kallene brushed a stray lock of hair that had escaped her ponytail behind her ear and continued running.

"I shouldn't have married Carson."

Kallene glanced sideways at her running partner, who matched her long-legged stride step for step. They were almost identical in size and body shape, though Linda's long, fiery red hair contrasted vividly with Kallene's shorter light-brown hair.

"I know you and Carson have been having problems, but I thought you were working them out."

"I don't think we'll ever work them out." Linda sounded defeated. "I thought I was doing the right thing when I agreed to marry him, but this latest stunt just proves he doesn't care about me or what I want. He only married me because of my resemblance to my sister."

Linda's twin sister, Louise, had died in a car accident almost three years ago. Her fiancé, Carson, and Linda had turned to each other for comfort, and they'd married a few months later. Their daughter, Macie, had arrived six months before Carson and Linda had purchased their home on the same street where Kallene had bought her own home a year ago in a new upscale neighborhood at the south end of the Salt Lake valley.

"That can't be true." Kallene shook her head. Linda had to be exaggerating the seriousness of the disagreement with her husband. "You're understandably upset over his job change, but once he settles into the new job . . ."

"There was nothing wrong with his old job. He earned a good salary, and he was in line for a promotion."

"But if he was unhappy with the work he was doing and was given a chance to change to a job he likes better, won't it improve your marriage?" Kallene's breath came in little gasps. They were coming up on their third mile, and the path up the canyon was growing steeper. Almost every morning, she and Linda ran the loop that went up one side of a canyon, crossed a footbridge, then returned to their neighborhood on the opposite side.

Kallene felt a little uneasy discussing Linda's marital problems. She couldn't help feeling that Linda and Carson should sit down and have a frank discussion with each other and that Linda shouldn't share her and Carson's problems so freely outside their marriage, even though Linda and Kallene were good friends.

"It's not that," Linda protested. "Of course I want him to enjoy his work, but he didn't even discuss it with me, and we can't afford the sharp drop in income. We're still paying medical bills from when Macie was born. Then there's Carson's college loans, which weren't worth it since he didn't finish school, and we can't afford the payments on the house with an income barely more than half what he was making from the job he quit. Why didn't I listen to Jon and my parents? They warned me I was making a big mistake."

"Is it really that bad?" Hearing a quick sob, Kallene turned to see tears streaming down Linda's face. Kallene was only a few years older than Linda, but sometimes she felt like she was the other woman's big sister. Moving closer, she put her arm around Linda's shoulder and led her to a low wall that bordered the path beside a steep drop-off. Early-morning light streamed through a thick copse of trees, and there were no other runners in sight along the dirt trail. "All right, maybe you need to get it all out."

"He's just so stubborn!" Linda gulped before making an unsuccessful attempt to laugh. "You sound like my brother. Jon said I should slow down and take the time to carefully go over our expenses with Carson, and I promised I would try. I had everything organized when I approached him last night. I showed him our bills and the budget I set up. It spelled out in black and white that our expenses are greater than the income he'll be bringing in. I even offered to go back to work. Macie is eighteen months old now, but Carson won't even discuss it. He says my place is at home with our daughter and that there's nothing to discuss."

Kallene hugged her friend. "I can see how frustrating that must be. Do you think he'd listen to a finance counselor?"

"Ha! I've suggested financial counseling, marital counseling, and even talking to Bishop Andrews, but Carson refuses to consider any kind of counseling. He says I just need to have more confidence in his ability to support our family and learn to manage our income better. I pointed out that I'm a qualified CPA; I know how to budget. He said my degree hadn't taught me anything about *real* money."

"Maybe you should get some counseling yourself if he won't go with you."

"I might do that, but nothing is going to change Carson." She brushed a red curl from her damp forehead. "I knew that before we got married, but I married him anyway. Stupid me! We weren't even friends before Louise died. Even when he and Louise were engaged, he made snide remarks about my career, clothes, and car. I think he resented the fact that I earned more than he ever would."

"I've heard some men are uncomfortable with women earning more than they do." The topic touched a sore point for Kallene, too. Before she'd married Carson, she'd been told by well-meaning friends on several occasions that her advanced degree and comfortable income were the reason she was approaching thirty and still single. Even her mother's frequent phone calls hinted that buying a house and driving an expensive car might make the men she met feel they couldn't measure up.

"Carson said I put too much emphasis on money and worldly things. We had a terrible fight last night when I tried to explain to him the basic facts of our finances. He said that from now on he'd handle our money and give me a *household allowance.* I mean, really! Who does that?"

"Is that how you got that bruise on your arm?" Kallene hadn't asked about the bruise when she first saw it, assuming Linda would bring it up. Linda was talkative and seldom hesitated to talk about any- and everything concerning her health, marriage, or adorable daughter, so Kallene had expected to hear all about the large bruise as they ran.

"Sort of." She appeared unusually reluctant to discuss the dark spot that stood out just below the short sleeve of her T-shirt. Linda was a striking redhead with a redhead's typical pale skin that showed every bump and bruise. After a long pause, she said, "I was really angry, and when he tried to brush past me to leave the room so he wouldn't have to talk about our problems, I reached for his arm, trying to get him to stay and talk to me. He shrugged me off, and I fell against the coffee table."

"And . . . ?"

"He didn't help me up or anything." Linda was crying again. "He went straight to the baby's room. He picked her up even though she was asleep and walked out of the house with her. I heard his car start, and I ran to the garage, but they were already gone by the time I got there. I was so scared he'd run away and I'd never see Macie again. He sold my car right after we got married, so I couldn't follow him." Linda had complained to Kallene before about Carson's insistence that they only needed one car and that the down payment on their house had been paid with the money he got from selling her car.

"He brought her back, didn't he?" She felt something of Linda's panic as she thought of her friend's daughter.

Linda nodded her head and searched for a tissue to wipe away her tears. Kallene handed her one from her own pocket.

"It'll work out," Kallene soothed.

"It was after midnight when he finally brought her back! I was so angry and scared that I didn't know what to do, so I just pretended to be asleep. There was no way I could control my temper if he said one word to me. And speaking of being angry, we'd better start back. If I'm not there with Macie before it's time for him to leave for work, he'll kill me." She stood, and Kallene followed.

They didn't talk much on their return trip, though Kallene couldn't get her friend's words out of her mind. She'd purchased her two-story home a little more than a year ago, and Linda and Carson Longdale had moved into a rambler farther down the street around the same time. They both missed their families and laughed when they discovered Linda's parents lived in Baltimore near Andrews Air Force Base, where Kallene's Air Force father had been transferred. Kallene found Carson a little odd, but she and Linda had hit it off immediately, and when they discovered a shared passion for running, their friendship was sealed.

"Helloooo, ladies." They didn't slow as the drawled greeting came from a truck they passed as they entered the subdivision. "I see I won't have to exercise today. Just seeing you two in running shorts has my heart beating double-time."

"Creep!" Kallene muttered under her breath. "I don't care how great he is as a handyman—I'd never hire him."

"Ditto," Linda agreed. "Darnell Gines might flatter some women with all those muscles and exaggerated compliments, but he makes my skin crawl."

A block past the handyman's truck, they slowed to a walk and turned onto their street. Rupert Meyer was on his porch reaching for his newspaper. Both women waved but received no response. Mr. Meyer never acknowledged their greetings, and they'd long since given up expecting any sort of friendly overture from him.

Brittany Adams waved from where she leaned against a rake, and Kallene and Linda waved back. They'd met Jeff and Brittany Adams a few weeks ago at church, right after the young couple moved into the gray house two doors from Kallene's house.

"We should invite her to run with us after her baby comes," Kallene mused. She'd talked several times with the bubbly young woman who was expecting her first child and found her to be funny and intelligent.

"I won't be here. I've made up my mind. I'm going to tell Carson I want a divorce."

Kallene stopped, and Linda paused beside her. Kallene was barely aware they were in front of her house. "Shouldn't Carson be the one to leave?"

"He doesn't earn enough to make the payments now, and until I find a job, I won't be able to either. I have to find a cheaper place. Marrying Carson was a big mistake," Linda continued. "Staying with him would be a bigger one. I have no intention of living the rest of my life as my shy, insecure sister. I was stupid to let Carson convince me it was my fault she died and that somehow I owed him the rest of my life. I shouldn't have let guilt override good sense."

"I didn't know you felt guilty about Louise's death. That doesn't make sense. You said she was alone when she died in a car accident."

"She was alone because I'd moved out of our parents' house, and our brother and his wife had moved to California. She called me and said there was something she needed to tell me. She sounded like she'd been crying, but I told her I couldn't get away just then and suggested she come to my apartment, even though she didn't like driving in city traffic. Because of her driving phobia, I knew she was afraid to drive the two miles, but I thought conquering her fear would be good for her." Linda held herself rigidly, as though she were in pain. "I'll never know why she wanted to see me badly enough to agree to drive to my place."

Kallene reached out to hug her. "Getting hit by a car that ran a red light could happen to anyone, anytime, and it wasn't your fault."

"I think I finally believe that, but the only way to straighten out the mess I've made of my life is to put as much distance as possible between Carson and me." She tilted her chin at a stubborn angle.

"He's not going to let you just walk away with Macie." Kallene couldn't imagine Carson calmly accepting Linda's decision, and he certainly wouldn't give up his daughter without a fight.

"I have a plan. I'll tell you about it in the morning." She began a determined stride toward her house at the far end of the block, leaving Kallene standing at the gate leading to her own house.

Kallene had just stooped to pick up her newspaper when she heard the squeal of brakes. Glancing up, she saw Linda sprawled on the lawn of a house halfway down the block and a car in the driveway with the driver's door flung open beside her.

CHAPTER TWO

DROPPING THE PAPER, KALLENE BEGAN to run. Before she reached her friend, Linda sat up. With both hands she dusted off her bright pink shorts. She exchanged a few words with a man attired in a crisp business suit, who climbed out of his car to stand beside her for a minute. He appeared impatient and lost no time returning to his car. He backed the rest of the way down his driveway, and his tires squealed as he sped down the street.

"I'm all right," Linda said when she saw Kallene's worried face. "Ted just brushed me. I forgot to watch out for him. You know how that idiot backs out of his garage without looking and tears down the street every morning as if he's driving the Indy 500 instead of merely being on his way to work. He's going to kill someone one of these days."

"Look out!" Kallene tugged her friend farther back on the grass. "Or Julie Grayson will finish the job her husband started." They watched as a gray sedan shot down the sloped driveway. The perfectly coiffed blonde driver never glanced their way. A small face pressed against the back window, and a child waved. Kallene lifted her hand. The driver gunned the engine, and the car shot down the street.

"You waved to her?" Linda raised an amused eyebrow. "I didn't think the great Julie Grayson condescended to acknowledge anyone on our street."

"Not Julie." Kallene laughed. "Parker—her son. He's only eight and has started attending Cub Scouts. He waved, so I waved back."

"Julie Grayson actually lets her son attend Cub Scouts?" Linda looked skeptical. "She probably considers it two hours she doesn't have to be bothered with him." Julie was a runner, too, but she ran competitively all over the world and had competed in the Olympic Summer Games twice. But she'd offended Linda and Kallene when she'd scoffed at their invitation to join them for their daily morning runs. Tall and lean, like both of them, she modeled fashionable running clothes for television ads and trained at a private training facility.

Linda glanced at her watch. "Uh-oh. I'm in trouble." She began to run. "I'll see you in the morning."

Kallene walked back toward her house. After showering, she prepared a light breakfast and left half of it sitting on the serving bar. Earlier she'd been anxious to finish her run and resume work on the portfolio she was preparing for a favorite client. She loved her work and had been thrilled when her college apprenticeship with a respected advertising firm had resulted in a job following graduation. She'd been with Benson & McCallister for four years and still looked forward to each day and the challenge of designing new campaigns. She enjoyed the flexible hours, too.

Most days she showed up at the company's downtown office for a few hours then did most of her design work at home. One of the advantages of the company's flex-time, work-from-home policy was keeping her contact with Ben McCallister to a minimum. His father was one of the partners who owned the company, and Ben was one of the project directors. She wasn't impressed by his artistic ability or his honesty—or more appropriately, the lack thereof—though he did exceptionally well at signing new clients. Unfortunately she'd been assigned to Ben's team, but she wouldn't have to see him for the rest of this week. With the new campaign and a tight deadline, he'd given her permission to work entirely from home on the project.

Her feet dragged as she made her way to the room she'd turned into a studio office, and she found herself staring out the window instead of turning on her computer. Her mind kept going over her earlier conversation with Linda. She knew her friend tended to dramatize, but she sensed Linda was serious about ending her marriage. She couldn't help thinking Linda was right— she shouldn't have married Carson— but on the other hand, since they were married and had a child, they should do as much as possible to make their marriage work. Right?

Growing up on military bases, Kallene had seen too many marriages end in divorce with children torn between parents because of divorce or long deployments of one parent. She could sympathize with Linda. In fact, she'd often wondered how vivacious, outgoing Linda had fallen in love with a man as rigid and controlling as Carson. But divorce? There had to be some way to persuade them to get counseling and give their marriage a chance.

As she stared out the window, she saw Darnell Gines's truck pull into the Graysons' driveway. She reached for the cord to close the blinds. Her mind flashed back to Linda's close calls with the Grayson vehicles that morning. The Graysons were snobs, but at least they seemed evenly matched, much more so than Linda and Carson. Perhaps she should be grateful she was single. She sighed and pushed the button that lit up her computer screen.

Shouting broke her concentration. She glanced at her watch and groaned. She may have had a difficult time getting started, but once she'd managed to shut out other distractions, she'd lost track of time, even missing lunch.

She frowned as she heard Mr. Haney shouting. He lived next door, between her and the Adams. Kids on their way home from school each day taunted him by stepping on his grass or pulling the petals off his flowers, and he responded by screaming threats at them.

Delbert and Martha Haney were older than most of their neighbors, and Delbert had no patience with the children. His poor wife seldom stepped outside her door and seemed to be more cowed by her husband's ranting than the children were.

It was a good thing his shouting had pulled her out of her work. There wasn't much time to get ready. She scribbled a couple notes to herself before saving her work and closing her file. She'd forgotten she'd changed den meeting from Friday to Monday this one time. She hurried to get ready.

Once all the Cub Scouts had arrived, she opened the sliding-glass doors leading to her deck and ushered eight Wolfs in blue Cub Scout shirts outside, where they would begin their painting activity.

For once they were all on time, even Parker Grayson with his ever-present khaki backpack over his shoulders. Though Parker lived on the same street she did, he seldom arrived on time. Both of his parents worked, and the boy spent after-school hours alone. There was something about the boy that always seemed out of step with the other boys, and

Kallene frequently found herself feeling sorry for the child.

They'd all remembered to bring the balsa wood airplanes they were working on. However, only a few of the boys had remembered to bring paint shirts, but after six months of preparing such activities, she had accumulated a pile of surplus paint shirts. While the boys were engrossed in their projects, she took one boy at a time aside to check which requirements he was ready to pass off.

"I'm done!" She looked up to see Parker holding up a lopsided airplane with paint dripping from its wings to the papers she'd spread on her picnic table and across the deck floor. The airplane was hastily made: the wing pieces were upside down, and there was a chip out of the nose of the craft. It wasn't the smooth masterpiece she might have expected had the boy's perfectionist father helped him with its construction. Being a sales representative for a major tool corporation evidently didn't mean Ted had any interest in actually using those tools to help his son build a model airplane. She supposed she shouldn't be surprised. Ted Grayson hadn't shown the slightest interest in any Cub Scout project yet, and he'd never even shown up for any of the pack meetings. Neither had Julie. She couldn't understand parents who showed so little interest in their son's activities.

"What is it supposed to be?" There was no mistaking the scorn in Davey's voice. Davey Sorensen was the undisputed leader of eight- and nine-year-old boys in the neighborhood. A titter of laughter followed from several of the boys. Davey's plane was the exact opposite of Parker's. Its smooth construction suggested Davey's father and an array of specialized woodworking tools had much more to do with building the plane than Davey had.

Kallene's eyes followed Parker's to the other sleek wooden airplanes strewn along the table by the other boys. Some were more polished than others, but all showed the unmistakable signs of adult involvement in their construction. His attention returned to his own clumsy project. Parker was only eight, but his face showed his keen awareness that his airplane didn't measure up to those the other boys were painting.

Parker was often rude and disruptive, and he didn't seem to have any close friends among the other boys in her den. His frequent outbursts wrought havoc wherever he went, so she wasn't surprised to see his face grow red as he scowled at the other boys. Fearing he might smash the other boys' planes in a fit of temper, she started toward him. Instead of brushing projects and paint from the table as she had expected, he stomped to the stairs leading down to the backyard, carrying his own plane. He screamed unintelligible words as he threw the plane into the air as hard as he could.

"Stupid garbage! Go to—" Kallene wrapped her arms around the upset child, muffling his angry words. Over Parker's head, she could see the clumsy craft float away. A slight breeze lifted it, making it appear almost graceful for a few seconds. It hovered in the air before dropping straight down into Delbert Haney's "Mr. Lincoln" red rosebush that grew several feet higher than the fence.

An angry snarl erupted from the Haneys' backyard. "What idiot threw trash into my yard?" Delbert Haney rushed into sight, waving his arms and shouting curses.

"The boys are making airplanes, and one got away." Kallene attempted to keep her voice light and cheerful while preventing Parker from bolting from her yard. "I'll get it."

Mr. Haney snatched the awkward model plane from his prize roses and broke it in his hands before throwing the pieces across the fence into Kallene's yard. The boys behind Kallene grew still, and she could feel Parker trembling.

In a sudden twist, Parker broke free of her hold. Running to the edge of the deck, he shouted, "I hope my plane broke every one of your stupid flowers. You're mean and ugly, and I hate you! It would serve you right if all your dumb flowers got smashed!" The boy's voice rose to a hysterical scream.

Parker dashed toward the gate in the fence, and Kallene barely caught him before he escaped. "Mr. Haney shouldn't have broken your plane, but being rude to him doesn't help anything." She tried to soothe him. "Now come back inside the house. Your mom and dad aren't home yet, and I have cookies."

Kallene went to bed that night still mulling over the disastrous den meeting. Though she'd been able to persuade Parker to stay, he was sullen and seemed bent on picking a fight with the other boys. It wasn't surprising that the other Cubs left without finishing off the plate of cookies she'd set before them. She'd walked Parker home so she could talk to his parents, but it didn't feel like discussing the incident with Julie had accomplished anything positive.

"It was just a few pieces of wood Parker found somewhere and stuck together. It's not like it had any value. He's got dozens of toy airplanes, and if he wants another one, he knows he only needs to ask, and I'll give him the money to buy any model he wants. I'm sure Parker has forgotten all about it by now. Now if you'll excuse me, I have a real plane to catch." She patted her blonde hair before closing the door, leaving Kallene standing on the porch and feeling foolish for her attempt to discuss the matter. She had made it clear she was uninterested in her son's interaction with others and annoyed by Kallene's attempt to explain the airplane incident to her. Perhaps it really wasn't as important as Kallene had thought.

"Perhaps if I had children of my own," she muttered to herself as she turned back toward her own house, "I might have handled Parker better." A familiar ache filled her heart. Since she'd been a little girl, she'd assumed that one day she'd be a mother, but with each passing year, that likelihood seemed more remote. She'd be thirty in a few months, and she wasn't any closer to finding a man she could love than she was to becoming a mother. She'd had ample opportunities to date and had even received a couple of proposals, but somehow Mr. Right, or even Mr. He'll Do, had never come along.

She had trouble falling asleep that night. Between Linda's confession and the disastrous Cub meeting, her mind went in circles. She tossed and turned several times more, and it occurred to her that Parker had been hurt most by the realization that the shabby little plane he'd thrown together didn't pass muster beside the poorest of the planes the other boys' fathers had helped them build. She wondered if he'd even asked his dad for help building the plane or if his father had been too busy to be bothered. Both Ted and Julie had high-powered careers that involved a great deal of traveling. Neither one seemed to have much time for Parker. In the morning she'd ask Linda for help in figuring out a way to get closer to the boy—and perhaps give him a little of the parenting she sensed the boy needed.

CHAPTER THREE

KALLENE OVERSLEPT, WHICH LEFT HER scrambling to pull on shorts and a T-shirt for her run. Linda would arrive any minute, and she didn't want to keep her waiting. With one hand she grabbed her running shoes, and with the other she fumbled on her dresser for her keys.

She glanced up the street to see if Linda was coming before settling on the top step to slip on her shoes and tie them. There was no sign of Linda, but in the soft predawn light, it was difficult to see all the way to the far end of the street. Kallene began a series of stretches and warm-up exercises. After several minutes she paused to look up the street again. It was growing lighter, but there was no figure hurrying toward her. She checked her watch again. With a frown, she resumed her prep routine.

The soft slap of running footsteps brought her head up once more. The sun was just peering over the horizon, enabling her to see both ends of the street. The runner she spotted across the street wasn't Linda but Rupert Meyer. He never glanced her way, but seeing him increased her concern over Linda's tardiness—a half hour late.

He wasn't the only runner on their street besides herself and Linda. With the convenience of the nearby trail, running was a popular exercise for many residents of the new subdivision, although it seemed most of the men ran earlier than her and Linda. They occasionally spotted Ted Grayson or Jeff Adams returning to their street as she and Linda were just beginning their morning run.

After another impatient glance in the direction of Linda's house, Kallene began an easy trot toward her friend's home. It wasn't like Linda to be so late, but if she and Carson had been arguing, she might have lost track of time. Before she pushed the doorbell, she could hear Macie crying. An uneasy feeling began to settle in the pit of her stomach, and she sensed something was wrong. Macie usually didn't wake up until after Linda and Kallene returned from their run. If the baby was ill, that would explain why Linda hadn't met her at her front step as she did most mornings, but it was unlike Linda to not call. Remembering Linda's words from the previous morning, Kallene acknowledged that a confrontation between Linda and Carson could have awakened the little girl. A chill wind sent a flutter of leaves scuttling across the grass, reminding Kallene that cooler weather was approaching and that she'd soon have to begin wearing sweats when she ran.

She pressed the doorbell again and added a solid hammering of the door.

The door swung open with an abruptness that caused Kallene to take a step back.

"It's about time . . ."

"Is everything all ri—?" Carson and Kallene spoke at the same time. They both paused, staring at one another. Carson appeared as startled as she felt. Slowly she took in his appearance.

She had never seen him so disheveled. His hair, still wet from his shower, was uncombed. Bits of tissue dotted his neck where he'd nicked himself shaving. There were dark splatters on his jeans, and he held Macie on one arm. Her little face was tearstained, and loud hiccups shook her small nightgown-clad body. The remnants of her breakfast made splotches down her gown, and her red curls were tangled in wet clumps against her head.

"Where's Linda?" Without waiting for an answer, Carson thrust Macie into Kallene's arms. "You'll have to watch the baby until she gets here. I'm going to be late for work." He left Kallene standing on the step, gaping, as he disappeared toward the garage.

"Wait!" she shouted. "I don't know where Linda is. I thought—" It was no use. She heard Carson's car engine catch and watched, unable to move, as his car backed down the driveway and disappeared down the street.

Macie's small body quivered, and Kallene became aware of the baby's soggy diaper. She feared Macie was about to begin screaming again, so despite feeling a little uncertain, she stepped into Linda's house. She stood in the entryway feeling confused. Carson seemed to think she and Linda had gone jogging and were returning late. He hadn't even questioned why they hadn't returned together.

She stared at the few shabby secondhand pieces of furniture and the absence of paintings on the walls. The room was clean and tidy, but clean didn't cover up outdated and worn furnishings that contrasted with the newness of the house. No wonder Linda was discouraged with her life.

Macie patted Kallene's cheeks and grinned her infectious smile. Kallene found herself smiling back at the toddler. The smile didn't last as she remembered she knew almost nothing about caring for an infant. She had no idea where Linda might be, and she had a major project that would require her full attention all day. It wasn't a good time to take up amateur babysitting.

"Do you want more breakfast?" she asked Macie as she headed toward the kitchen and Macie's high chair.

Macie's small face crinkled into a deep scowl and more tears threatened.

"All right, no breakfast," Kallene agreed.

"Cookie!" Macie smiled her cherubic smile.

"Why, you little manipulator!" Kallene couldn't help laughing. She dug through Linda's cookie jar until she found an oatmeal cookie, which she offered to Macie, reasoning the oatmeal made the cookie *almost* a nutritious breakfast.

She fastened the little girl in her high chair to eat the cookie and then surveyed the kitchen. It was a wreck. Cereal caked the sides of a bowl and was splattered down the side of the microwave oven. When she opened the door to the microwave, it became obvious Carson hadn't bothered to cover the bowl he'd used for cooking his cereal. Grease and egg yolk spatters speckled the stovetop, and cold cereal crunched beneath her feet with each step she took. A Disney Princesses cereal bowl rested upside down beneath the table. Spilled milk dripped from the tabletop to the floor. Catching sight of a clock mounted on the wall, she gasped. It couldn't be that late!

It was a whole hour later than she'd thought. It really was past the time she and Linda should have been returning from their run. Now the question was, where was Linda? Had she gone running alone when Kallene didn't join her? Had Kallene slept through the ringing of her doorbell?

Kallene reached for the dish cloth to wipe the table and stove top. The cereal on the floor was an annoyance, so she swept that up.

"Mok!" Macie banged her fists on her tray.

"Of course. What's a cookie without milk?" Kallene turned to the cupboard. She knew right where Linda kept her daughter's sippy cups.

While Macie drained her cup, Kallene puttered around the kitchen, finishing her cleaning. When she finished, she peeked through the kitchen window, wondering where her friend had gone. Even if she'd gone running alone, she should be back by now. Linda didn't have a car, so she couldn't have made a quick trip to the store.

Using a paper towel, she wiped Macie's face and hands before unbuckling her from her chair and carrying her to the bathroom for further cleanup. The only towel she could find in the bathroom was a crumpled wet one lying in a corner next to the trash basket where she assumed Carson had tossed it after his shower. It had spots of blood on it. She remembered the bits of tissue stuck to the razor cuts on Carson's face and tossed the towel back where she'd found it.

She was soaked by the time she carried the wet child to the nursery and found a towel to dry her. Diapering Macie included numerous trips down the hall chasing her with one side of the diaper fastened and the other dangling. At last Macie was dressed in a cute pair of coveralls with a white knit shirt trimmed with a narrow edge of lace. Her curls were combed, and little red sneakers were on her feet. She looked adorable.

"Now what?" Kallene wondered. There was still no sign of Linda, and she couldn't remain at her friend's house all day. She had a job to do. "I guess you'll have to come to my house." She spoke aloud to the little girl, who clapped her hands and gurgled something incomprehensible.

Only taking time to gather up a supply of diapers and scribble a note to leave on the kitchen counter for Linda, Kallene left the house with Macie, and a few minutes later she was almost to her own front door. Her attention turned from Macie to a police car parked in front of her house. Putting on a burst of speed, she sprinted forward, jostling Macie against her hip, which brought a ripple of giggles from her small passenger. As she drew closer, she noticed two officers standing in Delbert Haney's yard talking to him. She slowed her steps.

"That's her!" Mr. Haney shouted, pointing at Kallene. Both officers turned, and Kallene felt her face go red. She had no idea what her neighbor was accusing her of, but the accusation plus two police officers staring at her made her feel she must have done something wrong.

"Could we speak with you for a few minutes, ma'am?" The officer was polite enough, but the request made her feel self-conscious and a little guilty. Of what, she had no idea.

"This will only take a minute," the officer reassured as he stepped toward her.

"Oh, all right." She shifted Macie higher on her hip and gave the officer her attention.

"She heard him threaten me!" Mr. Haney waved his arms and pointed in her direction again.

"How about sitting on my front porch?" She motioned the officer toward the patio chairs on the long veranda that ran from the connected garage across the front of the house. Macie was growing heavier with each passing minute. Besides, she didn't want to be any closer to Mr. Haney than necessary. No matter what he was accusing her of, she preferred to put some distance between them. The officer made no objection, so she led the way.

When they were both settled in chairs, with Macie on her lap, she asked, "What is this about?"

Macie sat stoically watching the officer with wide eyes, her thumb in her mouth.

"He says someone broke into his yard sometime during the night and dug up his rosebushes. Whoever did it didn't steal them, just left them on the ground."

"He thinks I did *that*?" She couldn't believe anyone would make such a ridiculous accusation.

"No, he doesn't think you did it, but he says you know the boy who did. He says you had a group of young vandals in your yard yesterday afternoon and that one of the boys threw some rubbish in his roses, damaging several blossoms. He also said that when he reprimanded the boy, the little thug threatened to destroy all of his roses."

Kallene didn't know whether to laugh or cry. "I'm a den mother," she began. "Yesterday I held a Cub Scout meeting right after school on my back deck. Those boys are eight and nine years old, hardly juvenile delinquents. They were painting little airplanes they'd made out of balsa wood. One landed in Mr. Haney's roses, but I doubt it caused any damage."

"I used to make those little airplanes when I was a kid." The officer beamed, and Kallene realized it probably hadn't been too many years since the officer was a Cub Scout. She felt herself relaxing.

"Did the boy threaten Mr. Haney?"

"I don't recall what was said by the boy, but Mr. Haney was much more threatening than Parker was—he destroyed the boy's airplane without letting us retrieve it."

"The rosebushes aren't a complete loss," the officer told her. "The roots hadn't dried out yet, and Mr. Haney has already replanted them. Our main concern now is the missing tools. It seems the vandal who tore out the roses and ripped off a couple of boards from Mr. Haney's back fence also stole a small garden shovel or trowel and a length of rope."

"Parker is just a little boy. I don't think he would think of breaking into a garden shed to steal tools. He has a temper, but he's always seemed honest to me. Are you sure Mr. Haney hasn't just misplaced his tools?" It seemed to her the old man was creating an awful fuss and making accusations without sound justification.

"I don't know what to think," the officer frankly admitted. "Mr. Haney has called us out here before. He seems to have a lot of problems with kids trespassing on his lawn or pulling blossoms off his flowers—that kind of thing. Pulling out plants, especially roses with all those thorns, and stealing tools just doesn't sound like something an eight-year-old would do. Junior high kids maybe, but not the younger ones." He scratched his head and stared off into the distance for a moment. "You better give me the boy's name and address. I suppose I'll have to talk to him."

Kallene was reluctant to give the information to the officer but felt she had no choice. She had a feeling the Graysons would be furious. Mr. Haney wasn't a pleasant neighbor, and she regretted not meeting him before signing the contract for her house. It was true Parker hadn't behaved well the previous day, but he was a child. Certainly an adult Mr. Haney's age should have learned a little tact and know the futility of making a big fuss over minor irritants. She just hoped the incident wouldn't land Parker in trouble with his parents.

CHAPTER FOUR

By the time Kallene had moved breakables, and any object that might be dangerous for a toddler, from Macie's reach and had sorted through her kitchen drawers for utensils and plastic items to substitute for toys, the morning was half over, and the shower she'd planned on taking after her run was a forgotten dream. Assuring herself that stairs were blocked, all the doors were locked, and knickknacks were out of reach, she at last sat down at her computer.

Concentrating on her work wasn't easy. If the house grew quiet, she rushed to find her small guest. When Macie sang and played nearby, Kallene found herself watching the child's antics instead of concentrating on her work. Several times the baby tugged at her pants, attempting to crawl onto her lap. When Kallene picked her up, the child played havoc with Kallene's designs by hammering on the keyboard.

Lunchtime proved to be another area Kallene was unprepared for, but Macie seemed to be content with applesauce and a peanut butter and jelly sandwich, though Kallene had possessed no idea one small child could make such a mess of herself eating the simple meal.

When Macie appeared to grow sleepy, Kallene made her a nest of sofa cushions and blankets in the living room next to her office. She worked furiously while the baby took a much-too-short nap.

It was late afternoon when a knock came on her door. Linda! Kallene rushed to the door and jerked it open. Instead of Linda, Carson stood on her step. He walked past her to pick up Macie, who giggled and patted his cheeks.

"Da Da!" she cooed in delight, snuggling in his arms.

"Carson!" Kallene yelled when Carson had already started toward the door without a word to Kallene. She stepped in front of him. "Has Linda come back? Where did she go?"

"You tell me!" He pushed past her with Macie, and Kallene watched, feeling helpless, as he hurried down the street carrying his daughter home. At the moment, her sympathies were entirely with Linda. Carson was the most exasperating man she'd ever met! If she'd had the misfortune to have married him, she'd have demanded a divorce a long time ago. Short of running down the street yelling at him, she had no idea how to get answers to her questions.

She slammed the door a little too hard and took long strides toward her office. It took close to half an hour before she calmed down enough to resume work on her project.

* * *

Following a restless night, Kallene prepared for her morning workout. Without waiting for Linda to arrive, she set off toward the Longdale home. She and Linda needed a serious talk.

The sky was still gray, and the only people she saw were shadowy in the predawn light. All was quiet when she reached her destination, and she hesitated before ringing the doorbell. What if Linda hadn't come back? She'd mentioned several times that she usually set out for Kallene's house while Carson was in the shower and Macie was still asleep. She really didn't want to disturb either of them, but she felt an urgency to discover whether or not Linda had returned.

Chiding herself for her reluctance to push the doorbell, she jabbed her finger against the button. She didn't have to wait long for Carson to answer the door. He was dressed in jeans and a long-sleeved blue shirt. He stood in the doorway with bleary eyes, just staring at her for several seconds before saying anything.

"I'll get Macie." He turned away, but before he could take a step, Kallene reached out to touch his arm.

"She hasn't come back?" She spoke in a quiet voice. Carson's Adam's apple moved up and down a couple of times before he said no in an equally quiet voice.

"Do you know where she went?"

He shook his head.

"Have you called her parents?"

"I see no reason to bother them. She'll be back when she's through sulking."

"I know you were having problems, but I don't think Linda would go away without Macie, or without at least being certain some-one would be available to care for her."

"You're taking care of her, aren't you? When you came yesterday, I figured she'd asked you to watch Macie." Something close to a sneer crept into his voice.

"She never said anything to me about it."

"Are you sure?" The sneer had turned to a snarl of anger. "You've been sticking your nose in our marriage since the day Linda met you. I'm sure you know more about her whereabouts than I do."

Kallene felt the color drain from her face. How could she defend herself from such an absurd charge? Macie's high-pitched wail saved her from saying anything more. Carson appeared uncertain what to do.

"Go get her. I can watch her another day." She really had too much to do to spend another day entertaining a toddler, but Linda was her friend and Carson was behaving so irrationally she wasn't sure he'd watch her closely enough if he stayed home with her. Besides, he'd just started a new job and was probably afraid to ask for a day off so soon.

"Wait here!" Carson strode toward the child's room. He returned moments later with Macie in one arm and a diaper bag in the other. He thrust both toward Kallene.

As he prepared to close the door, Kallene's temper began to rise. "You're dismissing Linda's absence too easily. You should call the police."

His only response was a sharp bark of laughter. "There's no reason to waste their time." He slammed the door behind him, and once again Kallene stood on his doorstep holding Macie and watching his car back down the driveway and speed down the street. She felt an almost uncontrollable urge to throw something at the disappearing car.

She walked with angry strides back to her own house. Granted, Carson might know a side of Linda Kallene had never seen, but something wasn't right. "'Carson wasn't taking Linda's disappearance seriously enough. She could be in real trouble. Linda would not leave her daughter for two days without calling at least once to be certain she was being cared for.

What if something had happened to Linda? It's true there were only about ten houses between Linda's house and hers, but still . . . It had been dark, and she'd been late yesterday morning. Someone could have forced Linda into a car and driven away with her. Or she might have given up on Kallene and run alone. She might have fallen . . . No, she wasn't going to let her imagination go that route—but if something had happened to Linda, she'd never forgive herself for doing nothing.

By the time she reached her house and settled Macie on a high kitchen stool with a dishtowel securing her to the chair, Kallene had convinced herself that something needed to be done. If Carson wouldn't call the police to report Linda's absence, she'd do it herself.

"Here, sweetie." She handed Macie a Pop Tart and broke off several small chunks of a banana for her. Once the baby was occupied with her makeshift breakfast, Kallene picked up the phone. She started to dial the police then called her parents instead. She probably wouldn't be lucky enough to find Dad at home. His job on the Air Force base kept him terribly busy. But she'd welcome her mother's advice on how to care for Macie.

"Hello."

"Hi, Mom."

"Oh, Kallene, how are you? You're calling earlier than usual."

"I'm fine, but I need someone to talk to."

"Honey, you know you can talk to me about anything."

"I know, Mom. It's about Linda . . ." She explained about her friend's disappearance and her uncertainty about caring for Macie. "I'm not sure whether I should report Linda missing to the police or not. I think Carson should do it, but he won't, so do you think I should?"

"It might be best to call. As for your friend's little girl, you'd better block off your stairs and put breakables out of reach." She continued to talk for several minutes, sharing tips for temporary toys and foods for Macie.

"She's through eating and trying to free herself from the chair I put her on, so I'd better go."

Once Macie was happily playing with the contents of a bottom drawer in the kitchen, Kallene turned to the phone again. She wasn't certain whether this was a situation that merited a 911 call or not. She set the telephone down to dig through a cupboard drawer for the telephone directory.

Once she found the number for the police department, she pressed the numbers with care. After what seemed an eternal wait, someone came on the line. He asked for her name, address, and to state the nature of her problem.

"My neighbor has been missing for two days . . ."

"You'll need to speak to Missing Persons. I can connect you." The line went dead.

After a frustrating wait, she hung up and dialed again. This time she asked for Missing Persons. As soon as she explained to the woman on the other end of the line that her neighbor had been missing for two days and that she had become an impromptu babysitter for her friend's daughter, the operator informed her she should report the matter to DCFS.

When the dial tone again sounded in her ear, Kallene slammed the phone back on its cradle and stood glaring at it.

Some instinct nagged at her, telling her to try again. If she were missing, Linda wouldn't give up so easily. This time she dialed 911. After explaining the situation to the dispatcher, she received a promise that an officer would be sent to the Longdale home. She agreed to meet him there in twenty minutes.

A police car was sitting in the driveway when she reached Carson and Linda's house. Detective Scott Alexander introduced himself and showed his ID. He was close to six feet tall and was about her own age, maybe a little younger. She suspected he spent a generous amount of time in the gym. His blond hair gleamed in the sunlight, and his eyes were that amazing Paul Newman blue. Instead of a uniform, he wore gray slacks and a sports jacket.

"You're Kallene Ashton?" His smile almost caused her to forget to introduce herself.

"Yes." She managed a one-word answer. *Since when are police officers as good looking in real life as they are on TV shows?*

Macie began to squirm to get down, and Kallene welcomed the distraction the child provided.

"Perhaps we could sit down while I ask you a few questions?" She followed the detective's glance to the lawn chairs on the front porch of Linda and Carson's house. She nodded her head and led the way to the chairs. Macie wiggled free and was soon dropping plastic blocks she found behind a chair over the rail that circled the small porch. Each time a block disappeared, the little girl clapped her hands and squealed.

"It's the child's mother that is missing?" the detective began. "I know you explained this over the phone, but if you don't mind repeating . . ." His voice trailed off, and Kallene took that as her signal to begin.

"Linda and I run every morning at six," she began. "Two days ago, she didn't show up for our run and hasn't been seen since."

"Have you spoken to her husband about his wife's whereabouts?"

"He admits he doesn't know where she is but doesn't seem concerned, just angry."

"How would you describe their relationship?"

Kallene hesitated, uncertain if she should mention anything Linda had told her in confidence.

The detective seemed to understand her hesitation. He smiled in encouragement. "I respect your loyalty to your friend, but in order to investigate a reported missing person and determine whether a crime has been committed, the department needs all of the information possible." There was something about that little half smile that made her want to tell him anything he wanted to know. No wonder he made detective so young!

"They've had some problems," she admitted. "Linda tends to be a little dramatic, but she told me the last time we ran—on Monday, that she was going to tell Carson she wanted a divorce."

"Do you think she meant it?"

"I think so. Carson is pretty controlling, and he recently changed jobs to a much lower-paying one. Linda said they're having financial problems, but Carson refuses to consider letting her return to work."

"Is Linda's husband abusive?" The question caught Kallene by surprise, but it also made her feel a little defensive. She wasn't sure why. She didn't particularly like Carson, but since he was her best friend's husband, she found herself defending him.

"No. I think I'd know if he hit her or anything like that." She thought for a moment before adding, "I'm not sure you could call him emotionally abusive either. When they fight, Linda does most of the talking. He makes adamant decisions, then he just walks away and refuses to argue or even talk about their differences. Linda gets pretty frustrated over that."

"Do you think he'd oppose his wife's desire for a divorce?"

"Yes. Linda's brother and his wife got a divorce a couple of years ago, and Carson forbade Linda to have any further contact with him."

After a few more questions, Detective Alexander put his pencil down, leaned back in his chair, and appeared to be studying the neighborhood.

"Nice neighborhood," he commented. "The houses appear to be quite new."

Kallene let her attention wander down the street, seeing leaves on young trees beginning to turn to fall colors. Lawns were neat and tidy, with a profusion of flowers peeking from a generous number of flower beds. The subdivision was perched on a wide bench at the southwest end of the valley and boasted a magnificent view of the Wasatch Range to the east, with a rural feel added by the Oquirrh Mountains and a winding, little-known canyon behind it.

"The first houses in this neighborhood were built about two years ago, and this section of the subdivision was finished last spring."

"Ma Ma!" Macie hammered on Kallene's leg, intent on getting her attention. Kallene scooped her up and snuggled her on her lap. The little girl's thumb went in her mouth, and she stared at the detective for several minutes before her own eyes began to droop.

"Cute kid." The detective smiled, and Kallene felt her insides do a little dance. Chiding herself for reacting to a good-looking male like some silly teenager, she looked away to give herself a moment to compose herself. Her attention was caught by a familiar figure working in the yard next door. Darnell lifted a hand to wave. The wave was accompanied by a slow wink. Not wishing to appear rude, Kallene returned a feeble wave.

"Neighbor?"

"No. I don't know where he lives. He does yard work and odd jobs in the neighborhood." Kallene didn't say anything more, but she noticed that the detective sent speculative glances over her shoulder several times to look at Darnell.

Folding his notebook and tucking it in a shirt pocket was an indication to Kallene that the detective was ready to end the interview.

"You will look for Linda, won't you?" She was anxious for answers and was afraid the police might dismiss her concerns as easily as Carson had.

"I'll talk to her husband and a few other neighbors." He smiled his megawatt smile, but it didn't reassure her as it was meant to do. She wanted something done now. Carson had wasted too much time, and now this policeman didn't seem to be doing anything any faster.

"It's been two days! Someone should be looking for her. No matter what Carson says, Linda wouldn't leave her baby for two whole days without checking on her to be sure she was all right."

"If neither parent made arrangements with you to watch the baby, I could have Social Services pick her up." She stared at him, aghast. His eyes narrowed, but she couldn't guess what he was thinking. His offer seemed to ignite a fuse to her temper.

"Linda didn't ask me to care for Macie, but I know that if she's unable to care for her daughter herself, she would want me to do it. Even Carson assumes I should look after her. And I will. Macie isn't the problem; her missing mother is the problem." Kallene was almost shouting by the time she finished. Macie stirred and began to whimper. Lowering her voice, Kallene whispered soothing words until the baby settled into slumber again.

"I'm sorry. I didn't mean to upset you." The detective sounded more pleased with himself than regretful.

Kallene suspected he had somehow been testing her. He stood while she remained seated with the sleeping child on her lap. He hesitated a moment then suggested he give her a ride back to her own house.

"She's little, but even a sleeping baby gets heavy." He smiled and she couldn't say no. He helped her to her feet and ushered her toward the car parked in the driveway. It took only a few moments to drive the half block to Kallene's house.

When the car stopped, the detective hurried around the front of the car to assist her in climbing out of the vehicle with the sleeping baby in her arms. He walked beside her to the front door. "Is it locked?" he asked, reaching for the doorknob.

"It locks automatically when it's closed." She indicated the slender chain about her neck and found herself holding her breath as his fingers brushed her skin and drew it over her head. It only took a moment for him to unlock the door. She wasn't surprised when he followed her inside.

She was conscious of the officer standing behind her while she settled Macie in her makeshift bed in the corner of the living room. When she straightened, she noticed he was watching her.

"Very attractive." He waved his hand to indicate her living room, with its vaulted ceiling, a row of narrow windows, and a deep plush carpet dotted with leather chairs and sofas. Accent tables and a single, large painting completed the simple decor. Something in his voice hinted he was referring to more than the room.

"If you have any more questions . . ."

"I'll get started right away." He backed toward the door. Was it her imagination, or did he seem a little flustered? Dismissing the thought as vain and irrelevant, she watched him step casually toward the Haneys' house.

His car remained in her driveway for several hours, and she caught glimpses of him on different neighbors' doorsteps. When he drove away around noon, she wondered if Detective Alexander was on his way to interview Carson. She had a hunch Carson would be furious to have a policeman show up at his new job asking questions about his wife.

CHAPTER FIVE

Who knew shopping with a toddler would be so hard or take so long? Kallene carried Macie into the house first, planning to return for the groceries. She set Macie in the center of the improvised playpen she'd made by tying her dining room chairs together on their sides to form a lopsided square. Macie held up her arms at once, demanding to get right back out.

"Just a minute, sweetie. I have to bring the groceries in from the car." Before Macie's look of indignation could turn into tears, she handed the baby a cookie. "I'm beginning to understand American children's obesity problem," she added under her breath.

"Where do you want these?" Darnell Gines stood in the doorway to her kitchen with his arms full of grocery bags. What was he doing in her house!?

"I-I-you," she stammered.

"Okay if I just dump them on your island?" He walked past her to drop the bags on the broad granite surface. While struggling to pull her thoughts together, she remembered she hadn't taken time to close the garage door before carrying Macie into the house. She mentally kicked herself.

"Be back with the rest in just a moment." Darnell headed for the door.

"It's okay. I can get them." She started after him.

"It's no trouble." He was gone, and she was left feeling foolish standing in the middle of the kitchen floor. She considered slamming the door and turning the lock. Darnell Gines was the last person she wanted in her house. She'd be surprised if he was just being polite and

helpful. Before she could gather her wits to decide what to do, he was
back with the rest of her groceries.

"You look fine, more than fine." He leaned against the cabinet
with his legs crossed at the ankles. A wide grin spread across his face,
and his folded arms showed off world-class biceps. Kallene felt herself
begin to bristle. "I thought you might be sick, since I hadn't seen you
or your sidekick for a few days."

"I'm okay. I've just been busy. Thanks for bringing in my groceri-
ies." She was careful to keep the table between herself and Darnell.

"I see you've got the Longdale munchkin, so it must be the other
lady that's under the weather."

"Uh, I'm watching her for a few days. Her dad will be here to
pick her up any minute." She sounded like an idiot. What was it
about Darnell that raised her hackles and at the same time turned her
into a basket case?

"You got plans for tonight?" He moved closer.

"Yes." The only plans she had were to catch up on the work that
had fallen behind while she was watching Macie and worrying about
Linda, but she wasn't about to tell Darnell that.

"Too bad. I've a feeling we could have a real good time together."
His fingers brushed lightly down her arm where it rested against the
table. She jerked back just as her doorbell rang.

"All right, I'll see you around." Darnell sauntered toward the
open door leading to the garage. "Oh, by the way . . ." He paused.
Something in his eyes made her want to shiver. "You might consider
getting an automatic garage door opener, one with a remote clicker
so you can open and close the door without getting out of your car. I
could get you a good deal and install it for you."

"Hmm, I'll think about it." She moved around the table, anxious
to reach the front door, where someone was impatiently ringing the
doorbell again.

"You better get that." Darnell closed the door behind him. The
moment the door closed, Kallene darted forward to turn the lock
and drop the security chain in place before dashing toward the front
of the house. She opened the door to find Carson showing signs of
impatience on her doorstep. Under the circumstances, she was glad to
see him.

"It's about time," Carson said through tightly clenched teeth when she opened the door. "I was beginning to think you'd run off too."

Kallene ignored Carson's impatient greeting. "Have you heard from Linda?"

"No, and I don't appreciate you sending a cop to cause problems for me at work. If I lose my job . . . Where's Macie?"

"She's asleep over there." She pointed to the impromptu playpen. As angry as Carson appeared to be, she expected him to rush right over and pick up the sleeping child. Instead he knelt beside the chairs, untied one of the knots to slide two of the chairs apart, and slipped his hands beneath the baby. In one smooth motion, he rose to his feet with her cradled in his arms. Kallene hurried to the other room to collect the diaper bag.

"If I'm going to watch her tomorrow, perhaps you could bring her playpen and a few toys."

"That won't be necessary." He seemed to be struggling to keep his voice even. Not for her sake, she was sure, but to keep from waking Macie. "My dad will be here in a few hours, and he'll watch her. We'll be checking into a hotel while the police search my house and car."

"Oh!" What could she say? She supposed the search had to start somewhere, but it was quite obvious Linda wasn't at home, and if the police were searching her home and her husband's car, they must think one or the other might yield a clue to her whereabouts.

"Oh? That's all you can say? I spent all afternoon at the police station and will likely lose my job, but why should you care? There's nothing like accusing a man of murdering his wife to stir up a little excitement!"

"Murder? I never . . ."

"What else did you think that slick detective would think when you told him my spoiled wife had disappeared? Thanks to you, the police think I killed my own wife!" He reached for the door with one hand and made good his escape, leaving Kallene dazed. She gathered her wits in time to run after him with the diaper bag she still carried. Without a word, he slung it over one shoulder and continued toward a rental car parked at the curb. She watched it pull away and felt a wave of guilt. What had she done?

* * *

Kallene tried to work. Without the distraction of Macie, she should have been able to concentrate on the sketches before her, but her mind kept straying to her missing friend and her daughter. Being responsible for the toddler for two days had caused a severe dent in her productivity, but the thought of an old man who was a stranger to the baby taking over her care nagged at her thoughts. The little she knew about Carson's father had come from Linda, who claimed her father-in-law wasn't sociable; he lived alone on a boat near some small California coastal town; she'd only met him once a few months after her marriage to Carson; and Carson called him every Sunday evening at seven, no matter what. Wherever Linda was, Kallene felt certain she wouldn't approve of her daughter being left in the man's care.

She hesitated to even think about Linda, yet the suspicion that Linda might not be alive had flitted at the edges of her mind since she'd first learned of her disappearance. She couldn't force herself to think of Linda being dead, but what other reason could there be for a woman who lived for her child not checking once on her baby's welfare? Though Carson intimated that Linda was spoiled, thoughtless, and irresponsible, Kallene knew that Linda was none of those. Linda was the more responsible and realistic half of that couple. Carson seemed to believe they could live on faith and good intentions while Linda had argued that faith was fine, but work and common sense were necessary ingredients in life as well.

But dead? Murdered? She winced at the mere thought. She wondered if Deputy Alexander really did think Linda had been murdered and if Carson was a suspect. She shook her head as though that would clear her thoughts. She didn't particularly like Carson, and she'd never envied Linda's marriage to him, but she didn't think him capable of murder. He was overbearing, bossy, unrealistic, and often rude, but he also worked hard, adored his daughter, and devoted a great deal of time to service in their ward. Sometimes his strict conservative interpretation of how Church members should live was annoying, but she'd never doubted his sincerity. Of course, the police were just doing their job to question him. She'd heard somewhere that most murders are committed by someone the victim knows and trusts such as a husband or boyfriend. Not Carson.

"Arrgh!" She hit delete. She had to put a stop to such morbid thoughts. Every drawing she'd made in the past four hours was terrible. Ben McCallister had stressed over and over how important the Davidson account was to the company. He'd even hinted that a promotion was possible if the client was satisfied with her work. Anyway, she didn't want to turn in anything less than her best. She needed to clear her mind.

Rising to her feet, she walked the few steps to her kitchen for a glass of water, hoping that would help. She stood looking out of the window over her sink. The street was quiet with only porch and decorative lighting marking the presence of her neighbors' houses. She'd found something about the view of the street at night peaceful and calming ever since she'd moved into her house, but now she imagined something brooding and resentful hiding in the darkness. She hoped the city would soon get around to installing street lights as promised.

Making her way back to her desk, she wondered if Carson had informed Linda's family that she was missing. It seemed he'd notified his father, but did Linda's family know? Her cell phone sat on the desk near her computer. On an impulse, she sat down and made a few clicks on the computer to an online telephone directory. There were a dozen Adam Piersons in the Washington DC area, but only one Adam and Janet Pierson. She hesitated, wondering if she was overstepping, yet she couldn't dismiss the strong hunch that Carson had not notified Linda's family of her disappearance or the insistent conviction that they should be told.

She punched in the numbers then held the phone to her ear and listened to it ring. Too late she remembered the two-hour time difference. Eleven thirty in Utah was one thirty in the morning at the Piersons' home. Linda's parents were most likely asleep. She could try again in the morning. She started to cancel the call, but a voice suddenly roared in her ear. "This better be an emergency, or you're going to find yourself in big trouble!"

"Mr. Pierson?" Her voice squeaked. "This is Kallene Ashton. I'm sorry to bother you, and I apologize for forgetting the time difference, but have you talked to Linda anytime in the past two days?"

"Talked to Linda? Is this some kind of prank call? Wait, aren't you that friend of hers she runs with?"

"No, yes. I mean no, this isn't a prank call, and yes, we've been running together for almost a year. We've become close, and I'm worried about her."

"What's going on? What's this all about?" His voice had softened some, though he still didn't sound happy to be speaking to her. At least he hadn't hung up on her.

"Tuesday morning Linda didn't show up for our run. I haven't seen her since our run Monday morning. Carson says he doesn't know where she is either. He left Macie with me the past two days while he's gone to work. It's not like Linda to be gone two days without calling to check on her daughter." Speaking as though in a rush to get it all out, Kallene explained what she knew of Linda's absence and Carson's anger that she'd called the police to ask them to begin a search for Linda.

"Obviously it never occurred to that numbskull son-in-law to notify us that our daughter is missing!" Kallene jerked the phone away from her ear until the roar stopped.

Now she could hear another voice, a woman's scared voice in the background. "What is it, dear? Has something happened to Linda?"

"Now, dear, I'll get to the bottom of this." She assumed the words were meant to soothe Linda's mother.

"We'll get the first flight out there, so we should arrive sometime tomorrow. I have your number on the caller ID. Would you mind picking us up at the airport." It wasn't a question, and he broke the connection right after saying it.

Kallene stared at the phone in her hands for several minutes. Linda's father was certainly forceful. She couldn't blame him for being upset about being wakened in the middle of the night with bad news, but she couldn't help wondering if Linda had married a man like her father. Had she put up with Carson's domineering because she was accustomed to her father behaving the same way? Linda didn't seem like the type, but maybe she didn't know her friend as well as she thought she did.

Giving up on the possibility of getting any more work done on her project, she shut down her computer and turned off the lights. With so much on her mind, she suspected it was going to be difficult to fall asleep. After putting on her pajamas and preparing to climb into bed, she decided a few minutes relaxing on the deck might put her more in the mood to sleep. She did some of her best thinking on the second-story deck that looked out over the Salt Lake valley.

Settling in a deeply cushioned patio chair, she leaned back, reminding herself to relax and let the day's tension go. It was cooler outside than she had expected, and she was soon pulling her robe tighter around her shoulders as she stared up at the stars. In the distance a dog howled, and from somewhere farther down the valley a siren wailed. The solid wood fence she'd installed around her backyard blocked the view from the ground level of the street, and she was glad she'd insisted on a deck opening from the upper-level sitting room. Her gaze drifted to the north, where her next-door neighbor's house was dark, though she could see a faint glimmer of light coming from beneath the blinds where their two small boys slept. She assumed a night-light burned in their room. Next, her attention drifted to the south. Delbert Haney wasn't a pleasant neighbor. He was much older than Kallene and quick to find fault at every turn. They'd argued about the placement of the fence until she'd called a surveyor to make certain her fence didn't infringe on one inch of his property, then he'd complained that she'd planted trees too close to the fence. She'd seen his wife a few times, but she appeared to be timid and completely cowed by her domineering husband.

No lights—not even a porch light—lit the Haneys' yard, yet something niggled at her mind. She'd sat right there many times over the past year with moonlight and shadows alternating across both yards. Shouldn't she recognize if something was out of place? She didn't know what it was, yet something didn't feel right. Something was different. Suddenly she remembered. The rosebushes! She couldn't see the tops of the bushes over the fence, but hadn't the police officer said Mr. Haney had replanted them?

CHAPTER SIX

"Don't you live in Pine Shadows?" Lori Cassidy, a cute secretary, stuck her head through Kallene's door to ask.

"Yes." Kallene lifted her head from the prints spread across her work table. Without the responsibility of caring for Macie that day, she'd made her way to the downtown offices of Benson & McCallister that morning, hoping she'd be able to concentrate better. Ben hadn't seemed pleased to see her, but that was his problem. She'd shrugged off the disapproving scowl she received when she met him outside her office.

"I heard on the news last night that some woman there was missing, and her husband wasn't cooperating with the police investigation." It wasn't hard to guess Lori was talking about Linda's disappearance.

Kallene sighed. Lori was the fourth person who had mentioned the missing woman story to her since she'd arrived at the office. She hadn't watched the news the previous evening or turned her radio on that morning, so she hadn't heard the story firsthand, but she'd gotten plenty of secondhand reports. She felt certain the story was highly dramatized, and she wasn't comfortable with the speculation she heard behind the comments.

"I'm not sure that's accurate. As far as I know, he's sharing whatever he knows; he just doesn't agree that there's something odd about her disappearance. He seems to think she's just trying to cause trouble for him because they haven't been getting along well."

"You know her?" The secretary scurried inside the office to stand near Kallene. "Do you think her husband killed her?"

"No. Carson doesn't seem to me like the kind of person who would kill anyone."

"You never know." Lori lowered her voice as though confiding secret information. "It's usually the husband."

"I've heard that." She turned away, hoping to discourage the secretary who she suspected watched way too much TV.

"Are you going to help with the search tomorrow?" Lori persisted.

"Search?"

"I heard about it just a little while ago. Her brother is working with the police department to organize a search of the foothills behind Pine Shadows tomorrow. They're asking for volunteers. Jessica and I saw him on the television behind the counter while we were eating lunch. He's really cute."

"Thanks, I'll look into it." Kallene didn't want to encourage the gossipy young woman, but she was glad to hear that a search was going to be made. When she ran that morning, she'd found herself scanning the sides of the trail. She hadn't expected to see anything, but it had reminded her that three days had been wasted with no one making a genuine search for Linda.

"I might volunteer, too. That brother looks really hot." The secretary looked at one of the prints Kallene had been working on with a puzzled expression on her face before bustling out the door.

* * *

It was already growing dark, and she felt tired enough to drop into bed without eating dinner by the time she got home. She made certain her garage door was closed and left her shoes at the kitchen door. It took only a moment to punch in the security code for her alarm system. All she wanted to do was fall into bed, but she'd skipped lunch, so she had to eat something. After dropping her purse and portfolio in her office, she rooted through her cupboard for a microwavable soup bowl.

While her soup was heating, she flipped on the television to see if she could catch an update on the search for Linda. The broadcast was just starting. She stood still, ignoring the ring of her microwave, when a shot of Carson leaving the police station flashed across the screen. He turned his head away from the microphones and cameras as he made his way to a beat-up pickup truck parked at the curb. He showed no emotion, and she wondered if Macie was inside that truck with her grandfather. Even though she'd only cared for the little girl two days, she missed her so much her heart ached.

"No charges have been filed. The police department is still treating this case as a missing person . . ." She'd been so intent on watching Carson that she'd missed most of the announcer's words. The scene changed to a reporter putting a microphone in front of another man. This one was tall, dark-haired, and looked familiar, though she felt certain she'd never seen him before.

"What time do you expect searchers to begin arriving at the staging area?"

"We'd like them to arrive between five and six so they can be checked in and ready to go as soon as it gets light." Kallene guessed the man was Linda's brother. There was a distinct resemblance to her friend in the way he held his chin and the way he moved with a natural athletic grace as well as in his coloring, except for his dark hair.

"Thank you, Mr. Pierson." The reporter signed off, and Kallene shook her head. She supposed it was fatigue that had her spacing out, but she'd missed where the searchers were meeting. The high school and the church parking lot were the only areas close to their subdivision large enough, so she supposed she'd find the right place. She yawned, gulped down her glass of milk, and decided against reheating her soup. Sleep was far more important if she was going to be up before five.

Before plugging her phone into its charger and crawling into bed, she noticed the message light was blinking. She wanted to ignore it and just crawl into bed, but what if Linda had tried to reach her? She pressed the button and heard Linda's father announce they hadn't been able to get a flight until the next day but should arrive in Salt Lake a little after noon tomorrow.

* * *

Dressed in a nylon jogging suit and wearing her running shoes, Kallene chose to jog the few blocks to the church. From a block away she could see several large trailers parked and a row of tables set up in front of them. Kallene was pleased to see so many people milling about and lined up at the tables to sign in. She recognized some of her neighbors and a large number of people from her ward and stake. She acknowledged greetings as she waited in line to register.

"Hi!" She was surprised to see Brittany Adams seated on a folding chair behind the table. Her baby was due in a few months. "I knew you'd come." The other woman pushed a card toward her. "We just need your name, telephone number, stuff like that." She lowered her voice. "This must be so hard for you. I only moved in a few weeks ago, but I could see at once how close you and Linda were."

"Should you be here?" Kallene looked pointedly at the woman's prominent abdomen.

"I'm fine." Brittany's smile lit her small face. "I wish I could join the search, but this is all Jeff would agree to let me do. He teamed up with one of the guys from his work. Do you have a partner, or should I assign one to go with you?"

"No, I don't have a partner." Kallene looked around, wondering if Lori had come. She didn't relish the thought of pairing with the secretary, but everyone else she knew seemed to already be paired with a spouse or friend.

"She can come with us." She turned toward the speaker and was pleased to see Detective Alexander. He smiled as he addressed her. "Good morning, Kallene. Do you have any objections to joining me and Linda Longdale's brother?"

Jon Pierson brought a lump to her throat. He looked even more like his sister than he had last night on the news.

"Good morning . . . Kallene, is it?" The man standing beside the detective echoed his greeting. "I'm Jon Pierson. I understand you are my sister's friend and running partner. She told me quite a few times that you're a terrific friend. Detective Alexander said—"

"We might as well make it unanimous. I go by Scott," the detective said, while leading their small group to the side. "We might as well start. We've been assigned the dry gully that parallels the Pine Fork trail from the highway to the picnic area above the spring."

When they reached the gully, Scott instructed her and Jon to follow the slope about six to ten feet above and to either side of where he walked along the bottom of the gorge. They were to scan the area closely for any signs that someone had passed that way. "Most of the others will be assigned different parts of the hiking trail that run along the top," he told them.

Scott set a moderate pace, and there was little conversation as they walked. Kallene had run the trail at the top of the gorge many times and knew that the gully extended for almost two miles before it joined the main canyon.

The morning was bright and clear, and nearby she heard an occasional voice, though never distinct words. The grass growing along the side of the gully was long and brown. Water only ran in the gully during the early spring, when the stream in the canyon overflowed and occasionally after a heavy rainstorm. Once she passed over a blackened spot where it appeared a fire had started but had burned out before spreading. To her disgust, beer and soda cans along with snack wrappers appeared frequently, caught in clumps of the dry grass. The higher they climbed, the more often she encountered bare rock and small boulders instead of grass. In some places the terrain was steep and the dry, tangled growth made passage difficult.

A wooden footbridge marked the end of the gully. Kallene scrambled up a rocky path leading to the trail above and moved more rapidly toward the picnic area. A few minutes later, she crossed the footbridge to join Scott and Jon at one of the picnic tables. The small picnic area was sheltered by large trees with leaves that were beginning to turn red and yellow. She knew without asking that they'd found no more clues than she had.

"Look at it this way," Scott was saying to Jon. "Not finding her in the gully is a good indication she didn't fall from the trail above. In the past we've had to rescue a few runners who slipped from the trail and were injured falling into the gully."

"I don't think Linda fell anywhere. She might have been pushed, but she didn't fall." Jon made his view clear. "Linda is a superb athlete."

"I agree with Jon," Kallene added. "Linda is an experienced runner and is sure-footed. Besides, I don't think she was running here or on any of the other trails that morning. We always ran together, and even though I was late, she wouldn't have started her run without me. There have been a few times she arrived before I was ready, but each time she rang my doorbell and waited for me."

"What did your crime scene people find at the house?" Jon's abrupt question sent chills down Kallene's spine.

"I can't answer that," Scott hedged.

"Don't give me that," Jon shot back. "We're talking about my sister."

"So far there's nothing concrete. The lab is doing some testing, but I haven't heard of anything suspicious." Scott seemed to be explaining that he really couldn't give any answers—not that he wouldn't.

"What about his car?"

"Same answer."

Kallene's phone rang, sending a symphony blaring through the still air. She fumbled at her belt to unlatch the carrying case, feeling embarrassed, though she couldn't have said why. She opened the tiny silver flip-top.

"Hello?"

"We've landed. We're just waiting for our luggage. How soon can you get here?"

"Mr. Pierson?"

"Of course."

"I'm some distance from the airport. Some of Linda's neighbors are doing a walking search of the canyon behind our subdivision, and I volunteered to help." She felt a hand on her arm and looked up to see Jon mouth, "Dad?"

She nodded her head.

"Let me talk to him." She handed the phone to him.

"Dad, Kallene is needed here. Rent a car and go to the Comfort Inn in Sandy. I've already checked in, and I reserved a room for you and Mom. I'll meet you there as soon as I can, but it might be late afternoon." He listened for a minute.

"Yes, I have my phone. Call me in an hour or so." Jon closed the phone.

"How'd Dad get your phone number?" Jon asked as he handed her phone back to her.

"I called him when I realized Carson probably hadn't notified Linda's family that she was missing or even checked to see if she might be visiting her parents."

"That's Carson. I'll never figure out what either of my sisters saw in that guy."

"I take it you're not close to your brother-in-law," Scott said.

"'Not close' is putting it mildly." Jon's voice betrayed a hint of contempt. "Carson and I were missionary companions for three miserable months. He did everything by the book but found fault with everything I did and looked down his nose at anyone he didn't think had the proper attitude."

"You expressed some negative feelings for Carson Longdale, too." Scott turned to Kallene. "Is that how you see him?"

"I'm not sure," she answered with a bit of hesitation. "In a way, I think I'd call him a reverse snob. He seems to think anyone with money or nice things isn't living their religion. I don't think he wanted to buy a house in this neighborhood, and he objected to Linda's spending money on clothes or furniture or having her own car. Their furniture and most of their clothing came from secondhand stores. He reminds me of that old joke about being proud of how humble he is."

"He's a cheapskate!" Jon said.

"No, I don't think he's a cheapskate," Kallene argued. "He's just committed to a minimal lifestyle for himself and his family, but he's generous to other people."

Scott looked back and forth between them for several seconds then checked his watch. "I'm supposed to be back at police headquarters in forty minutes. That just gives me time to hike down the trail and drive in. Do you two want to go on searching, or are you ready to head back with me?"

"I'm going on up to the springs. There's a narrow trail that winds up to the top near there. It's easy to miss, and not many people know it's even there, so I'm not sure anyone has been assigned to check it," Kallene said.

"I think I'll stick with her," Jon volunteered. "I don't think anyone is supposed to search alone."

"Okay, I'll see you both later." Scott rose from the picnic bench. "Kallene, you might need to come down to the station later to give a formal statement. I'll let you know."

Kallene watched Scott disappear down the trail where she and Linda had frequently run during the past year. She'd loved the canyon since her first run there, but she wasn't sure she'd ever feel quite the same way about it without Linda.

"Shall we get started?" Jon was standing now, too, and seemed impatient to continue the search.

Feeling uncertain how she felt about Jon inviting himself to accompany her up to the spring, she rose to her feet. After a slight hesitation in which Jon indicated she should lead the way, she started up the trail that led from the picnic area to the spring. Trees and thick undergrowth lined the trail. A layer of fallen leaves rustled beneath their feet. The deep peace she usually felt when hiking or running in the mountains evaded her. It could have been because of the serious nature of this hike, or it could be because of the stranger, who didn't seem like a stranger, walking beside her.

"It's hard to tell if anyone left the path along here recently," she commented.

"Don't worry about it too much," Jon said in a tight voice. "There's not much chance Carson carried her this far. He's not in good enough shape for a trek like this."

"Do you really think Carson killed her?" Kallene stopped to face Jon.

"What other possibilities are there? Their marriage was on the rocks, and Carson must have gone ballistic when she mentioned divorce. Divorce is one of the worst sins imaginable according to my brother-in-law. He refused to allow Linda to even speak to me after my divorce."

"I know. She told me about that." Kallene remembered their discussion of the matter. Kallene thought there were far too many divorces, too, but she conceded that under some circumstances divorce was the only viable solution to a bad situation.

"We both know Linda wouldn't walk out on her marriage without telling you or her family," Jon said, adding with a touch of sarcasm, "and there's no way she'd take off, leaving Macie in her husband's 'tender' care."

Kallene stopped and turned to face Jon, who was several inches lower on the trail, bringing them almost to eye level. "I won't pretend I like Carson, but I just can't believe he'd kill her. Linda was always pretty open with me in talking about Carson, and I never got the impression Carson was ever violent toward her or Macie."

"He's a strange duck, but I wouldn't have thought him capable of murder either until now." He motioned for her to keep moving.

"If you think this search is a waste of time, why did you organize it?"

"I don't think it's a waste of time. I just think he disposed of Linda's body somewhere accessible by car. The gully was a good possibility. That's why the detective and I chose to start there, but anywhere in the west desert is just as likely to be where he dumped her or in any of the other dozen or so canyons around here. Organizing a search is important for eliminating places close to home, for alerting the public to be on the watch for the missing person, and to jog the memory of someone who may have seen something the night she disappeared."

The sound of falling water caught Kallene's ear. They were almost to the spring. The trail grew wider, and Jon closed the distance between them to emerge at her side into the clearing that surrounded a small pool. A slender column of water dropped thirty feet from the rocks above the pool, and a six-inch trickle of water slid between rocks to form a stream that nearly disappeared on its way to a larger creek several miles away. A man in running shorts and a T-shirt leaned on a large, smooth rock near the water's edge.

"Find anything?" Jon stepped toward the man.

The man started as though he hadn't heard their approach. A wide grin spread across his face when he noticed Kallene standing a few steps behind Jon. "It didn't take you long to find a new running partner."

"Darnell." She knew he ran regularly in the canyon, but she hadn't expected him to join the search. As far as she knew, he didn't live in the neighborhood, and she was surprised he would show up on a busy Saturday.

Jon looked back and forth between her and Darnell. "I take it you two know each other?"

Darnell's leering grin made her want to throw something at him.

"Kallene and I have known each other for a little more than a year," Darnell replied.

Kallene frowned. Darnell made it sound like they were friends, maybe more than friends.

She took a step closer to Jon. "Mr. Gines works for the Pine Shadows Homes contractor. He makes repairs for the builder and hires out to do private handyman projects for homeowners as well."

She turned to complete the introduction, gesturing toward Jon. "This is Jon Pierson, Linda Longdale's brother."

"Sorry about your sister." Darnell's words were meant for Jon, but he never took his eyes off Kallene. She was glad she was wearing a jogging suit instead of her running shorts.

"Are you helping with the search?" Jon asked Darnell, though he didn't seem to pay attention to the introduction. His eyes were busy scanning the clearing.

"It didn't start out that way. I was just out for my morning run when I met up with a bunch of folks along the north trail. They told me about the search, and I decided to come on up here for a look around. Besides, I thought there might be a chance of partnering with a good-looking chick who often runs on this side of the canyon. I heard she was in the market for a new running partner."

"I'm not looking for a partner." It was fun running with Linda and together she'd felt braver about trying new trails she wouldn't have run alone, but running with an egotistical flirt was not in her plans. She had known for months that Darnell was a frequent runner. She and Linda had often seen him near the end of their run. And as a frequent visitor to the canyon, he probably knew the trails as well as she did. But those attributes alone did not help his case for becoming Kallene's new running partner.

"We better be on our way." Jon surprised her by touching her arm in a motion that indicated she should lead.

She was glad when Darnell brushed past her with a familiar pat to her shoulder before disappearing down the trail she and Jon had just left.

She wasn't certain why she hesitated a moment, feeling a strange reluctance to follow the almost hidden path instead of heading toward the more worn one that connected the two major canyon trails.

They hiked in silence for about ten minutes before Jon brought up their encounter with Darnell. "How well do you know that guy?"

"Not as well as he insinuated, and not as little as I'd like," she snapped back.

Jon held up his hands, palms out. "Easy, I didn't mean anything by asking. I just found it a little odd that he was out here alone when I heard Scott order officers to block the bottoms of both trails and not let anyone past without signing in and having a partner."

"I don't know how he got past. Maybe he started up the trail before it was closed off. There are even a few routes that lead over the mountain into other canyons. He and several of my neighbors all run here, though most start earlier than Linda and I do." Mentioning her friend's name brought an ache to her heart. She couldn't be as sure as Jon that Linda was dead, but with each passing hour, the likelihood of ever seeing her friend alive again was growing fainter.

"He seems a little . . ." Jon hesitated.

"Creepy," Kallene filled in.

"Well, yeah, I suppose that term fits."

"He fancies himself a ladies' man. He's always flirting, dishing out extravagant compliments to women, and he has a bad habit of showing up uninvited to offer assistance." She explained about Darnell bringing in her groceries two days earlier. "I'll admit that I would consider help carrying groceries a kind gesture coming from other neighbors, but Darnell's assistance creeped me out."

"Do you think there's a chance Linda went running with him when you were late Tuesday morning?"

"No way. Linda wouldn't cross the street with Darnell Gines if a bear was chasing her."

"Okay, I get it, but the guy is muscular and tough, and there are a lot of women who would welcome his attention."

"Wait! Hold on a minute." She walked back a few steps. "It looks like someone left the trail here."

Jon stopped beside her. "You could be right. The ground is scuffed, and there's a heel mark beside that clump of drooping flowers. Be careful not to step on it." Kallene stooped to examine the spot in more detail. They scrutinized the immediate area without finding another footprint.

Jon stepped his way around the spot. Kallene followed. Taking care to disturb the ground as little as possible, they walked on pine needles and dry leaves beneath tall trees for a considerable distance, checking for further signs. They searched for any indication that the ground had been disturbed but found nothing.

"We better check under any firs or pines with low branches," Kallene suggested.

"You check under the trees, and I'll tackle this thicket of brambles." Jon stood before a patch of wild roses.

"Be careful," Kallene warned. "Those things aren't like roses in most gardens. I swear, they jump out and grab you if they get a chance."

Jon chuckled but waded into the thick patch anyway.

After almost an hour of fruitless searching, they returned to the trail. Jon had a couple of long scratches down one cheek, and both of his arms evinced a thorough search of the wild rosebushes.

"Probably some guy just stepped off the path to relieve himself," he muttered. Kallene nodded her head in glum agreement.

They walked for another thirty minutes until they reached a bluff overlooking the well-worn path on the opposite side of the canyon from their starting point that morning. Kallene sank down on a large boulder, and after a moment Jon sat beside her. Below them a panorama of pine and aspen carpeted the valley. Patches of fall colors lingered in hollows and at the lower elevations. Where they sat, most of the deciduous trees had already lost their foliage. Beyond the mouth of the canyon, the rooftops of Pine Shadows could be seen, and in the distance they could see the haze marking the city.

"It's beautiful," Jon said in a quiet voice. "It's the kind of place I can imagine Linda loving."

"She loved this canyon. She said it was the one place where she felt truly free. Carson's restrictions cut her off from so many things she longed to do and places she wished to go. She couldn't even window-shop at the mall unless she went with me and I drove. Without a car and almost no bus service out this far, it's no wonder she felt isolated."

"I guess I was so involved with my own problems that I never really realized how difficult her life was. We talked on the phone as often as we could, but she never said much about her marriage. I wanted to see her, but she felt she was already being disloyal by just talking to me after Carson ordered her to have no contact with me."

"She talked about you often. The two of you must have been close." Kallene regretted that she'd never been as close to her brothers as Jon and Linda were to each other. She loved her brothers, but they didn't often call each other. They were content to mostly keep in touch through their parents.

"We were close, especially when we were younger. I should have seen she needed more than an occasional telephone call."

Kallene stared out over the canyon, thinking back over her relationship with Linda. "I saw her almost every day and had no idea her situation had become so bad. She talked about her problems, but she never mentioned wanting to end her marriage until the last morning we ran together. I'll admit I had thought a number of times that they were an oddly matched couple, but I missed understanding how deep their problems ran."

Jon plucked a long blade of dry grass and shredded it between his fingers as he talked. "I don't know what possessed Linda to marry Carson. Linda and Louise looked alike, but they were nothing alike in personality or interests. Sometimes it was almost like Linda was more my twin than Louise's. We both went out for track and basketball in high school and got scholastic scholarships to good universities. Louise didn't finish college, and she didn't like any sport; she met Carson and lost interest in finishing school. They both dropped out. She never was adventurous, but in the two years she and Carson dated, she almost stopped driving and gave up her cashiering job, becoming more isolated. She adored Carson and spent every possible minute with him. Linda and I used to snicker over the way she waited on him and how every sentence she spoke started with 'Carson said' . . . or 'Carson wants' . . ."

"Grief and guilt push people into doing uncharacteristic things sometimes."

Lapsing into silence, they watched people gathering where the trail ended below. Without anyone saying the words, Kallene knew their search had been as fruitless as her own. Most of the searchers rested a few minutes before beginning their return trek down the canyon.

The day was warm for late October, and with the sun beating down on her back, Kallene took off her jacket and wrapped the sleeves around her waist. Removing her water bottle from its holder at her waist, she took a long swallow. Noticing Jon didn't have a water bottle, she asked, "Would you like a drink?" She held out the bottle to him.

He nodded and accepted her offer. "I brought boots but didn't collect the rest of my gear before leaving San Diego. I was so upset that after Dad called, I threw stuff in my car without giving it much thought and drove straight to the airport, where I was lucky enough to catch a flight into Salt Lake."

Kallene watched Jon's throat move as he drank from the bottle that moments earlier had touched her own lips. The gesture seemed oddly intimate. Jon was an attractive man, but it seemed out of place during the search for his missing sister to entertain such thoughts. She rose to her feet.

"Ready to move on?" Jon asked.

"Yes." She moved toward a stair-step of boulders that led from their lofty perch to the main trail below. She stopped as she saw three familiar figures who arrived at the trail end below. "I thought children under eighteen wouldn't be allowed to join the search."

"A couple of Scout troops offered to help. They and their leaders were given some of the flatter areas to cover where the Scoutmasters could keep an eye on the boys."

"There's a boy down there who's in my Cub Scout pack. He's with his parents, but he's only eight."

Jon shrugged. "Someone must have made an exception since he's with his parents."

Jon stood beside her, and his gaze followed hers. "They don't look like they're together; they seem to be sitting as far apart as they can get."

"They're not very affectionate. To be honest, I don't think I've ever seen all three of them together in one place before. Parker, the boy in my Cub Scout den, has few friends and receives little attention from his parents, who both have demanding careers. His parents just don't seem like the type who would volunteer to search for someone they barely know." Kallene was angry with herself for almost saying "they barely *knew*." She lowered herself to the next rock.

"This sort of thing brings out the best in a lot of people." Jon followed her down the randomly spaced rocks and ledges that formed a giant staircase.

When they reached the trail, the Graysons were gone. Kallene indicated the well-worn trail, and Jon followed.

"In some of the research I did, I learned that other searches have found it helpful for searchers to take a different return route," he said.

The sun disappeared behind clouds, and a cold breeze swept down the canyon before they reached the staging area. Kallene pulled her jacket back on, and they walked faster to ward off the chill.

Kallene's mood matched the gloomy weather. "I don't think anyone found anything," she said before they reached the end of their search.

"I would have been surprised if they had," Jon responded in a neutral voice. His slumped shoulders told another story. He was disappointed and discouraged. After spending more than six hours with him, she knew him well enough to know Linda's disappearance was causing him a great deal of pain.

"What are you going to do now?" she asked.

"The police search will go on, and there may be some clues when the lab report comes back. Dad said he and Mom were going to spend the day calling all of the friends and relatives they could locate to see if there's any possibility any of them have heard from her."

"Scott told me yesterday that the police department would do another house-by-house canvas of the neighborhood to see if any of the neighbors saw or heard anything unusual."

The church parking lot was teeming with people. In addition to the two police department trailers, a large television station truck was parked at one end, and a catering truck was dispensing drinks and sandwiches to weary searchers who were sprawled on the lawn or sitting on the curb.

A pretty, young reporter hurried toward them with a microphone. Jon stopped and, taking Kallene by the arm, whispered, "I can't dodge reporters. Their help is needed. But if you hurry, you can avoid this one. My parents want to meet you. Could I bring them over to your house later or meet you somewhere?"

"My house will be fine. I'll be working at home the rest of the day. I gave your dad my address, and they've been to your sister's house before, so they shouldn't have any trouble finding mine."

"Mr. Pierson," the reporter called when she'd almost reached them.

"I'd better go." Kallene slipped behind a row of parked cars and began edging toward the far side of the parking lot. She had no desire to be on television.

"Kallene, wait a moment." She'd just reached the sidewalk, and all she wanted to do was go home and take a shower. Looking over her shoulder, she saw Scott hurrying toward her. She stood still and he stopped beside her.

"Is there any news?" she asked before he could speak. She looked into his face and felt a pang of sympathy. He looked as tired as she felt.

"No, nothing conclusive, but I wanted to warn you, our office ran some checks on people in your neighborhood and came up with some information that might or might not have a bearing on this case. Not long ago one of your neighbors was released on a legal technicality from prison in another state, where he was serving a life sentence for rape and homicide. Until we have more information, though, I can't release his name—it should be posted on our sex offender list before too long. He may be harmless, but you can never be too careful."

CHAPTER SEVEN

THE THREE-HOUR MEETING BLOCK THE next day seemed to drag. No matter how hard she tried, Kallene couldn't concentrate on the speakers or teachers. Her mind kept going back to Scott's bombshell warning. He wouldn't tell her which neighbor was an ex-con—only that he'd failed to register as a sex offender when he arrived in Utah, which meant she couldn't even look up his name. She tried not to speculate, but that was difficult. An uneasy glance around left her feeling chagrined. Church attendance was no guarantee of anyone's innocence, and though the young fathers carrying screaming infants to the foyer or scooping up spilled cereal wasn't a positive indicator of innocence, it seemed unlikely that any of them attending church with their wives and children could be guilty of a heinous crime. The fact that some of her neighbors didn't attend church and weren't friendly didn't automatically make them suspect.

She didn't want to think of Linda in terms of a possible victim to a sexual predator. She couldn't believe Carson could be the murderer. It was hard to accept the general assumption that Linda was dead, but with the passage of each day, it was becoming impossible to remain hopeful that she was alive.

Glancing at her watch for the fortieth time, she tried once more to turn her attention to the points the Relief Society teacher was making. Sister Conley wasn't the best teacher, but Kallene usually gleaned something from her lessons. Today, though, she'd have a hard time even recalling which lesson the teacher gave. When the meeting ended, she meant to make a quick dash for home, but several women in the ward stopped her to ask if there was any news of Linda. A few voiced their suspicion that Linda's husband knew more than he was admitting.

When she got home, she checked the roast in the Crock-Pot then hurried to set the table. She and the Piersons had spoken on the phone the previous evening, and they had agreed that meeting at her home for dinner after church would be the best time to get together. Removing four of her best plates from her china hutch, she placed one on each place mat she'd set at one end of the long table in her dining room. She was setting napkins in place when the doorbell rang. Her guests had arrived.

"Come on in. I'm Kallene Ashton, and you couldn't be anyone but Linda and Jon's parents." She welcomed the older couple who stood with Jon on her doorstep. She was amazed at how Jon and Linda resembled their father, Adam, while their long-lashed eyes were clearly inherited from their mother, Janet.

"Hello, Kallene. It's really kind of you to invite us for dinner." Janet stepped forward and shook her hand. Her husband repeated the gesture.

"It's nothing fancy, just a Sunday Crock-Pot roast."

"It smells wonderful," Jon said as she ushered them toward the dining room.

"Your home is lovely," Janet complimented. "Linda told us you're an artist and that your home reflects your artistic taste."

"Thank you. I'm actually a graphic artist, and I do ads for various products. Most of my work is done by computer and involves sketches and photography. I like working with color and design. I've never studied interior design, but I have strong ideas on what I like and dislike."

"She paints, too. I caught her signature on that great landscape in the living room." Jon grinned at her, and she hurried to the kitchen to hide her flushed face and to dish up their meal. The compliments pleased her and started dinner on a pleasant note.

Kallene hadn't expected to feel so comfortable with Jon's parents. Perhaps because of her friendship with Linda, they seemed like old friends. She'd expected some awkwardness entertaining Jon in her home, but the easy relationship they'd established the day before continued, and she couldn't help hoping they would have further opportunities to become better acquainted.

They avoided speaking of Linda while eating, but as soon as dessert plates were cleared away, Jon said, "We need to get out posters with Linda's picture and build up a better web presence to get people looking for her."

"What good will that do?" Janet's voice was filled with emotion. "Nothing we do is going to bring her back. We should be concentrating on getting custody of Macie. We haven't even seen her since Easter, when we made a quick two-day trip out here."

"Surely Carson wouldn't refuse to let you see your granddaughter!" Kallene said. Carson might be difficult, but she couldn't imagine him preventing Linda's family from seeing Macie.

"We don't know where he is," Adam explained. "He's not staying at his house. He hasn't been there since the police took him downtown for questioning."

"They didn't keep him, did they?"

"No, but he didn't return to the house," Jon pointed out. "And the police won't give us any information. They haven't charged him, so he could be anywhere now, even in another state. And he wouldn't dream of using a cell phone."

"I saw him on TV after he left the police station two nights ago, getting into an old pickup truck. He told me his father was coming to help him with Macie, and they'd be staying at a hotel until the police finish searching his house." After a moment, Kallene turned to Jon. "If you have a photo of Linda, I can design a poster and run it off tomorrow at my office."

"I just can't see how any of this is going to help." Janet wiped at her eyes, and Adam placed an arm around her shoulders.

"I'm sorry, Mom." Jon leaned forward to touch his mother's hand that rested on the table. "Whether Linda is alive or not, we have to know what happened to her. The more ways we can get her name and face before the public, the better our chances will be that someone will remember something that could help."

"He's right, dear." Adam gave his wife's shoulder a reassuring squeeze. "We need to move quickly, too, before people have time to forget important details that may seem insignificant. Until we know what happened to our daughter, we won't get anywhere with a petition to claim our granddaughter."

"Then we might as well get started." Janet rose to her feet, and the others followed. She retrieved her purse from the front room and handed Kallene a photo she took from her wallet. Kallene felt a twinge of pain as she looked at her friend's face. It had been less than a week since she'd last been with her, but in many ways it seemed like a lifetime ago. Something cold settled in her heart, confirming what she'd been denying from the start. Something terrible had happened to Linda, and she wasn't coming back.

* * *

With a thick quilt wrapped around her shoulders, Kallene sat on her deck. The nights were getting cooler, and it was already time to cover the deck furniture and put it away until spring. She'd always found something both restful and mind-clearing about sitting beneath an open night sky watching the stars appear one by one. She wrapped her hands around the mug of hot chocolate she'd carried to the deck and appreciated the warmth it gave her fingers. Lifting her face skyward, she marveled at the beauty and majesty of the night sky.

Thoughts of Linda intruded, and she found herself reviewing the things she and Jon's family had accomplished that afternoon. She was pleased with the flyer she'd designed, and she agreed that both the website and the message-board appeals Jon had set up were a good idea.

She wished there were something more she could do. In a way, she wished Carson had left Macie in her care. Though the little girl made working difficult, she missed the tiny girl's demands on her time and attention. She missed her infectious smiles and her little hands patting her cheeks, too. She loved her work, but more and more she found herself wanting to be a wife and mother.

She leaned back, closing her eyes while admitting to herself that she was tired and should go to bed. Linda was gone, possibly murdered. It still didn't seem real. Tears escaped to run down her cheeks. She swiped at them; she wasn't a crier. Maybe it was real, and she was just having a hard time facing it. Grief swelled in her heart, and she couldn't stop crying.

A faint scraping noise brought her head up. She wasn't sure when the sound began, but she felt she'd been hearing it for several minutes. It came again. Using a corner of the quilt, she wiped her face and rubbed her eyes. Had a shadow moved in the Haneys' backyard? She strained for a better view. She didn't remember being able to see into the neighboring yard so clearly before. A cold wind had come up, and the sound was probably just a branch, pushed by the wind, scraping against the fence.

She almost stood then thought better of it. If a burglar *was* prowling around the neighborhood, she didn't want him to see her. The detective's words came back to her. The prowler might be someone much more dangerous than a house burglar.

Gathering up her quilt and crouching low, she made her way to the door leading into the house. With trembling fingers, she pressed the lock before making certain the rod that kept the door from sliding open was in place. She checked the alarm system and set it before retiring to her bedroom. It was a long time before she fell asleep.

* * *

Kallene was up early Monday morning. She pulled on her sweats and scraped her hair back with a wide band that covered her ears. Before leaving the house, she drew on a pair of thin nylon gloves that fit snugly and left her hands feeling unencumbered. Even on chilly mornings, it was only her ears and fingers that got cold.

It was still dark out, and she hesitated over which route to take. With a sigh of resignation, she turned toward the high-school track. It wasn't as enjoyable as the canyon trails, but for someone running alone, it was safer.

She nodded to several runners she recognized as she looped around the oval track. She might have imagined it, but it seemed to her that the track was more crowded that morning than usual. She supposed she wasn't the only one who had become nervous after Linda's disappearance, though she'd disappeared before their run even began.

"Running on a track is a pain." A runner caught up to her. She turned her head and wasn't completely surprised to see Darnell. He seemed to appear everywhere she went. An unwelcome thought entered her head. Could Darnell be the ex-con Scott had warned her about? As far as she knew, Darnell didn't live in her neighborhood, but he ran in the canyon and worked for the company that built the subdivision, so it stood to reason he didn't live far away. He did handyman chores in the area, too, so he must live nearby. She gave a nervous glance around. At least a dozen runners were on the track, and the high-school cheerleaders with their adviser were holding a practice in front of the grandstand. Off to the far side of the track, a maintenance worker was mowing grass. Not even a criminal would attempt to harm her with so many witnesses around. She relaxed a little and at the same time increased her speed. Darnell kept pace with her. He was a far better runner than she'd expected.

"You're good," he complimented her. "Those lovely, long legs are good for more than being a pleasure to look at."

She gritted her teeth and attempted to ignore him. He didn't seem to notice. "How about running with me tomorrow? We could give the canyon loop one last shot for the season," he invited.

"No, thanks. I'm planning to run here until I can find a gym with an indoor track." She didn't relish bumping into Darnell every morning, but that would be better than being accosted while she was running one of the lonely stretches in the canyon.

"Well, if you decide you want to branch out, I'll be around. I've dreamed for a long time of having you . . . for a running partner." She didn't appreciate the slight pause he made after "having you."

If she increased her speed, he did, too. If she slowed, he followed her lead. Deciding she couldn't shake him, she veered off to the side.

"Quitting already?"

"Yes, I've got a lot of work to do today."

"I've got my truck. I'll give you a ride."

"No, thanks!" She cut across the grass. The last thing she wanted was a ride in Darnell's truck. As she left the grass and stepped onto the sidewalk, she found herself glancing over her shoulder to assure herself Darnell wasn't following. She hoped she could find a good indoor track soon.

* * *

Kallene entered her house and headed straight for the shower. She'd meant to arrive early at her office, but now she'd have to hurry to be there by nine. Standing under the hot spray, she remembered the events of the previous night. Had the sounds she'd heard and the shadow she thought she saw been her imagination? Or had they been the vandal who'd torn up Mr. Haney's roses? Maybe the vandal was Darnell. He seemed to be everywhere she turned and the only one she could think of who might steal garden tools. Had he returned to cause more mischief? Should she mention the incident to Scott? But she hadn't actually seen anything, had she? She'd feel silly calling him back and saying she'd heard something scratching on the other side of her fence and a shadow might have moved. And just because she didn't like Darnell Gines didn't mean there was any evidence to back up her suspicions.

She switched off the water and reached for her towel. She was becoming paranoid. It was time to concentrate on work and forget how much Darnell annoyed her. She was meeting Jon later to put up posters. It was a task she wished wasn't necessary, but she was glad she'd have another chance to spend time with Jon. Linda's brother stirred something inside her unlike anything she'd experienced with other men she'd dated.

* * *

"I think that's all for today." Jon picked up the flyers and the supplies they'd been using to post the flyers on fences and poles. They'd taped the flyers to store windows and bulletin boards all across the city as well. "Let's stop for something to eat, then I'll drop you off at your house." He set the supplies in the back of the SUV he'd leased for the time he'd be in Utah.

"Sure," Kallene agreed, though she was so tired, she wasn't certain she had enough energy left to eat dinner. She and Jon had been putting up posters for almost a week as had Jon's parents. She'd spoken with Scott several times as well. He'd assured her that the posters and flyers were a good idea and that the police department had received several hundred calls. So far none of the calls had resulted in any productive leads, but Scott felt certain one of those calls would eventually bring the break they needed in the case. Though both Scott and Jon were optimistic they'd get the lead they needed, Kallene felt discouraged. How could a grown woman just vanish as Linda seemed to have done?

"Where would you like to eat?" Jon asked as he started the SUV.

"There's a Burger Barn just across the street. I'm too tired and grubby for anywhere but a burger joint."

"Okay, but I promise that when this is over, I'll take you to the classiest restaurant in town."

"Do you think this will ever be over?" she asked in a subdued voice. It had been almost three weeks since Linda disappeared, and no one seemed to know any more now than they'd known at the beginning of their search.

They went through the drive-through then parked at the back of the small parking lot to eat their burgers. A large weeping willow hung over their parking spot, sheltering their eyes from the fiery glow of the setting sun. Neither seemed inclined to talk until their fast food supper was nearly finished.

"How soon do you have to return to work?" Kallene asked. Jon and his parents had arrived just over two weeks ago. She was well aware most people couldn't afford to take off work indefinitely. Adam was retired, but she wasn't certain about any limits Jon might face. She'd been working mostly from home, starting early and stopping around two to help Jon with the posters.

"There's no hurry," Jon said. "I'm pretty caught up on my work, and if something important comes up, I can work from anywhere. In that respect, your work as a graphic designer and mine as an architect are a lot alike."

"Sometimes I have to meet with clients or with other members of my design team, attend photo shoots, or put in an appearance at meetings."

"I do, too, but I asked my partners to take any new clients for a while. If something comes up that I need to return to the office for, I can be there in a few hours. Right now, nothing else is as important as finding Linda."

"Maybe I'm just tired, but right now I'm feeling discouraged. Do you really think she is going to be found?" She reached through the open window beside her and stripped the last lingering leaves from the willow branch that hung near the window. Absently, she shredded the leaves between her fingers.

"I doubt we'll find her alive after this long," Jon admitted. His voice hardened. "But I want to see Carson punished for her death, and I want her body recovered. My mother needs the closure of a proper funeral." He started the engine.

"I think you do, too. And your father. It's not too long ago they went through this with Louise." Kallene's voice was whisper-soft. She missed Linda. Their friendship had been one of those special, rare relationships that only comes along once or twice in a lifetime. They had both been a long way from family and the friends they'd grown up with and had each found something in the other that filled a deep need.

"I suppose I do." His hand left the wheel and settled over hers for a comforting moment.

When he pulled into her driveway and cut the engine, she considered inviting him in, but before she could speak, he asked, "Where are you running now?"

"The high-school track."

"Would you mind if I join you in the morning? The hotel has a great weight room, but I'd rather run."

"Sure. That would be great." She meant it. She was tired of the sameness of the school track and looked forward to having a running partner to talk with. The fact that it was Jon offering to run with her made the prospect that much better.

"I'll pick you up at six." He smiled and was out of the SUV to open her door before she could say anything more. He held out his hand to help her alight, a gesture that made her want to giggle. She wasn't exactly a helpless damsel, and their being together wasn't a date, but it was a nice gesture anyway. He kept her hand in his as he walked her to the door.

After unlocking her door, she turned to say good night and found him standing much closer than she expected. A flutter like butterfly wings between her ribs left her feeling light headed. She felt an urge to lean closer, and she wondered if he would kiss her if she did. His head moved toward hers.

The sound of an approaching car broke the spell. Jon straightened. "I'll see you in the morning." He turned toward his SUV.

Kallene turned the dead bolt and hurried to shut off the alarm before pulling off her jacket and sinking down on a kitchen chair. Did Jon almost kiss her? Did she want him to kiss her? She didn't know if the quick affinity she seemed to share with him was real or if it was just the product of their shared grief and concern for his sister. Maybe she was just one of those silly women who hadn't had a real boyfriend for so long that she imagined romance where there was none.

The ringing of the door chimes startled her. *Perhaps Jon forgot something.* Peering through the small window set in the door, she found Scott standing on her front porch.

She released the dead bolt and opened the door.

"Hi!"

"Hi, yourself." The detective grinned, looking a little sheepish. "Mind if I come in?"

"Oh, no." She stepped back, ushering him to enter. "Have a seat." She gestured toward the sofa. He sat down, and she took the chair across from him.

"This isn't an official visit, but you've been concerned from the start, and I thought I should let you know."

"Know what?" She leaned forward.

"We got the results back from all of the lab tests on the Longdale home and car. There's nothing that raises any alarms."

"There must be something. Linda couldn't just vanish."

"We're not giving up." He sounded slightly defensive. "Someone is going to remember something or discover a bit of evidence."

Kallene felt a stab of guilt. "I didn't mean to sound critical. I've just become so discouraged."

"That's understandable. Losing a good friend is never easy, and I've seen how you've thrown yourself into the search for Linda Longdale." He paused and pulled at his tie. "There's one more thing I wanted to talk to you about."

"Would you like to go out on the deck? The house seems a little stuffy to me."

"Yes, that sounds great." He stood to follow her to the deck.

When they were both seated again, Scott looked around, admiring the view as city lights twinkled to life below. "Quite a view!"

"It was the major selling point when I looked at this property." Kallene sighed and leaned back on the padded deck chair. It would be so easy just to drift to sleep.

"One of your neighbors called me today to report she'd seen a U-Haul truck in the Longdale driveway this afternoon."

"What?" Her eyes jerked open, and she leaned forward.

"There's absolutely no evidence we can hold Carson on. We may consider him a person of interest, but without any evidence to back up a charge, there's nothing we can do. He can take his daughter and leave the state at will."

"What about the job that was so important to him?" She couldn't keep the bitterness out of her voice.

"The company let him go. I spoke with his boss, who said keeping Carson wasn't doing their company's image any good."

"That hardly seems fair." Scott gave her an odd look. "I'm not defending him," she was quick to add. "It just seems to be contrary to all that until-proven-guilty stuff I've been taught all my life. If there's no reason to keep him in jail, then he should be able to work to support himself and his daughter."

"I have to agree with you, but I've learned over the years that life doesn't always live up to the lofty standards of justice it ought to. I've got a feeling that whatever happened to your friend wasn't just or fair either."

"Is Carson going back to California with his dad?" The prospect of never seeing Macie again troubled her.

"That's our assumption, but I plan to do a little discreet checking to make certain he doesn't just disappear." Scott's voice was terse, and he sounded angry enough that Kallene suspected her friend's case had become personal to the detective.

"Is there any possibility Janet Pierson can see her granddaughter before Carson takes her away?" Kallene stood and walked to the rail.

Scott stood also, joining her at the rail overlooking the Haneys' yard. He stood so close his shoulder brushed hers.

"My heart goes out to that woman, but there's nothing I can do officially. The U-Haul truck is still parked in the driveway, so he hasn't left yet. If I were you, I'd suggest to Mrs. Pierson that she leave her husband and son behind tomorrow and spend the day with you. When there's some activity at the house, the two of you might wander down there. He might be more cooperative if the request for a visit comes directly from Macie's grandmother without any threatening backup from Adam and Jon."

"Jon and Adam wouldn't threaten Carson!"

"Not intentionally, but they're both large men and they're angry. Neither has made a secret of their conviction Carson is responsible for his wife's disappearance. I think it would be wise to keep some distance between Carson and the Pierson men."

"I don't understand why Carson isn't more concerned about Linda's disappearance. They've been married three years, and he knew her for several years before that. He knows she wouldn't simply run out on him or their daughter." Her hands moved restlessly on the rail in front of her.

Scott slipped a hand over one of hers as though he meant to comfort her. "I'm not convinced he ever really knew his wife at all. When I talked with him, I got the impression he has her mixed up in his mind with her sister, and unraveling the two is more than he can emotionally deal with."

Kallene let the words sink in bit by bit. They made sense in a way. Carson had loved Louise, and Linda had confided her suspicion he'd never gotten over his first love. Was it possible Carson had substituted Linda for Louise because they looked alike and had closed his mind to their real differences? Had Linda's request for a divorce dissolved Carson's fantasy, releasing a storm of anger and grief? She couldn't help wondering if loss and disappointment had pushed him over the edge.

"I'll call Janet Pierson first thing in the morning," she promised.

Scott didn't release her hand, and she made no movement to pull away. A large harvest moon shined down in all its brilliance. Above, uncountable stars created a panorama of lights across the night sky. The only unnatural light was the one over the Haneys' back door.

That's odd. All summer she'd enjoyed her deck but had never had such a clear view of her neighbors' backyard. Suddenly she knew what was different.

"The roses! They're gone."

"Roses?" Scott appeared puzzled by her sudden outburst.

"Sorry," she apologized. "I haven't spent much time on my deck during the past few weeks, but I came out here the night after Linda disappeared. I couldn't sleep, so I wrapped up in a quilt and sat out here for a long time. I kept thinking something was different, and I just now realized what that difference is."

"The roses?"

"Yes. There was a thick hedge of rosebushes that reached several feet higher than the fence. They're gone. I know someone pulled them out, but I thought Delbert Haney had replanted them."

"I think Mr. Haney moved his roses to the other side of his yard."

"Those flower beds look kind of odd, almost like—"

"Graves," Scott finished for her. She winced when he said the word aloud. "The similarity occurred to me when I was in his yard a few weeks ago. While I was contacting the neighbors on this street, he told me about someone stealing a few things from his shed and insisted I see how he'd had to move his roses to the other side of his yard."

"You don't really think—?"

"No. I ran a check on him and he's clean. He's filed a few nuisance complaints against neighbors over the years, but he's never been in any kind of trouble. Besides, he's eighty years old and not in the best of health. From what I've learned about your friend, she could have held her own against someone like him."

"Could someone else have buried a body there?"

"Not likely, but if it will make you feel better, I'll have someone bring a cadaver dog by."

She was about to ask if the missing tools had been found when the Haneys' back door opened, and Delbert Haney stepped out onto his patio. He settled himself in a chair and turned toward them. Kallene couldn't be sure if he could see her and Scott on her deck, but something about the way his attention seemed to be directed toward her made her uncomfortable. Delbert sat beneath a strong porch light while she hadn't turned on an outside light, yet she still felt she was being scrutinized.

Moving her hand from under Scott's, she turned toward the door. He followed her without speaking until they were back in her house. She locked and barred the door before drawing a curtain across the sliding doors.

"Have a seat." She indicated a small sofa and several chairs in the small sitting room. He declined the invitation but issued one of his own. "I have tickets for the Jazz opener. Will you have dinner and go to the game with me Saturday night?"

"I'd love to." She felt like breaking into a childish happy dance. She was pretty certain Scott liked her, but she hadn't dared hope he'd ask her out on a real date.

"Good. I'll pick you up at five, if that's okay." She nodded her head, and he added, "I'd better be going now."

"Thank you for letting me know about Carson and Macie." Her own words broke the spell that had momentarily surrounded her at his invitation, reminding her of the loss that had dominated her thoughts and emotions for three weeks. She watched him until his car pulled out of her driveway. As his tail lights disappeared down the street, she felt a chill. Stepping back inside, she closed the door and locked it. Leaning back against the closed door, she thought, *In the spring, I'll plant bushes on my side of the fence.*

CHAPTER EIGHT

JANET ARRIVED WITHIN HALF AN hour of Kallene's call.

"Adam wasn't happy about my coming here alone," Janet said with a sigh as the two women lingered over cups of warm chocolate. They sat on Kallene's front porch bundled in heavy coats. They'd chosen the front porch as a place to watch for activity at Linda's house, which was far enough away they couldn't see details, but they could tell the U-Haul was still parked in the driveway. So far they'd seen no activity.

"The forecast is for freezing temperatures tonight and snow by the weekend." Kallene pulled her coat tighter. "Perhaps we should wait inside and just take turns going outside to check."

"But what if we miss them?"

"We won't. Carson's father's truck just pulled up in front of their house."

"Let's go." Janet rose to her feet. She squinted, trying to get a better view of the far end of the street.

Janet's steps made a sharp staccato beat as she marched down the street. She looked as though she expected the battle of a lifetime. Kallene hoped Carson wouldn't see them coming and leave.

"Janet," Kallene said, "remember we have to be careful. No matter what we may suspect about Linda's disappearance, the police found no evidence Carson had anything to do with Linda's disappearance. He has every legal right to Macie and to take her to another state. You're going to have to calm down. If you anger Carson, he can keep you from Macie permanently."

"You're right." Janet took a deep breath. "I promise I'll keep this about Macie. I just need to be sure she's being cared for properly."

"Two men probably aren't caring for her the way Linda always did, but Carson loves her, and I'm sure he's doing the best he can."

"I'll try to remember that."

They reached the Longdale home in time to see Carson and his father carrying a sofa from the house. They placed it in the U-Haul, and as Carson stepped back onto the sidewalk, he noticed the two women.

"What are you doing here?" He glanced toward the house then gave the women a suspicious look. His father hurried into the house.

"Carson, I want to see my granddaughter."

"You're not taking Macie. She's all I have left." Carson assumed a belligerent stance.

"I have no intention of taking her, but please don't cut off the only part of my girls I have left. I need to see Macie grow and be happy. My daughters are both gone; can't you share Macie just a little?"

Kallene ached for Janet as she pleaded with her daughter's husband. She remained quiet, feeling uncertain whether adding her pleas to Janet's would help or hurt Janet's cause.

Carson, for once, appeared uncertain. "She's in the house. You can go in." He looked around as though making certain they were alone then followed them inside. They heard Macie before they saw her.

"No! Nonono," she screamed.

"Come on, Princess, just try one." The old man's voice sounded tired. Macie began to scream in earnest.

Janet scurried into the kitchen with Kallene and Carson right behind her. Kallene was relieved to see the baby was securely strapped in her chair. She struggled to hide a smirk when she saw the old man trying to persuade Macie to eat the bits of dry cereal scattered across her tray. Janet hurried forward, and Kallene winced at the sound of cereal crunching underfoot. Kallene followed more slowly.

"Mama!" Macie stopped in midscream. Ignoring her grandmother, she held out her arms to Kallene. Kallene unclasped the harness that confined the baby to her chair and lifted her into her arms. "Mama!" Little hands patted Kallene's cheeks, and she snuggled her head into the curve of Kallene's neck.

"She calls you mama?" Carson sounded angry.

"Macie knows Kallene isn't her mother. She only associates her with her mother because Linda and Kallene were together so much. Sometimes children Macie's age call all women Mama and all men Dada." Janet answered before Kallene could think how to answer.

"Better put her back in her chair. She hasn't eaten any breakfast yet," Carson's gray-haired father said.

Kallene's lips twisted in a wry smile. "Macie won't eat that cereal no matter how hard you try to persuade her. The cold cereal is Linda's. This little girl is like her daddy: she expects a cooked breakfast. She will make an exception for cookies, though."

"I'll be danged!" The old man chuckled. "And here I thought she might get sick eating my flapjacks and bacon."

"Bacon?" Janet said.

Kallene nudged Janet, hoping she'd get the message to not make an issue over Carson's father feeding her granddaughter bacon. Janet nearly choked, but she didn't pursue the subject. Instead she offered to watch Macie while the two men loaded the truck.

"I don't know." Carson looked around as though he expected trouble.

"Carson, she's hungry," Kallene pointed out. "Let me take her to my house where she'll be warm. I can feed her, and she'll have a chance to spend time with her grandmother."

When he didn't answer, she continued. "If you don't trust me, I can go fix her some breakfast and bring it here, then her grandmother and I can play with her in her room and keep her from getting in your way."

"The utilities are already turned off, and we've checked out of the hotel." He seemed to be thinking aloud. A gust of wind swept through the open door. He came to a decision. "So long as you don't take her anywhere but to your house." He turned to his mother-in-law. "Don't talk about her mother or me. And don't think that once you get her to Kallene's house, Adam and Jon can take off with her. We'll only be a couple more hours, and when we get through, she's going with me."

"Thank you, Carson. I promise we'll do nothing to interfere with your right to raise your daughter. When she's older, I hope you'll trust us enough to let her come visit us during her vacations from school."

Kallene knew it wasn't easy for Janet to acquiesce to Carson's demands or refrain from saying anything in her own defense.

They walked quickly with Macie clinging to Kallene's neck, but rain was pelting them before they reached her house. They hurried inside where Macie squirmed to get down. Once on the floor, she scurried toward the drawer where Kallene kept her plastic containers. She flung them about the room with happy abandon.

Janet wiped away a tear. "She's so much like her mother was at this age."

"It must have kept you busy trying to keep up with two like her."

Janet laughed and Kallene joined her. Soon Janet was sitting on the floor beside her granddaughter building towers for Macie to knock down while Kallene prepared French toast for the baby.

Macie insisted on feeding herself, which resulted in every surface within her reach being liberally smeared with maple syrup. When she finished eating, Janet took her to the bathroom to clean her up while Kallene wiped up the kitchen. When they returned to the living room, Janet pulled a small cloth doll from her purse and offered it to Macie. Macie squealed and hugged it to her.

"Be-be," she said.

Kallene seated herself on a chair, leaving entertaining Macie to her grandmother. After a few minutes, she ran upstairs to retrieve her camera. She snapped several pictures of Janet and Macie. She'd make prints for Janet to keep. Perhaps she'd give copies to Carson to give to Macie someday.

Both the older woman and the toddler were absorbed in their play when a knock sounded on the door, followed by the peal of the doorbell. She felt something twist in her heart to see Janet slowly rise to her feet, a stricken look on her face. The older woman picked up Macie, holding her in her arms while the little girl continued to cuddle and sing to the doll, oblivious to the emotions playing across her grandmother's face.

"Da-da!" Macie shouted when Kallene opened the door to reveal Carson waiting impatiently on the porch. He pushed past Kallene to pull the little girl from Janet's arms. Kallene sensed Janet was fighting an impulse to hold the child tighter rather than let her go.

"See!" Macie thrust the doll in her father's face. "Be-be."

"Give it back." Carson attempted to remove the doll from his daughter's grasp and return it to Janet.

"No!" Macie hugged the doll tighter and glared at her father.

"It's hers. I made it for her," Janet said in a soft voice. "It might help to keep her entertained on your trip."

Carson glowered but made no further attempt to take the doll from his daughter. He turned toward the door.

"Just a moment." Kallene reached out to touch his arm. "I care about Macie, too, and I'm going to miss her." She stepped closer and leaned forward to kiss the baby's cheek. Janet did the same.

"Bye, sweetheart," Janet whispered in a choked voice.

"Bye-bye." Macie waved with one hand, the doll clutched in the other, as Carson walked out the door and bolted toward the U-Haul now parked in front of Kallene's house. The beat-up pickup truck idled behind the bigger truck. They watched Carson strap Macie into her car seat that had been set in the U-Haul truck cab.

The two women stood in the open doorway until the trucks were out of sight. Several minutes passed before either spoke.

"Will I ever see her again?" Janet sank onto a nearby chair, and the tears she'd struggled to keep at bay streamed down her face.

Sinking to her knees beside the chair, Kallene took Janet's hands in her own. "Perhaps you should lie down for a while. Let me show you to the guest room."

"No, I promised I'd call Adam when I was ready to return to the hotel. He'll be pacing the floor by now."

"All right. You can use the phone in the kitchen when you're ready."

No more than twenty minutes passed before Kallene heard a car pull into the driveway. Janet rushed into her husband's arms. When she tried to speak, only sobs came out. Adam held his wife, patting her back and whispering quiet words in her ear.

Kallene was glad to see Jon had accompanied his father. He looked at her and seemed about to explode. "What happened? Did Carson refuse to let her see Macie? Is Macie hurt or neglected?"

Kallene wiped away a few tears of her own. "We both saw Macie, and Carson let us bring her here for a little more than an hour. She's fine. It was just hard for your mother to tell her only granddaughter good-bye without any assurance that she'd ever see her again."

"How can he be so selfish and unfeeling? It's not right to keep Mom from seeing Macie or even knowing how to contact her!" Jon clenched his fists. "Why didn't you tell me? I would've . . ."

"That's why I didn't tell you. Carson is scared. He knows everyone assumes he killed Linda. I don't know if he still thinks she's playing some cruel trick on him, but he's been questioned extensively by the police, and he's terrified someone will try to take Macie from him. If you had been with us, there's no way he would have let your mother have that one precious hour with her granddaughter."

It took considerable effort, but Jon relaxed his angry stance. "I suppose you're right, but I can't understand why the police are letting him leave the state and take a helpless child with him."

"The police can't hold him or charge him without any evidence that suggests he's done something wrong, but you can be sure he isn't going to just disappear," Adam said. "The detective assured me there's no way he can keep his destination a secret."

"Thank you." Janet reached for Kallene and gave her a hug. "You don't know what it means to me to have this memory of little Macie to help me through losing a second daughter."

"I'm glad it worked out and that I got to see her, too. Because of my friendship with Linda, Macie has been part of my life since she was six months old. I'm going to miss her." She swallowed hard and dabbed at her eyes. "What will you do now? Will you be going back to Baltimore?" Kallene returned Janet's hug and wished she could do more for her.

Janet looked at Adam, who nodded his head. "Yes, we'll be going home in the next few days—tomorrow if we can get a flight. There's really nothing more we can do here, but we'd like to stay in touch with you. Even though the police have promised to keep us informed and let us know if there are any breaks in the case, we'd still like to hear from you if you hear anything about Linda—or Macie."

Kallene promised she'd contact them if she heard anything. She wondered if Jon would be leaving, too, but he lingered behind as his parents made their way down the sidewalk to their rental car. They looked older and more tired than when they had arrived three weeks earlier. Kallene wiped away a tear as she watched the gentle way Adam seated Janet in the rental car and fussed with her seat belt before walking with stooped shoulders around the vehicle to take his place behind the wheel.

"Could I take you to dinner tonight?" Jon asked. The sudden question took her by surprise. "There's something I'd like to talk to you about."

Her voice failed her, and she simply nodded. Dinner dates two nights in a row with two different men? This would be a first for her.

CHAPTER NINE

Kallene wasn't certain what to wear for her date with Jon. Finally she decided on a tailored, gray wool skirt and a light sweater. She debated between dressy boots or heels. The heels won. It wasn't often she went out with someone tall enough that she felt comfortable in the stylish, stiletto heels she'd purchased on a whim several months earlier. When Jon arrived wearing a coat and tie, she was glad she'd dressed up.

"I hope you don't mind riding Trax." He gave her a wry smile. "I'm still trying to find my way around Salt Lake, and I'm hopeless at finding parking downtown."

"No problem. I hate finding parking downtown, too. I only drive back and forth to my office because parking is provided, and sometimes I have to meet with a client who isn't near a bus or train stop."

The bump and sway of the train proved to be fun and distracting from the worry and concerns of the past weeks. Dinner at the Garden Restaurant at the top of the Joseph Smith Building was all it was reputed to be, and since they were seated near the windows, she found looking out over the temple grounds peaceful and a much-needed rest from the past stressful weeks. She felt a moment's regret that the Christmas lights weren't on yet.

As if by agreement, they never mentioned Linda, Carson, or little Macie. Instead they talked about their shared passion for running and the different running events they'd each competed in.

"I haven't run a full marathon for several years," Kallene said. "I've found I enjoy the 5- and 10K runs more."

"I try to do a marathon at least once each year. I haven't had a lot of experiences with the shorter races, but I've been thinking of trying a 10K. I've heard that the Twenty-Fourth of July celebration here in Utah includes both a full marathon and a 10K. If I'm still here next summer, I think I'll register for one or the other."

"That's almost eight months away. Do you think you might still be here then?" Thinking of Jon still being in Utah the following summer gave Kallene a happy boost.

"That's something I want to talk to you about." He picked up his water tumbler, took a small sip, then twirled it by its stem a couple of times before returning the glass to its place on the table. "I'm a partner in an architectural firm two friends and I started five years ago. We've done well and have been thinking of branching out, maybe taking on another partner, but definitely hiring a couple more architects to work with us. I'll need to go back to San Diego soon, and I've been thinking of presenting a proposal to my partners that we open a permanent office here in Salt Lake."

"Wonderful! I think you'll enjoy it here. I certainly have until . . . I'm sorry. I wasn't going to mention anything about Linda."

"I know. I tell myself I need to get back to my own life." Jon closed his eyes for a moment. "It's hard to think of anything else. I lose myself in my work for an hour or two, then without warning her face, her baby, this whole sorry mess is back in my head, and I come close to doubling over with the pain of it all."

Kallene reached out to place her hand over his. They sat that way for several minutes, saying nothing but taking comfort from each other. Jon cleared his throat and reached for his glass, taking a deep swallow this time. "If my partners approve, I'll be looking for office space and an apartment over the next few months." He resumed their earlier conversation.

The possibility of Jon moving somewhere close by was the best news she'd heard in a long time. She liked him—a lot. And she looked forward to having a chance to learn whether their relationship might go beyond their shared search for Linda. They seemed to have a lot in common, and she was more comfortable with Jon than she'd been with any other man she'd ever dated.

"I have reservations to fly back to San Diego in the morning," he told her. "If all goes well, I'll be back in a week. I'll be bringing my own car and more of my belongings. When I get back, I plan to begin searching for an apartment that will double as a studio until I can find a building that can be turned into a branch of our firm."

They lingered over dinner, discussing Jon's plans for his business, and Kallene confided that she was working on a major promotion campaign for a client that would air on national television and would include layouts in six major magazines.

"How did you get into advertising?" Jon asked. "I noticed the landscape in your living room was painted by you. It's very good."

"I discovered in college that as much as I enjoy painting, I have an equal passion for other types of art. I like mixed media, and it's fun to dabble in caricatures. I really enjoy taking a concept and giving it a face. I know many people dismiss advertising as a lesser art form than oil painting, but I enjoy the challenge."

"I didn't mean to imply that advertising is less important or fulfilling—I just wondered why you chose that field."

"I didn't take your question as criticism of my career choice. I saw it as an opportunity to share with you my feelings for what I do. I don't often try to explain, but since you're an architect, which is also an art form in its own way, I felt you'd understand." She wiped her lips with her napkin and pushed the remainder of her dessert a few inches back. "I'm so full, I can't take another bite, which is almost unbelievable considering how much I love boysenberry pie."

Jon chuckled. "I understand. Both of my partners get excited over designing huge buildings, but I prefer designing homes. Office complexes and high-rises draw more public attention, but I like the feeling I get from designing living space to suit a particular family's lifestyle and dreams. As for dessert, I'm afraid I've met my limit, too. How about a slow stroll around Temple Square before we catch the train back?"

Oops! I should have worn the boots. She smiled and took the hand he held out to her. She wouldn't let four-inch heels prevent her from enjoying a stroll across the plaza and around the temple grounds with her hand in Jon's.

* * *

Kallene was tired from a couple of hours of rushed housework and the remainder of the day spent finishing up the project that was due Monday.

A small blister on her right toe didn't help any. No heels for her date with Scott! This time she chose dressy pants and a knit top. She tried several pairs of shoes before settling on a comfortable pair of slip-ons.

Scott arrived in a sporty, small pickup truck and was dressed casually. She couldn't help noticing how good he looked in designer jeans and a polo shirt.

At a small restaurant near the basketball arena, they joined a table of Scott's friends, most of whom were also police officers, some with dates and some without.

"This is Kallene." He made a general introduction. "These are my friends from work. I won't bother with running through all their names."

"Actually, he just doesn't want to embarrass himself by demonstrating his poor cognitive skills," a burly man with a blond crew cut said.

"Forget that loser and come sit by me." A tall, dark-haired man patted the vacant chair beside him.

A boyish young man with shaggy hair, a thin goatee, and a single earring glinting in one earlobe said, "Alexander always gets first dibs on the good-looking babes."

"Poor baby." One of the women leaned across her date to pat the boyish officer on the head. "You might be able to get a date if you didn't look like one of your own perps."

Scott found chairs for them, and Kallene found herself laughing and enjoying the banter and conversation that flew back and forth across the table. She also enjoyed the steak piled high with mushrooms and onions that a waitress set before her.

Following dinner, the entire group went to the arena for a basketball game and sat together in the upper balcony. Kallene had never taken an interest in professional sports, but she'd played enough high-school and rec basketball to understand the game. She soon found herself clapping and cheering along with the rowdiest fans each time the Jazz scored.

"Go, man!" Scott stomped his feet and broke into an improvised dance when Jazz player Gordon Hayward sank a three-pointer, sending Kallene into a fit of giggles. The camaraderie and laughter of Scott's friends were contagious. She laughed with them and discovered there was something healing in the laughter, a much-needed release from the pressures and sadness of the past weeks.

Scott clasped her hand and swung it between them as he walked her to the door later that night. A feeling of calm settled over her.

"I had a good time," she said.

"That bunch can be a little overwhelming." He sounded half apologetic.

"Your friends were fun, and I think I needed to laugh and let all the worry and pain go for a few hours."

"Most police officers feel that way. Sometimes our work is so intense, I think we might explode if we didn't release our tension by laughing too hard at crummy jokes or cheering too wildly at sporting events. Some people use alcohol the same way to release tension, but it's my opinion a rousing Jazz game burns up the adrenaline and releases tension better than anything else."

"It's certainly a good excuse to shout and scream until laughter turns to tears." She glanced sideways at him.

"Well, yeah. I guess I got a little carried away."

"I think I did, too."

"I think I'm getting carried away again." His arms went around her, and he pressed his lips against hers. She kissed him right back.

* * *

Sunday morning came much too soon. Ordinarily she liked the nine o'clock starting time for her ward's block of meetings, but she could have used another hour or two of sleep this morning. Kallene groaned as she stumbled out of bed and made her way to the shower. Not only did her toe still hurt, but her throat was raw from all the screaming she'd done the previous night. Still, a smile tilted her mouth when she looked in the mirror. She wouldn't trade the past two evenings for dates with anyone else in the whole world. Her date with Jon had been romantic; her date with Scott had been exhilarating. She couldn't help breathing a small sigh. How could she ever choose between two such men! A dose of practical reality brought her back to earth. Her relationships with the two men weren't anywhere near the "make a choice" stage. Long before that stage, either or both could decide to dump her.

The church was just a few blocks away, so Kallene slipped a light jacket over her dress and stepped out the door. She was looking forward to sitting with Brittany again through Relief Society and was grateful for the younger woman's overtures of friendship.

"Sister Ashton?" She checked her steps before stumbling over Parker Grayson, who was sitting on the top step of her porch.

"Goodness! You startled me. What are you doing here so early?"

"I'm in big trouble."

"Uh-oh, why do you think you're in trouble?" She sat down beside him.

"You know those old rosebushes of Mr. Haney's?"

"Uh-huh." She nodded her head and prayed silently that the boy hadn't damaged the bushes further.

"I dug them up just like he said I did, but I told that policeman I didn't because I didn't want to get in trouble."

"Did you tell your parents?"

He hung his head. "No."

"Do you think you should?" She'd never had much experience dealing with children, but it seemed reasonable that the boy should talk over his attack of conscience with his parents. He shook his head.

"Mom wouldn't care. She'd just say the smart thing to do is to keep my mouth shut, and anyway, Mr. Haney can't prove I was the one who did it." Her heart sank. She couldn't tell a little boy his mother's attitude was wrong. Neither could she encourage Parker to follow the advice he expected his mother would give him.

"What about your dad? Perhaps he could help you apologize to Mr. Haney and think of a way to make up for digging up the roses." She should be on her way to church, but talking with Parker was more important.

"I can't let Dad find out I sneaked into Mr. Haney's yard that night!" A look of panic crossed his face, and he started to rise.

"Okay." She reached out as if she would prevent him from jumping to his feet, and he settled back on the step. "Do you have a plan?"

"I was going to put them back where they were, but when I dug the holes, I found these." He opened a plastic shopping bag she hadn't noticed before, lying at his feet. Several large flower bulbs lay in the sack. "I don't know what they are. I thought maybe old man Haney planted bombs, and they'd blow me up to get even for what I did."

"Oh, Parker! They're not bombs. Mr. Haney is cranky, but he

wouldn't actually hurt anyone." She hoped that was true. "Those are called bulbs. They're big seeds that will grow into plants in the spring with beautiful flowers on them. I think you should give them back to him."

"He'll yell at me."

"Probably."

"Will you go with me?"

A confrontation with Mr. Haney wasn't how she wanted to start her Sunday morning, but she'd probably already missed sacrament meeting, and something told her too many people had let Parker down in his short life. She nodded her head and reached for his hand.

CHAPTER TEN

KALLENE WASN'T SURE WHO WAS the most nervous—her or Parker—as they approached Delbert Haney's door. Since she had one hand free and Parker was carrying the bag with the bulbs, she pressed the doorbell. Martha Haney answered the door. Seeing them, she cast a nervous glance behind her and called in a quavering voice, "Delbert."

The old man approached the door, and as soon as he saw the two of them standing on his front step, he began to frown. Seeing her neighbor's face turn dark and the perpetual scowl he wore heighten, Kallene hurried to get in the first word. "Before you say anything, I want you to know Parker is being very strong and brave to approach you. He has something important to say, and the least you can do is be courteous enough to listen."

"She's right, dear." Martha's timid voice seconding her statement was a surprise.

The old man's mouth fell open, and Kallene nudged Parker, who stammered the first word or two then spoke as fast as he could, as though in a race to get all of his words in. "I did it, Mr. Haney. I dug up your bushes. I'm sorry. I was going to put them back, but when I dug the holes for them, I found these things, and Sister Ashton says they're big seeds. I'll put them back in the dirt if you want me to." He held up the plastic bag.

Mr. Haney stared at Parker, speechless for once. Finally he squeaked, "You dug up my daffodil bulbs?"

Parker nodded his head. "I didn't mean to. I was going to put the bushes back."

"You were going to put the bushes back? Those bushes have been moved enough! You had no business coming . . ."

"Dear, the doctor said you shouldn't get excited. Why don't you take the boy in the backyard and show him how to put your daffodil bulbs back in the ground?" Martha's hands quivered, and she glanced with anxious eyes from her husband to Parker and Kallene.

Delbert muttered something under his breath before stomping toward a closet where he collected a tattered, thick sweater. Kallene stood beside Parker, feeling uncertain and out of her depth. "Meet you 'round back," the old man barked and turned toward the back of the house.

She accepted her cue to step off the porch and lead Parker around the house to the backyard. He knew the way and only needed her for moral support. She almost smiled to see his sagging shoulders and the look of a condemned man on his face.

Delbert took the bag holding the bulbs from Parker and lined the bulbs up in a row next to the mound of dirt, which had once been a rose garden and more recently had been designated a spring bulb garden. He examined each bulb with care and seemed pleased to find none had been harmed in the digging process. He eyed the holes Parker had dug.

"Here!" He handed one of the bulbs to Parker. "Fill the hole back in until it's only three times as deep as the size of that bulb, then put three of these in the hole, pointy side up. Be sure to space them about a hand's width apart before covering them with dirt."

Parker pulled a small collapsible shovel from his backpack and began following Delbert's instructions. Kallene checked her watch and considered whether she might still make it to church in time for Sunday School and Relief Society. Seeing the worried but determined expression on her young friend's face and the watchful-suspicious one on the old man's face, she decided against leaving them alone.

The soil was soft, and Parker was soon covered in mud, but she felt proud of him as he stuck to the task. When he finished, he stood and began folding his digging tool until it was only about ten inches long and compact enough to fit in his backpack. Before he could get the pack zipped shut, Delbert held out his hand.

"Let me see that trowel."

Parker froze and a look of panic crossed his face. He turned toward Kallene, seeking her help.

"Mr. Haney wants to see your shovel," she explained.

Parker, with a show of reluctance, handed the small tool to Mr. Haney, who looked it over. He appeared puzzled. After a few minutes, he said, "This is a good, solid trowel. Must've cost a pretty penny. Why did you take my shovel instead of using this one the first time?"

"I didn't take your shovel. This is the one I used to dig up your roses. It belongs to my dad, and he's going to be mad if I don't put it back where it belongs." He reached out to reclaim the trowel. "Anyway, mostly I just dug a little bit around those bushes. The dirt was real soft. After I dug a little bit, I pulled on them and they came right out."

"Did you tie a rope around them to pull on them?"

"No, sir. I knew those bushes were covered with stickers so I brought gloves."

"You're sure about that?" Mr. Haney didn't sound like he believed Parker, but he didn't come right out and say he doubted the boy's story.

"I'm real sorry, Mr. Haney." Parker's voice trembled as he repeated his earlier apology.

"It takes a man to own up to what he's done wrong." Delbert didn't quite look at Parker as he spoke. "Just don't come messing around here again." He handed the shovel back to Parker, and the sternness was back in his voice.

Parker crossed his heart, grabbed the shovel, and bolted toward the street.

"What about your fence?" Kallene asked.

"I already fixed it."

"Thank you," Kallene said before she turned to follow Parker from the Haneys' backyard.

Parker was already halfway to his house by the time Kallene reached the street, and she decided not to follow him. She looked at her watch and felt a stab of disappointment. She'd be late for Relief Society if she didn't hurry to church right now. But she couldn't just go; her shoes were muddy, and her hands needed washing. By the time she finished cleaning up, and even if she drove instead of walking, she'd be lucky to get there in time for the closing prayer. She was sorry to have missed her meetings and hoped Brittany would understand, but she couldn't help thinking of the time she spent backing up Parker as "getting the ox out of the mire time" or at least being of service on the Sabbath.

* * *

Kallene awoke early the next morning. Though the sun wasn't up yet, the day promised to be clear and unseasonably warm. As she pulled on running clothes, she felt the ache that preceded all of her morning runs now—Linda wouldn't be there to enjoy the movement and exhilaration of their morning run. Jon wasn't back yet either, leaving her without a running partner. She began her stretch routine, at the same time debating whether or not to run at the high school or do the canyon run. Darnell had shown up several times recently at the high school, and she didn't want to be stuck running with him again. Besides, several of her neighbors ran in the canyon as did a few other people from her ward. She'd stay alert and keep other runners in sight.

A block before she reached the trail, she spotted Jeff Adams starting up the first steep incline. She called out to him, but he didn't acknowledge her, and she assumed he was wearing earphones. Most runners ran with an MP3 player or small radio of some sort. She increased her speed, hoping she could catch up to him. It soon became apparent that his long-legged gait surpassed hers for speed. Soon she could no longer catch even glimpses of him rounding the curves in the trail ahead of her.

The sun sent long streamers of light over the nearby mountain, and birds sent up a cacophony of sound. There was a crispness to the air, and the trees, except for the few pines, were almost stripped of their bright fall foliage. Patches of frost glistened in dark recesses. It was the kind of morning she and Linda had treasured.

Hearing the steady pounding of footsteps behind her, she felt her muscles tense. Kallene was almost to the bridge that crossed to the other side of the canyon and the path that would lead her back to the subdivision. She increased her pace, hoping Jeff might have chosen to rest a moment at that midway point, as many runners did. She clattered across the bridge and felt a stab of disappointment to find no one in the small picnic area.

The footsteps were closer now, and as the other runner moved up beside her, she took a quick peek from beneath her lashes. Darnell Gines! Something about him made her nervous at best, but finding herself alone with him on a secluded mountain trail shot her fear meter into overdrive. She hoped he'd pass her and keep going. No such luck.

"Hey, babe! You're a hard lady to catch up with."

She attempted to ignore him, hoping he'd go away.

"I don't see that California dude. You two have a spat?" She didn't feel the question should be dignified with an answer.

"Oh well, his loss, my gain." He nudged her arm, and she moved to the far edge of the path.

Though the trail was wide enough for two to run abreast, Darnell moved in so close his swinging arm occasionally brushed hers, much to her annoyance. "I haven't seen you for a week or more at the school track and thought for sure I'd be out of luck until spring. Lucky for me, I saw you leave your house just as I drove by on my way to the track. Didn't take two seconds to decide to catch up to you. I figured you'd found that gym with a good indoor track you said you were looking for."

"I'm still looking." Though she didn't like Darnell, she didn't want to be rude or antagonize him. However, she didn't want to give him more information than necessary.

"Most of the newer high schools have indoor tracks they let the public use before classes begin or in the evening. The one out here should have had one, but with money so tight, the board voted against it."

"Thanks, I'll look into that."

"Oops!" Darnell stumbled. "My shoe's untied. It'll just take a minute to fix it."

Thanks for small miracles, she thought. "See you later."

"I'll catch up," he called after her.

Not if I can help it! She once again increased her speed.

Feeling certain she'd put at least a quarter mile between herself and Darnell, she slowed to negotiate a steep slope. Water glinted on the trail ahead, and she had to stifle a groan when her ears caught the unmistakable slap of running shoes behind her. How had he caught up so quickly?

She turned her head as the runner drew alongside her. She opened her mouth in surprise. Instead of Darnell matching her step for step, she met Ted Grayson's eyes. He smiled and gave a faint nod. He might be an aloof snob, but she was glad to see him. She didn't trust Darnell, but she felt reasonably certain he wouldn't try anything with Ted around.

"I didn't think you still ran here." Ted's voice was friendly but impersonal. She noticed a small backpack on his shoulders, similar to the one his son was never without.

"I haven't been here much lately. Too many memories. And it's getting cold, so I'll probably move to an indoor track soon," she said.

"It doesn't get that cold here. I was in Anchorage last week. Now *that's* cold. Winter is a great time to run outdoors here. The paths aren't crowded and the view is grand."

"Linda and I ran here last winter and loved it. It just wouldn't be the same without her."

"Hey! Kallene! Wait up!" Darnell moved up behind them. Thank goodness they were almost to the end of the trail. She expected Ted would leave her now and she'd be stuck with the annoying handyman for the rest of her run.

Her assumption proved wrong with Ted matching her strides all the way to her driveway. Darnell didn't give up, though, and she was further irritated to see his truck parked in front of her house.

"See you!" She waved to both men as she dashed to her front door. No way was she going to let Darnell follow her inside.

While standing in the shower, letting the hot water sluice away her aches and black mood, she remembered Scott's warning. If the person he'd referred to had failed to register, surely that had been remedied by now, perhaps with a bit of persuasion from the police department. She'd go online to see what she could find. If Darnell Gines was the man Scott said had been released from prison where he'd been serving time for a rape/homicide conviction because of a technicality, she intended to find out. She turned off the shower and reached for a towel.

Ten minutes later, dressed in jeans and an oversized T-shirt, she gave her hair a few flicks with her brush, applied a quick swipe of lip gloss, and hurried to her office. It took only a few moments to find the registered sex offender list for Utah. She was appalled to see how long the list was. Once she'd narrowed the list down to a half-mile radius, she began searching the names. She went over the list twice before conceding Darnell's name wasn't on it. She wasn't sure if she felt relief or disappointment.

Could it be possible he still hadn't registered? That seemed unlikely since Scott knew someone in her neighborhood should be on the list. She decided to google Darnell's name. Nothing! Four results came up, but none were the Darnell Gines she'd come to think of as a thorn in her side. It was hard to believe he hadn't done one thing in his life that merited a google mention.

She was about to close the program and head to the kitchen for breakfast when a familiar name caught her attention. A chill went down her spine. She'd never suspected Rupert Meyer!

CHAPTER ELEVEN

KALLENE STARED AT THE SCREEN, feeling certain a mistake had been made. Rupert Meyer lived across the street from her and pretty much kept to himself. He didn't have a wife, was never seen with a girl-friend, and had never to her knowledge paid attention to any of the women on their street. He wasn't friendly, but he'd never done any-thing to make her think he was anything other than a neighbor who valued his privacy. He seemed perfectly normal.

Of course, that word *normal* might mean a lot of things, and she had no idea what a homicidal sex offender was supposed to look like. Obviously they looked like everyone else, or they'd all be locked up.

The list with his name gave little information. She hadn't had any luck googling Darnell's name, but if Rupert Meyer had been involved in a high-profile murder case, she should be able to access news sto-ries that would tell her more. There was a possibility he'd changed his name, but she began typing anyway.

There were more than eleven thousand entries! It would take a month to scroll through them all. She considered closing the site and forgetting the search, but she couldn't. It took only a few minutes to find "Prisoner Released on Technicality."

Pulling up the page, she recognized a well-known newspaper from Seattle. She read with a heavy heart about Rupert Meyer, a recent parolee, who had been convicted of raping and killing a young woman in a forested area south of Seattle. He'd been released from the Washington State Prison because of improper collection and storage of evidence. The headline was followed by details of the crime, which occurred three years earlier. The blood on Meyer's clothes and skin had matched the victim's, and he'd been arrested at the scene of the crime. He'd already served two and a half years of a life sentence when his lawyer won his release on the grounds that the rape DNA evidence had never been collected or matched against his client, though there had been numerous requests to do so. At the end of the article, a brief sentence reported that Meyer's previous conviction had been for the statutory rape of a seventeen-year-old girl he'd picked up in a bar while on leave from the Navy and that he claimed she'd told him she was twenty-one.

The picture that accompanied the article was grainy, but Kallene felt certain she was looking at a younger version of her neighbor. With shaking hands, she shut down her computer and walked on stilted legs toward the kitchen. She stared at the refrigerator for several minutes then turned toward the stairs.

Feeling a slight queasiness in her stomach, she questioned whether she should go to the office that morning or not. Breakfast was out; she couldn't bear to think about food. She had an assignment to turn in, and she needed to find out which theme another client had settled on. Perhaps it would be best to spend the day downtown, away from any possibility of running into either Darnell Gines or Rupert Meyer. This hadn't been a good morning.

In the interest of time and her mutinous stomach, she collected her car keys and portfolio and headed for the garage. Traffic was heavy on I-15, requiring her full attention, and the underground parking lot reserved for Benson & McCallister employees was full, so it took extra time to find a parking space. When she walked through the door with her portfolio under one arm and her computer bag and purse held by the other, the receptionist looked up with round eyes, a startled expression on her childlike pixie face.

"I didn't expect to see you today," said the secretary at the front desk. Her smile looked nervous, like she was hiding something. It was probably just the bad morning she'd had that intensified the annoyed feeling the young girl often provoked in her. She tried to think of the secretary's name—Kennedy? Madison? Some dead president.

"Why not? I usually make an effort to be here for Monday morning staff meetings."

"Didn't you get the memo?" The secretary glanced at the closed boardroom door then back at Kallene.

"What memo?" Kallene suspected the young woman behind the desk knew something she'd rather Kallene didn't know.

"Ben said you weren't coming, and since there were several important matters to discuss, he sent out a memo on Friday moving the ten o'clock meeting to eight."

She had a niggling suspicion her name had been deliberately left off the list of those who should have received it. It was probably just paranoia because of the awful morning she'd had. Anyway, there was no use standing in front of the silly girl, loaded down like a pack mule, discussing the matter. The receptionist was so infatuated with Ben she couldn't see straight, and if Ben left Kallene's name off the list of those to be notified of the time change, the girl wouldn't go against his wishes or even check to see whether or not the omission was deliberate.

On reaching her office, she rested her portfolio against a tall easel in the corner and shoved her purse in a drawer. She might be late, but she meant to walk in on the meeting and act surprised to see it already in progress. Stepping into the hall, she discovered it was too late. Everyone was filing out of the boardroom.

"I'm glad you're feeling better," a designer commented as she swept past Kallene. Before she could respond, she noticed two coworkers who seemed to be pretending *not* to see her. Ben, his father, and Mr. Benson emerged from the board meeting with broad smiles on their faces, heading toward the front door.

I suppose I'll learn what the meeting was about sooner or later. She turned back to her office and called her client. Half an hour later, feeling good about a productive conversation with the client, she decided she might as well get started on the new project. But before getting immersed in a first draft, she carried her completed project to Ben's office for final approval. His office was empty, so she left her sketches and discs on his desk. On her way back to her own office, she was greeted by Lori.

"Hi," she said back to Lori.

Lori started to say something then stopped. She bit her lip then thrust a thin stack of papers toward her. "Since you missed the meeting this morning, you might want to read the article I wrote for the newsletter from my transcribed notes. You can keep that copy; I have another one."

"Okay." Before she could say anything further, Lori hurried toward the business office.

Curious, Kallene began reading as she made her way to her chair. A rush of excitement buoyed her as she learned the company was being awarded a prestigious award at the end of the week in New York for the Davidson project she'd finished two months earlier. Ben would be flying to New York to accept the honor, which included a large cash bonus in addition to a trophy.

Kallene felt a twinge of envy. That project had been her baby from start to finish, except for the text, which had been written by Trent Sawyer. Shouldn't she, or both she and Trent, be the ones to accept the prize? It was only natural, she supposed, to send their department manager, but it would have been nice to have at least been present for the staff meeting and been recognized by her peers.

She continued reading and felt disappointed by the high praise Ben had received for his brilliant work. There was no mention of the work she had done and only a brief mention that Trent had assisted with the text. A feeling of gloom settled over her as she recalled the work she'd put into the project at the same time her best friend had disappeared. Had she been so distracted that she'd made errors Ben had needed to correct? She'd only caught a quick glimpse of the ad when it played on a local television channel, but since she'd watched little television during the past few months and no changes had caught her attention, she'd assumed it had run as she'd submitted it.

She stared at the boards she'd laid out for a preliminary draft of the new project and failed to feel the excitement she'd felt for the project just half an hour earlier. She began gathering up her notes and supplies. Perhaps by the time she got home, she'd be in a better mood.

"Leaving?" The receptionist wasn't even attempting to hide a smirk.

"Sort of." Her smile was deliberately bright and breezy. "I'm meeting Ben's wife for lunch then going shopping. Chelsea wants something glamorous to wear to the awards presentation when they go to New York next weekend." She waggled two fingers at the receptionist and walked out the door.

An immediate bout of guilt struck her. She'd lied. Though she knew Chelsea and got along well with her, they weren't going to lunch or shopping together. She couldn't even justify the lie by claiming her intentions were pure even if the infatuated receptionist did need a reminder that Ben was a married man. She'd struck out at the girl simply because she was hurting and wanted to hurt someone in return.

A wave of shame swept over her, and she considered going back to apologize. Doing so could make matters worse. She didn't want to risk what would amount to accusing the woman of behaving improperly. And maybe she was just taking the cowardly way out, but in the future she'd try to be extra kind to her—and even learn her name.

Her cell phone rang just as she exited the parking garage. Hearing Jon's voice lightened her spirits. She pulled over to the curb so she could concentrate on the call.

"I'm in Salt Lake! Are you up for lunch and apartment hunting?"

"Absolutely!" She welcomed a chance to skip work for the rest of the day. "I just left my office. Where would you like to meet?" They settled the details and Kallene turned toward Trolley Square in much better spirits.

The restaurant was crowded, but it didn't take long to locate Jon. He was seated at a table at the far side of the room. As she made her way toward him, she heard someone call her name. She felt a flush of heat when she recognized Chelsea McCallister. As she walked past the table where Ben's wife and another woman sat, Chelsea reached out a hand and caught Kallene's.

"Kallene, I just want to say thank you. Ben is so excited about that award. When I watched the commercial with him, he mentioned that you helped with it." She stood to hug Kallene. Kallene wasn't sure what to say.

"Oh, this is my friend, Dixie Nash." She introduced the woman who was still seated in their booth. "Dixie, this is Kallene Ashton. Kallene is an up-and-coming artist for my father-in-law's firm."

"Nice to meet you," Kallene managed to say.

"Dixie and I have been shopping. I found the cutest . . . I'm sorry. I'm sure you're anxious to join that young man who is staring daggers at me over there." She giggled and waved in the general direction of the table where Jon sat watching. "By the way, don't mention to Ben that I had lunch with Dixie. For some silly reason he doesn't approve of our friendship." Chelsea sat back down, and Kallene was amused to see the face Dixie pulled behind Chelsea's back.

"What's that silly grin for?" Jon said when she slid onto the chair across from him.

"I think I just got saved from a lie." Seeing the puzzled look on Jon's face, she explained. "There's a woman at work who is aggressively chasing my boss. I was annoyed with her and upset over him taking credit for something I did, so when I left today, I told her I was meeting my boss's wife for lunch. The woman you saw me talking to is the wife, and, well, we are eating in the same room."

Jon chuckled. In a moment Kallene's grin faded. "I shouldn't have lied. I pride myself on my honesty, and I'm embarrassed and disappointed in myself for fibbing."

"Don't be too hard on yourself." Jon reached across the table and placed his hand over hers. "We all disappoint ourselves at time. It's only a problem if we continue to make the same mistake or if we refuse to admit to ourselves that what we did wasn't right."

The waitress appeared to take their order, and after she left, Jon said, "My partners are enthused about opening a Salt Lake office. We spent a lot of time figuring out what equipment and staff will be needed and setting up a budget."

"That's great news!" There was something satisfying in knowing Jon would be taking up permanent residence in the area.

Their orders arrived, and they busied themselves with eating for several minutes before Jon continued the conversation. "In time, I'd like to design and build a home in a location similar to the subdivision where you live, but for now I only need a small apartment. Even though I'm looking for a downtown location to set up a business office, eventually I'd prefer to live farther out."

"When I first arrived in Salt Lake, I found an apartment near Thirty-Ninth South," she told him. "It was nice, but as soon as I was offered a permanent position and had saved enough money for a down payment, I began house hunting. I never meant to look so far out as Pine Shadows, but when I saw the house and the view, nothing else I looked at after that measured up."

"I don't expect to find something as nice as your house, but if this new branch of our business is as successful as I'm hoping it will be, it won't be long before I'll be able to build my dream house."

The waitress reappeared to ask if they'd like to order dessert.

Kallene declined, and Jon ordered a small piece of pie. While they waited for the pie, Jon set a photograph on the table. Kallene leaned forward for a better view and gave a slight gasp. The picture was of a small girl with a mop of red curls wearing an orange life vest over a ragged pair of denim shorts. Her face was smeared with something unidentifiable, and she was sitting on a heavy coil of rope. Behind her was a vast expanse of blue water.

CHAPTER TWELVE

"Macie! How did you get this picture? Did Carson send it to your mother?"

"No. But it is the reason I'm a day later returning to Salt Lake than I'd anticipated. I picked up a newspaper to read while I was eating breakfast. A short article on an inside page caught my attention when the name Carson Longdale practically jumped out at me."

"Carson's in San Diego?"

"No, but he is in a small waterfront town not far from there."

"You found that out from a newspaper article?"

"Some fishermen found a woman's body weighted down with rocks in a small, rocky cove near the town where Carson's father's boat is docked. The local police department, it seems, was aware of Carson being a person of interest in a murder investigation here in Utah, so they hauled him in for questioning. They kept him overnight until a judge ordered him released, since there was insufficient evidence to hold him."

"You don't think . . . ?"

"No. I'm pretty sure Carson had nothing to do with that woman. You suggested once that Linda's death might have been an accident. To be fair, I can't rule out that possibility."

"Macie looks healthy and even happy." Kallene continued to study the snapshot. "Did you speak with Carson?"

"No. I wandered down the pier looking at the residence boats until I spotted Macie sitting on the deck of an old bucket that appeared to be in pretty good condition. An old man was fiddling with something nearby. I watched for a bit and snapped several pictures but didn't attempt to contact Carson or his father. I was afraid that if they knew I'd found them, they'd pull up anchor and go somewhere else, and I might not be able to find them again."

* * *

Kallene's feet hurt, and the apartments they'd toured were a blur by the time they decided to call it a day and head back to her house to review their notes.

"Whew! I didn't think it would be this hard." Jon stared at the papers strewn across Kallene's dining room table. "I need space to work until I have an office. Every place we looked that's big enough has poor lighting. The ones with proper lighting are in inconvenient locations or are no bigger than a postage stamp. I think I'll make a few calls and set up some appointments for tomorrow. Are you available for another round of apartment hunting tomorrow?"

"Sorry." She regretted having to decline. "I promised to meet a client at the office tomorrow morning to go over rough drafts for some ads he wants to run in several nature magazines. I do most of my work at home and set my own hours, but I always meet new clients at the office."

"I'll miss your help. I have a few pieces of furniture and my drafting table arriving at the end of the week, so I don't have much time to find a place."

"While you make your calls, I'll fix us something to eat." Kallene made a mental inventory of her cupboards. Taking time to shop for groceries hadn't been high on her priority list lately.

"Please don't go to a lot of bother. I'm not terribly hungry after the big lunch I ate."

"I'll keep it simple," she promised.

From the kitchen she could hear the rumble of Jon's voice talking on his cell phone as she pulled out a pan of Rhode's frozen orange rolls and slipped them in the oven. Then she turned to preparing omelets. As she worked, she wondered if she should tell Jon what she'd discovered about Rupert Meyer. Even with all that had happened since her discovery of Meyer's past that morning, she'd never succeeded in putting it completely out of her mind.

"Penny for your thoughts." Jon stepped up behind her and lightly set his hands on her shoulders. She leaned back a little, enjoying the touch.

"I'm not sure my thoughts are worth a penny right now." She deftly flipped the first omelet. "I learned something disturbing about one of my neighbors this morning, and I've debated whether or not to tell someone." She added cheese, peppers, and crumbled bacon to the omelet.

"I'm a good listener."

"I know you are." She turned her head to smile up at him. "Hold that plate for me?" She slid the omelet onto the plate and turned her attention to preparing the second one. "Scott told me the day we searched the canyon that one of my neighbors was a sex offender who failed to register when he moved here. This morning I found Darnell Gines particularly annoying. Not for the first time, I wondered if he was the man Scott meant."

"I'd certainly consider him strange but probably harmless. Did he attempt anything that made you think otherwise?"

Kallene turned to face Jon.

"No, it was just that I saw Jeff Adams start up the canyon trail and decided on an impulse to follow him or even catch up and run with him. He's a nice guy who moved into my ward a few months ago, and his wife, Brittany, has become a good friend. I couldn't catch up to him, but Darnell caught up to me and was so persistent about running with me, I got nervous. When I got home, I checked the sex offender list. I didn't find Darnell, but I did find Rupert Meyer, from across the street." She removed the second omelet just as the timer for the oven buzzed.

They were almost finished with their simple meal when Jon asked, "Is Meyer the ex-con Scott mentioned?"

"I'm pretty sure he is." She told him about the newspaper article she'd read online. "I was so sure he meant Darnell that I never once thought Rupert Meyer might be a criminal. He's not friendly, but I've never thought of him as threatening in any way."

"That doesn't sound good. I hope you're being vigilant about keeping your doors locked at night and when you're here alone. You're a grown woman, and I won't presume to tell you what to do, but I'm hoping you won't run alone again. If a trusted friend isn't available to run with you, please go to a gym or the high school, where there are other people around."

"Don't worry. Darnell scared me enough this morning to make me swear off solo runs in the canyon. I've also ordered a new garage door opener with a remote control and asked the alarm company to upgrade my alarm system."

"Good!" He leaned forward to press a quick kiss on her lips. The kiss ended so quickly that she had no time to respond, but she couldn't help wishing he'd lingered a bit or hoping he'd kiss her again in the very near future.

* * *

Kallene approached her agency's front doors with some trepidation the next morning and was surprised when the receptionist greeted her with a polite good-morning. She noticed Ben's office was empty when she walked past his open door. She learned later from the talkative Lori that Ben and his wife had decided to leave early for New York so that Chelsea could shop for a suitable dress there for the awards ceremony.

Her appointment with her client went well, and she hummed as she began making rough sketches on her storyboards. She was interrupted by the ring of her cell phone. It was Jon calling to let her know he'd found an apartment. "I have a lead on a promising location for my company's offices and studio, too. I'm going to be kind of busy for the next few days finalizing agreements and confirming business details, but can I count on you for a run Saturday morning along with some help arranging my apartment? I'll even cook dinner for you."

"It's a deal." They chatted for a few more minutes before saying good-bye.

When a tap came on her door, she looked up expecting to see Lori. Instead it was Scott. Her breath caught for a moment as it always did on seeing him. "Any chance I can interrupt your work long enough for you to share lunch with me?"

"Lunch? You said the magic word. I'm starved." She set her pencil aside and pulled her handbag from the bottom drawer of her desk. Scott crooked his elbow. Grasping it, Kallene left the building with him.

Scott took her to a tiny restaurant where the hamburgers were fabulous. The heavily bearded and tattooed man who manned both the counter and the grill had greeted Scott like an old friend. Before she was half finished with her hamburger, Scott had finished his as well as his fries and was nibbling at hers. He kept her laughing with funny stories, supposedly true, of the misadventures of his days as a uniformed officer before being promoted to detective. An idea began to form.

As she wiped away sauce that was leaking toward her chin, Kallene asked, "Scott, would you come to a den meeting and talk to my Cub Scouts?"

"When is your next meeting?"

"Friday at four. If that's too soon, we could plan for another week."

"Friday. Sure, I can do that."

She couldn't believe it was that easy. She'd been thinking of inviting someone to one of her Cub Scout meetings for a while to talk about honoring the law. Scott would be perfect.

They returned to the agency, and Scott said farewell with a promise to see her Friday at her house. Kallene strolled inside and managed to hide a grin when Kennedy—she'd learned the young woman's name from Lori—asked if Scott was her boyfriend. "He's *so* good looking!" Kennedy practically drooled.

"He's just a friend," Kallene said in a nonchalant voice, but when she reached her office, she found herself staring in a vacant fashion at the sketch on her easel. Scott was good looking, probably the handsomest man she'd ever dated. He was fun and thoughtful, too, but that didn't make him her boyfriend. She wasn't even certain she wanted him to be her boyfriend. What about Jon? Was he her boyfriend? She'd never enjoyed a friendship with any other man quite like what she shared with Jon. He was attractive, too, though he didn't have the heart-stopping good looks Scott had that made women turn their heads. There was something about being with Jon she couldn't quite describe, but it was definitely good.

* * *

Parker was the first of the boys to arrive for Cub Scout meeting. The others soon followed. It didn't take long for Scott to establish a rapport with the boys. After explaining a little about the requirements for becoming a police officer, he launched into the dangers of experimenting with drugs. He finished by encouraging the boys to respect the property and rights of other people. She made a hasty glance toward Parker, but he seemed absorbed in Scott's message and showed no signs of being upset by the gentle reminder. When Scott finished speaking and started answering the boys' questions, Kallene brought in a plate piled high with cupcakes and was amazed when the boys showed more interest in peppering Scott with questions than in devouring the cakes.

When the last boy closed the door behind him after the meeting, Scott sprawled across an armchair in a dramatic fashion. "You do this every week?"

She laughed. "Every week, but don't tell me you weren't having as much fun as the boys."

"Got me!" He sat up and snagged her hand, pulling her down beside him on the arm of the chair. "Now, young lady," he said in a mock-severe voice, "anyone who works as hard as you do then rides herd on ten eight-year-olds deserves a little pampering. I already ordered pizza." He made a big show of checking his watch. "It should arrive in five minutes."

Kallene shook her head and grinned. "Sometimes I think you're no more than a kid yourself."

"Guilty as charged."

The doorbell rang, and Kallene rose to her feet, but before she could reach the door, Scott was there. He paid the delivery man and handed Kallene a two-liter bottle of root beer while he carried the huge pizza to the table.

"Scott." He turned toward her, a question in his eyes, as though he'd sensed from that one word that she had something serious to say. She'd meant to bring up the subject earlier, but the time had never seemed right. "I looked up the sex offender list on the Internet and found Rupert Meyer's name. Do you think he might have killed Linda?"

Scott shook his head.

"Why are you so sure Rupert didn't kill her?"

"We ran a background check on him and had him down to the station to talk. He hasn't made a wrong move since he got out of prison, and there are some legitimate questions concerning his trial. And that first conviction was a railroad job. He was just a kid who made a stupid choice. Chances are the girl did lie about her age. The bartender served her, so why wouldn't a guy assume she was of age? She admitted there was no force involved, but the judge decided to make an example of him anyway."

"Just because there were irregularities with his trial doesn't mean he's innocent of the charges. He still might have killed that woman, and if he killed her, he might have killed Linda, too."

"We don't know for sure that Linda is dead," Scott reminded her.

"But you think she is."

"Yeah, I do, and off the record, I feel certain her husband killed her. The chief isn't ready to arrest him, but he's making an announcement to the press in the morning, naming Carson Longdale officially a person of interest."

"You found something—?"

"It might be nothing. Anyway, I can't talk about it."

CHAPTER THIRTEEN

SLIDING THE GLASS DOOR OPEN, Kallene stepped onto the deck and stared at the bare trees in her backyard. They weren't large trees, but they'd done well since she'd planted them a year ago. Grass and a few trees were as far as she'd gotten with landscaping. Next spring she'd add some flowers. What her backyard really needed was a swing set, a sandbox, and children. She'd only cared for Macie two days, yet since the little girl had gone, Kallene often found herself staring off into space, imagining children of her own running through the house and interrupting her work.

She wrapped her arms around herself, surprised by the sharp chill in the air. It was only a week until Thanksgiving, and she'd noticed frost on the grass a few mornings lately. Still it seemed too soon to be thinking about winter. Almost against her will, her eyes strayed to the side. Though she'd promised herself she'd ignore Mr. Haney if he was on his back patio, she couldn't help glancing toward his yard. The chair where he sat the night Scott had been with her was empty, and she breathed a little sigh of relief. She'd seen little of him since she and Parker had visited him to replant the bulbs the boy had dug up, and she wasn't anxious to tangle with him again.

Delbert Haney was a fussy old man but harmless. She should be more charitable. It was sad, really, that he had so little to do with his time that he made a big production of hassling kids and neighbors. He probably wasn't spying on her, but she felt uneasy every time she caught him staring into her yard, and she didn't like the way he'd positioned his chair, giving him a front-row seat for watching her deck. Even during the recent rainstorms, she'd noticed his nose pressed against a window staring toward her house. It wasn't that she had any big secrets; she just didn't feel comfortable being watched by a nosy neighbor.

With the foliage gone, she was surprised by how clearly she could see into her neighbor's yard. On the far side, she could see where the roses had been moved. Mr. Haney had brought in additional soil, and she noticed a raised section of dirt beneath the bushes that had been pruned back to little more than stumps. The raised mound of earth brought a shiver to her skin in spite of the bright sun that had at last chased away almost two weeks of rain. There was something about the shape and size of that dirt mound that resembled a grave a little too much, even though Scott had assured her there was no body under those roses. It was a silly idea anyway.

She was being paranoid. The events of the past few months were causing her to see something twisted everywhere she turned. Instead of imagining someone breaking into her house with every strange sound in the night, speculating on why her ex-convict neighbor had moved to her neighborhood, or imagining that her eighty-year-old neighbor was burying bodies in his flower garden, she should be basking in the attention of two charming, handsome men. Scott had asked her out twice during the past two weeks, and she saw Jon almost every day.

Jon's move to Salt Lake had gone well, and he'd rented an apartment with a generous-sized studio in the Avenues. Negotiations were underway to sign a lease for office space and to announce the opening of the new branch of his architectural firm. Her own office was only a few blocks away from his proposed office, and already they were planning to meet often for lunch. They'd discussed joining a gym that was fairly close to both of their offices, where they could run in the mornings before beginning work.

On Saturday mornings, when the weather permitted, running the canyon trail together had become a regular routine, but once snow filled the canyon, there would be few days they could run there. During the recent rainy spell, they'd met several times at a local high school with an indoor track, and they'd discussed exploring new running venues. For some time she'd been thinking of trying the trail at the new Legacy Parkway north of Salt Lake on a Saturday when they could both get away. They'd agreed they might have to wait for spring, or at least a stretch of better weather, to attempt running in the wetlands park.

Until meeting Jon and Scott, she hadn't dated much since buying her home. When she'd lived in an apartment in Holladay, she'd attended a singles ward where she'd become painfully aware that there were few attractive, intelligent single men her age. The best ones were already married, and the few who were left were single for obvious reasons. The older singles group didn't meet her needs either. Caught in the in-between age group, she hadn't bothered looking for a new singles group and had her membership records transferred to the family ward a few blocks from her new home after moving into Pine Shadows. Kallene felt guilty that the loss of her best friend had brought two wonderful, eligible men into her life.

Scott had the kind of good looks any woman would find attractive. He was fun, hard working, and thoughtful. Almost the same could be said for Jon. Lately she'd noticed a stiffness in Jon's demeanor anytime Scott's name was mentioned and knew he was aware she'd been seeing the handsome detective. She didn't want to complicate the relationship between the two men as they searched for clues concerning Linda's disappearance. She was reaching a moment of decision and was dreading it.

With one last look at the sparkling, clear morning, she stepped back inside her house. It was time to get to work. If she was going to be ready when Jon arrived at six, she didn't have time to be dawdling over the view from her deck or daydreaming about men.

Once she sat down in her studio, she became lost in her work, forgetting even to pause for lunch. She was critically eyeing a sketch, wondering if it needed just a little more shading, perhaps a brighter shade of red, when her doorbell rang. Ignoring the sound, she studied her palette of colors, wondering which would best draw attention to the logo. The bell rang again. Giving up, she rose to her feet, hoping she could soon get rid of the caller and get back to work without losing her train of thought.

Taking reluctant steps and hoping the caller would give up and leave, Kallene moved toward the door. Recognizing that the caller wasn't going to go away until she answered the door, she opened it, belatedly remembering Scott's admonition to first check her visitor's identity through the small pane in the door. Swallowing her annoyance at the intrusion and her own forgetfulness, she opened her mouth to send the caller on his way. Instead of a salesman, Parker Grayson stood on her doorstep, but he didn't look like himself. The knees of his jeans were caked with leaves and dirt. His face and hands were grubby, his eyes wide, and he looked as though he'd been crying. She hoped he hadn't gotten into another confrontation with Delbert Haney.

"You have to come." Parker's tear-stained face looked up at her.

"What's the matter?" She attempted to keep annoyance out of her voice.

"You have to come." He reached for her hand.

"Can't you just tell me what's wrong? I'm working on a big project right now."

"No, I can't tell anyone. You have to see."

"You can't even tell your mom?"

He shook his head. More tears slid down his cheeks, carving furrows in his dirt-grimed face. His panic was evident.

"It's cold out, and the weather man said it might snow tonight."

"Please, Sister Ashton. It's really important."

She could see the boy was trembling. He almost seemed in shock. At first she'd thought he was shaking from the cold since he only wore a sweatshirt for a jacket, but now she could see he was scared. "Parker, are you afraid of something? Did someone threaten you?" Suddenly she felt fiercely protective. "Where are your parents?"

"Mom is on one of her business trips, and Dad just got back from Detroit. He worked out for a long time then fell asleep."He pinched his lips together and continued to watch her face with pleading eyes.

"All right. Come inside while I get my coat." She turned back to pull a fleece-lined windbreaker from the hall closet. She grabbed a second jacket and tossed it to Parker. Parker shrugged out of his backpack, letting it slide to the floor, while he pulled on the jacket. Once more he reached for her hand and tugged her toward the door.

This better be good. She'd encouraged the boys in her den to talk to her, and she'd believed she was making progress with Parker. He seemed eager to accept the friendship she offered. He was even getting along better with the other boys and causing fewer disturbances during their den meetings. *But* she was working on an important project and on a tight deadline, and she still needed to organize a photo shoot. Another look at the boy's face, however, told her that whatever had upset him was more important than her project or her date with Jon that evening.

As soon as she pulled the door closed behind her, Parker gripped her hand tighter, urging her to hurry. He led her down the street toward the trail beginning a short distance behind the church—one of the routes leading into the canyon.

"I'm not sure we should go up the canyon, Parker. It will be dark soon, and the sky looks like it might snow." She didn't want to get caught in the canyon during a storm.

"It isn't far." He tugged harder on her hand and glanced around in a furtive gesture that raised alarms in the back of Kallene's mind. She hoped he hadn't been playing in the canyon alone and been frightened by older kids. She knew it wasn't unusual for teenagers to hold keg parties or mess with drugs in the various canyons that surrounded the valley.

"All right." She'd come this far, so she'd go the rest of the way. Whatever had upset Parker needed to be dealt with and his fears put to rest. Hopefully there would still be time to make a few calls and finish the sketch she was working on before Jon arrived to pick her up for their date. She wished she'd taken time to leave him a note. Perhaps if Parker paused to catch his breath, she could give Jon a quick call.

The trees were bare and skeletal. Thick pockets of dirty brown leaves filled cracks and formed mounds beneath shrubs. It had rained the day before at the lower elevations, leaving the trail slippery. If they climbed high enough, she suspected they would find snow. She wished she had her running shoes on since they would give her better traction. Slip-ons weren't designed for climbing mountain trails.

"Does your mom know you're playing up here?" she asked. They'd traveled much farther than an eight-year-old should be allowed to roam on his own.

Parker shook his head. "Mom's still in Chicago." His grip on her hand never relaxed, and she suspected from his increased tension that they were nearing whatever he wanted her to see. Without warning, he veered from the trail onto a rocky slope. Letting go of her hand, he climbed over a good-sized boulder then waited for her to follow. She was glad she'd decided to wear jeans that morning. She usually dressed up to go downtown to her office, but since she was working at home that day, she hadn't bothered to dress up.

Using her hands to help her scramble over the rock, she at last stood beside Parker—but only for a moment before he started down a shallow cut filled with rocks. Thorns and twigs tugged at her clothing as she attempted to follow Parker. He seemed to have a destination in mind, but she could see no indication of any sort of trail.

The cut ended at a ledge that hung over a five- or six-foot drop. Peering over the edge, Kallene could see a narrow ledge surrounded by trees. Parker lay on his stomach and inched his way backward over the drop.

"Wait!" she tried to caution him. Too late, he slipped over the edge to land in the tiny clearing below. He looked back at her, motioning for her to follow.

"How do we get back up?" she asked. The clearing appeared to be poised on the edge of a cliff.

"It's not too hard." Again he motioned for her to follow. With some reluctance, she followed. It wasn't a difficult drop for her, and she landed safely on her feet. Looking around, she could see the clearing was no more than ten feet by six, surrounded by a jumble of rocks, trees, and brush. Below, she could just pick out the church steeple through the thickly bunched trees. She'd had no idea such a place existed, but she could see how a young boy would delight in the secret hideaway. In the summer, when the aspen trees were in leaf, it would be impossible to guess the ledge existed and that it concealed a hidden clearing.

An unpleasant odor seemed to linger in the small space, and a sense of unease tightened the muscles at the back of her neck. She'd heard stories of wildcats and an occasional bear being spotted in the canyons. What if this hidden spot was some wild animal's lair?

Parker moved more slowly now to the edge of the clearing, where a large fallen fir tree blocked one side of the minuscule clearing. He knelt down to pick up a small shovel that lay on the ground and began to dig at the leaves and debris packed against the log. Suddenly he sat back, wrapping his arms against his knees, his head bowed. His shoulders shook, and she heard great, gulping sobs.

Hurrying to him, she knelt to put her arms around him. That's when she saw it. An arm with an outstretched hand lay in the shallow hole he'd dug. Familiar rings on the third finger told her Parker had found Linda.

She didn't scream. She simply held the child, and together they rocked back and forth, too numb to speak.

Kallene had no idea how long she held Parker before the reality of the situation began to creep in. She needed to call Scott. And Jon.

"Parker, I have to call the police." He moved a few feet away and sat with hunched shoulders while she made the calls. When she finished, he looked up at her with tear-swollen eyes.

"I found this place a long time ago. I didn't tell anybody because it was my place. After a while there was a bad smell, so I didn't come anymore, then I started coming again, and it didn't smell so bad anymore. I knew someone else had found my secret place, because over there," he pointed to the opposite side of the clearing, "I found a dirty towel and this shovel. Someone fixed a better way to get down, too. There's a rope fastened to a tree over there." He waved in the general direction of the opposite side of the ledge. "I think the shovel is the one someone stole from Mr. Haney."

"You'll have to tell the police all that. They'll want to know why you didn't tell someone sooner."

"Mrs. Morris, my teacher at school, said lots of animals die during the winter because they can't find enough to eat, and they don't have a place to keep warm. I saw a rabbit one time when I came here, and so today I was going to dig a cave for it under that tree and leave some carrots. When I started digging, I found her."

CHAPTER FOURTEEN

CLOSING HER MIND TO ANY kind of thoughts, Kallene sat on the curb that encircled the church parking lot, staring into space. She couldn't even cry. After a few minutes, Scott came over and sat down beside her. His arms went around her, and he pulled her against his chest. A slow drizzle of cold rain left a sheen on the asphalt and the parked vehicles. Her wet hair was plastered to her head, but she didn't care.

"I'm so sorry you lost your friend in such a horrible way." His voice was a soft murmur. "I made note of all you told me, and of course, your call to 911 was recorded, but I'm certain the captain will want you to go to the station and make a formal statement soon."

"I can't. Not now."

"I know. Go home, shower, and sleep for a few hours. That will give you a chance to pull yourself together and collect your thoughts and impressions."

"What about Parker? His mother is out of town, and I don't know how to contact his father. Wait! Parker said his dad had just returned from a business trip and was sleeping." She felt something akin to guilt for not going with the boy when a female officer led him away.

"He told me that when he first found the rope and used it to climb down the perpendicular drop from that ledge, he used a towel he found up there to protect his hands from rope burns, but it wasn't much help, so he threw it in the Dumpster behind the church. He said it had brown stains on it. The stains might have been blood. If you could find it . . ."

"It has already been collected and sent to the crime lab." Scott attempted to soothe her. "The stains are blood, and we'll soon know if they match our suspect."

A profound sadness settled deep into her bones. She lifted her head and whispered, "I should have gone with Parker. He's just a little boy and he'll be scared."

"He's not your worry. The social worker who took him will prepare him to make his statement and contact his father. Come on. I'll give you a lift to your house." Scott helped her to her feet, and with his arm around her, he led her to an unmarked car.

Seated in the car, she looked up the side of the mountain, following a straggling line of brush and aspen trees to the thick grove hiding the ledge where Linda's body had lain hidden until the officers carried it down to a waiting vehicle from the coroner's office a short time ago.

Jon had been furious when Scott wouldn't let him climb up to the ledge. Perhaps she shouldn't have called him, but she hadn't wanted him to receive the news from some stranger who couldn't share his hurt. He'd arrived right after the police, and she'd watched him pace like an angry tiger and had felt helpless to comfort him. She'd seen someone who looked like a reporter approach him and witnessed his impatient rebuff of the eager young man. He'd gripped Kallene's hand like it was a lifeline as the body bag was lowered down the steep slope. Moments later he'd informed her that he was following the hearse to the coroner's office and that he'd call her later.

"Do you want me to come get you in a few hours?" Scott asked, and she became aware they were parked in front of her house.

"No. I can drive myself." She reached for the door. He touched her arm in a caring gesture. His eyes told her of his real concern for her. "I'll be okay," she whispered before exiting the car and hurrying inside. Stepping into the foyer, she stumbled against Parker's backpack. He'd forgotten to put it back on after donning the jacket she'd given him. She eyed it a moment then set it inside the coat closet to return to him later.

She went to the bathroom and caught a glimpse of herself in the mirror. She was covered with mud. Twigs and dead leaves clung to her hair. Her wet clothing clung to her skin. She didn't care; she was past caring about her appearance. When she closed her eyes, she saw only Linda's decaying hand and the rings that should have symbolized eternal love.

She stood under the hot shower spray for a long time, becoming aware in a vague way of the sharp sting of the water hitting numerous scratches on her face and hands. Not all of the water streaming down her face came from the overhead shower fixture. At last she shut off the water and toweled herself dry. Dressed in clean jeans and an over-sized T-shirt, she threw herself onto her bed. Sleep didn't come, but the shock seemed to diminish, and she thought of dozens of questions she should have asked Scott.

Carson's face filled her mind, and she sat straight up on her bed. Had he been told Linda's body had been found? Had he known all along that she was dead? And Macie? What would become of that dear child, growing up without a mother? Macie wouldn't even remember her mother. The tears began again, and Kallene cried for Macie, for Jon, for Adam and Janet, and for herself. When at last her tears subsided, she slid off the bed, found her shoes, stopped for a moment in the bathroom to apply a cold cloth to her eyes, then searched for her purse, phone, and a warm coat.

The sun was low in the west when she backed her car out of the driveway. She ignored Mr. Haney, who stared at her from his front-room window. At least she was no longer worrying about a body buried beneath his roses. She felt embarrassed that she'd considered for even a moment that possibility.

Not wanting to think about death or anything remotely related to that day's grisly discovery, she studied the houses as she drove down the street. A man with a large dog running beside him came toward her, and she recognized him as Rupert Meyer. He was bundled in a heavy fleece jogging suit, the black dog trotting beside him. She wondered when he'd gotten a dog. She'd never seen him with one before. She liked dogs, but this one seemed to be an unusually large German shepherd–Labrador mix. She'd never seen her reclusive neighbor running in the evening before either. Perhaps she wasn't the only one who had changed her running routine since Linda's disappearance. Or had he known all along about the body hidden on the mountainside? Had he been watching its recovery from some hidden vantage point?

She bit her lip to divert her mind. She'd go crazy if she allowed herself to dwell on the gruesome corpse of her friend.

At the police station, she was escorted to a cubicle office to write down everything she could remember from the time Parker rang her doorbell until the police arrived. When she finished, she was surprised to find Jon instead of Scott waiting for her. Her heart went out to him the moment she saw the pallor of his face and the pain in his eyes.

"Jon." She reached his side and threaded her arm through his. His arms closed around her, and he held her like she was his last hope. "Are you all right?"

"Yes. I thought I was prepared, but it's harder than I could begin to imagine. I bawled like a baby when I talked to Dad." His eyes were red and swollen, and the desolated look in his eyes bore witness of his grief.

"When are your parents coming?"

"They're not coming. I've already identified her body, and there's nothing they can do here. Dad says coming here would be too hard for Mom, and he wants Linda buried next to Louise in Baltimore, but it may be a couple of weeks before the coroner releases the body. State law requires an autopsy. Anyway, Carson will have the final say where she will be buried." The last was said with more than a little bitterness.

"Has Carson been notified?"

"I don't know. The police won't tell me anything, but I think you and I need to talk. I need to know what you saw."

"Come over for breakfast in the morning," Kallene said.

"I'll do better than that. I'll be there early to run with you. I suspect I won't sleep much, and a good, hard run will clear some of the tension for both of us."

Jon reached to hold the door for her. As Kallene passed through, she caught a glimpse of Scott standing in a doorway farther down the hall, watching them with a scowl on his face.

* * *

The run did help in spite of the thin layer of snow that had fallen during the night. It was cold and wet, but neither one minded. They decided to go to the high-school track. After their run, they lingered over waffles and berries at Kallene's kitchen table. Neither one was anxious to bring up the subject on both of their minds, but after their plates were emptied, Jon pushed his back a few inches and began. "I need to know everything you can tell me. Why was that little boy digging around on that ledge, and why did he have a shovel? I heard the detective say the two of you descended from the ledge on a rope; where did the rope come from?"

Kallene set her fork down and said, "It was already there. Parker said he found that ledge last spring while he was playing on the canyon trail. His parents both work and are out of town a lot. I think they leave him alone more than they should. Even when one or both are around, I don't think the boy is supervised well, and he doesn't seem to have any friends. He said he hadn't gone to his secret place for quite a while because it became too hard to push past the wild bushes with all of their thorns, but when he went there again recently, he found the rope attached to a tree at one end of the ledge."

"Did he say why he decided to go there again?"

"He said as soon as he arrived on the ledge, he knew someone else had been there. He last visited the spot right after school started in the fall, and the rope and shovel weren't there then. He found a towel, too, poking out of the leaves near the rope."

"The towel might be a clue."

"Scott said the towel had been found earlier in a Dumpster and has been turned over to the crime lab."

"But why did Parker go there yesterday?" Jon asked.

"Parker said his teacher told his class some animals have a hard time finding food and shelter in the winter, and he remembered the shovel lying on the ground at his secret place. He decided to use it to dig a little cave for wild animals to shelter from the cold. He even took along some carrots for them to eat." She blinked away tears.

"I can't believe she was so close . . . and when I think of all the times we ran near there . . ."

Jon's hands went to his head as he took several deep breaths.

"When he started digging, Parker said he wondered if the shovel was the one Mr. Haney had accused him of stealing. He was afraid if he took it to Mr. Haney, the old man would be sure he'd been the one who took it. He'd only been digging for a few minutes when he saw Linda's hand. He covered it back up and came to get me. He was in shock when he came to my door."

"And was it Mr. Haney's shovel?"

"Scott said the police would contact Mr. Haney today to ask if he could identify either the shovel or the rope. It's probably safe to assume they are his, but after almost three months of exposure to the weather, it will be hard to make a definite identification."

Kallene picked up her fork again and twisted it between her fingers. After a few moments, she resumed the conversation. "You spoke with the coroner and identified the body. Did you get any idea how she died, and was she . . ." That wasn't an appropriate question to ask Linda's grieving brother.

"Her neck was broken, and the back of her skull was crushed. Until the autopsy is complete, the coroner won't speculate on whether it was an accident or if she suffered other trauma. He did indicate there was evidence she'd been struck by a heavy, blunt object about the face, but the crushed skull wasn't caused by the same object."

A commotion erupted next door. The shouting could be heard, even though Kallene didn't have any windows open. Kallene glanced at the kitchen clock. It wasn't time for school children to be passing Mr. Haney's yard. Wondering what had set off her neighbor's tirade this time, she glanced toward the window. The loud barking of a dog answered her question.

Rising to her feet, Kallene hurried toward the front door with Jon close on her heels. Mr. Haney stood in his driveway waving a snow shovel at a large black dog. The dog took a step toward the indignant old man. The dog's lip curled back, revealing a frightening set of teeth. She remembered seeing the dog earlier with Mr. Meyer, but now she wondered if it was a stray. She reached her driveway just as a sharp whistle sounded.

The dog stopped. It lifted its head and gave a series of sharp barks before turning its attention back to Mr. Haney, who had crept closer with his shovel.

"Put the shovel down!" Rupert Meyer shouted. Mr. Haney ignored him and lifted the shovel higher.

"I'll teach him to come in my yard!"

"No! Put the shovel down!"

Kallene hurried toward the altercation, unsure how she could possibly help the old man if the dog attacked.

"Kallene, wait!" Jon yelled. She stopped a few feet from her neighbor's front yard.

A car screeched to a halt in front of her, and a police officer scrambled out, pulling a club free as he ran and holding a leash in the other hand. Kallene's heart beat faster.

"Don't hurt him!" Mr. Meyer yelled. "The dog won't hurt him unless he's attacked. He sees the shovel as a threat!"

"Lay your shovel down," the officer ordered.

Mr. Haney hesitated, and Kallene thought he was going to obey. Instead he swung at the dog, and the animal became furious. With agility, he leaped toward Mr. Haney, grasping his arm, pulling him toward the ground, and sending the shovel clattering against the driveway.

"Help! He's going to kill me!" Haney's bravado was gone, and he screamed in terror.

Before the officer could do anything, Kallene dived toward the struggling pair. She heard both Jon and the police officer shout a warning, but she could only think of her neighbor's bad heart.

Her hand grasped the leather collar around the dog's neck. She tugged, and to her surprise the dog released his hold on Mr. Haney. He took a bristling stance in front of her, baring his teeth and moving his large head back and forth between Mr. Haney and the police officer.

"Raider! It's all right." Rupert Meyer knelt in the melting snow that covered the lawn and reached out to the dog. The hair on the dog's ruff slowly relaxed, and the dog gave a happy little yip and rubbed his head against Rupert's shoulder.

An arm settled around her waist as Jon attempted to pull her away from the dog. The dog noticed Jon, and he began to sink into a crouch.

"Knock it off!" Mr. Meyer commanded the dog. He snapped a leash to the dog's collar and spoke soothing words to him. The dog continued to eye Jon with suspicion but obeyed his master.

The officer turned from where he knelt beside Mr. Haney. "Fortunately, this man isn't injured. The dog's teeth didn't break the skin, though he tore a few small rips in his jacket."

"That dog should be shot!" Haney was back in form. Kallene saw his hand snake toward the shovel he'd dropped. The officer saw the movement, too, and moved to set his foot down on the shovel's handle.

"I wouldn't advise that," the officer warned. The dog watched the men with alert intensity. "I'll have to cite you for allowing your dog to run loose," he said to Rupert Meyer.

"My dog isn't a bad dog," Meyer protested. "He's a trained guard dog. He only goes after men who provoke him by threatening him with a gun or club. He's protective of those he's assigned to guard as well. He never would have gone after Mr. Haney if Haney hadn't come over to my place, where I was in the process of constructing a dog run, waving that shovel around and shouting at me for making so much noise. My dog interpreted his actions as a threat and chased him back to his own property."

"I'm pressing charges!" Mr. Haney shouted.

"Fine! Press charges." The officer sighed. He wrote out something on a piece of paper and handed it to the irate man. "I'm happy to let a judge work this out." He wrote something more on another piece of paper and handed the paper to Rupert before hurrying back to his car.

"Come on, Raider." Rupert Meyer led his dog back across the street. Kallene and Jon followed. "Thanks, Kallene." It was the first time he'd ever spoken to her, and she was surprised he knew her name. "He really isn't a bad dog, and he'd never hurt you. We've been separated for a while, and I just recently located him and was able to bring him home yesterday. I appreciate the way you stepped in to help." She hadn't actually. If she was thinking at all, it was of keeping the dog from tearing her cranky neighbor apart.

"Look, I think he's taken a liking to you." The dog had moved closer and was sitting, gazing up into her face. "Hold your hand out to him, palm down, and let him sniff your fingers."

She was reluctant to have all those big teeth so close to her hand, but she did as instructed. The dog sniffed, then his big, pink tongue swiped across her hand. "I think he smells the sausage I cooked for breakfast." She gave a nervous laugh then felt compelled to reach out and pat the animal's head.

"Why don't you try it, too," Rupert said to Jon. After the dog sniffed him several times, appearing bored, Rupert stuck out his hand. "Rupert Meyer."

"Jon Pierson." The two men shook hands.

"He seems like a nice enough fellow," Jon remarked as he and Kallene returned to her house.

She chuckled and rolled her eyes. "He bought that house six months ago, and this is the first time he's ever spoken to me. And by the way, he's the ex-convict I told you about earlier."

Jon turned to stare after the man who was just disappearing around the back of his house with the dog. "I've noticed him a few times when we've been running—but without the dog."

"That dog is going to take some getting used to." She shivered. "I don't think I'd want to run into him on the canyon trail, and I can't help worrying about the kids who walk by his house every day on their way to and from school. Some of them tease Delbert Haney, and he yells at them; if that dog thinks the kids are being threatened, there could be real trouble."

CHAPTER FIFTEEN

KALLENE SPENT THE MORNING AT the office attending a meeting and receiving several new assignments. She spent a few minutes updating the information she wished to take home with her and downloading it to a flash drive. When she finished, she decided to drop by the police station on her way home to talk to Scott about Parker. Almost a week had passed since Linda's body had been found, and she'd seen nothing of the little boy. She didn't even know if his mother was back in town. Whenever she drove past the Grayson house, there didn't seem to be any indication that she or anyone else was there.

Luck was with her when she reached the police station. Scott was in his office, and a welcoming smile spread across his face as he stood to greet her. "This must be my lucky day."

"I hope you've got time for lunch."

"I think I could manage that." She smiled in return but felt a pang of guilt. She enjoyed being with Scott but knew she couldn't go on seeing both Scott and Jon. She had strong feelings for both men and knew she wasn't being fair to either of them. "But I only stopped by to see if you have any information about Parker Grayson. He was so upset over discovering Linda's body, and I haven't been able to get my last glimpse of him walking away with that police officer out of my mind. He looked so lost and alone. I haven't seen him since that day, though I've dropped by his house several times and tried to call. I feel guilty that I didn't stay with him until one of his parents arrived."

"He was interviewed by someone from the DA's office who specializes in working with children connected to major crimes. She's an assistant DA and is very sympathetic to children. I don't know if any of his testimony will be used, but I can tell you his father picked him up from her office."

"He didn't show up for Cub Scouts this week, and I haven't seen him around the neighborhood. I hope he's not ill or still coping with shock."

"I'm sure there's nothing to worry about," Scott said. "Parents tend to be protective after a child has suffered from trauma. They may have taken him on a trip to distract him, but I'm sure the DA's office will keep tabs on him." He stood and reached for her arm in a courtly gesture to steer her toward the door.

When they walked into the restaurant, Kallene couldn't help noticing how many women watched Scott as they made their way to a table. She was also aware that Scott knew the effect he had on women and enjoyed the attention. For a moment she basked in being the envy of the adoring women who made it clear they'd love to trade places with her. She felt chagrined by her thoughts. She wasn't the shallow kind of woman who played games like that, was she?

Over lunch Scott turned the conversation toward almost every subject except the case. They laughed a lot, and Kallene discovered she felt in much better spirits after he kissed her cheek and walked her to her car with a promise to call her if there was any news about Parker or about the murder of her friend.

She meant to drive straight home, but on an impulse, Kallene pulled into the Grayson driveway. Ted and Julie were probably both at work, but it wouldn't hurt to check. She pushed the doorbell and heard it echo through the house. When no one came to the door, she tried again. After a few minutes, she heard a shuffling sound, and after waiting several minutes more, the doorknob turned, and the door opened a crack.

"Parker?" She hardly recognized the boy. His pupils seemed oddly dilated, and his face wore a flat, emotionless look.

"Parker, are you all right?" He looked ill, and she wasn't certain he even recognized her.

"I'm fine. Just tired. My mother said I don't have to go to school today." The words sounded memorized.

"All right. Go back to bed. We can talk when you come to Cub Scouts next week."

The door closed, and Kallene stared at it, feeling uncertain. The boy wasn't acting like the Parker she knew. She wondered if he'd been given sedatives to soothe his nerves. If so, she suspected he'd been given a heavier dose than needed. She'd have to watch for another opportunity to check on him and speak to his parents.

* * *

Kallene felt at loose ends when she reached home and found it difficult to settle into working on any of her projects. Thinking a little fresh air might clear her mind, she stepped out onto her deck. Trees and bushes rattled their branches as a crisp wind blew across the hillside where her home was perched. The sky appeared dark and menacing, and a haze hung over the valley, obscuring the view. She shivered. A few lazy snowflakes drifted toward the ground. There would likely be measurable snow on the foothills and perhaps even in the valley before morning.

It was too cold to stay outside for long. She turned to step back inside but not before she saw a movement beside her garage. She concentrated on the spot but saw nothing. *Probably just a stray bit of trash caught by the wind.* Nevertheless, she took a hurried step into the house, locked the sliding door, and put the bar in place. For good measure, she pulled the blind that covered the glass double doors.

Settling in to work was harder than usual. She found herself sending frequent glances toward the window. She got up to get a drink of water and noticed that the few fluttering snowflakes had turned to a steady onslaught. It took a while, but in time she started work and was so absorbed she forgot dinner until she heard the doorbell ring. She saved her work and dashed to the door, flipping the light switches as she went.

"Brittany, get in here!" She reached for her neighbor's coat sleeve to pull the young woman inside her cozy living room. "It's snowing out there and is much too cold for a pregnant lady to be wandering around. Are you all right?"

"Isn't it beautiful?" Brittany turned to watch the large flakes caught in the glow of Kallene's porch light slanting toward the ground. A thin coat of white covered the lawn but wasn't yet sticking to the driveway or road. The predicted snowstorm had arrived. There was a note of excitement in Brittany's voice. "I'm twenty-three years old, and this is the first time I've seen snow actually falling. The little storm we had earlier fell while I was asleep and melted before noon the next day. Jeff showed me banks of dirty snow in the mountains last month when we drove up to one of the ski resorts to look around, but I've never seen it clean and new like this before or felt it land on my face and hands."

"I'm surprised Jeff didn't object to your going out on a night like this."

"Jeff isn't home. He had to fly to Seattle this morning to give a demonstration for his company and won't be back until tomorrow. I wanted to feel the snow and touch it and share it with someone. I thought maybe you . . ." She lifted a box she held in her hands, which Kallene hadn't previously noticed. She caught the aroma of pepperoni pizza and laughed.

"Sounds great! Take off your coat and come into the kitchen. A girls' night sounds just right for a night like this. It'll only take a moment to mix a pitcher of lemonade." She led the way into the kitchen. "Do you like strawberries in your lemonade?"

"Uh, sure."

Kallene dumped a can of frozen concentrate and some frozen strawberries into her blender then added water and several handfuls of ice. When the drinks were ready, she set them on the table.

"Oh! That's good!" Brittany sighed as she took her first sip.

"This is good, too." Kallene reveled in the melted cheese and warm pepperoni that filled her mouth. They ate in silence for a few minutes with Brittany's attention drifting toward the window, where she could see the snowfall increasing in intensity. A shadow seemed to cross Brittany's face, and she gave a little sigh.

"Are you all right?" Kallene asked. What would she do if the young woman seated across from her started having labor pains or her water broke? If she remembered right, Brittany's baby was due some-time near Christmas.

"I'm fine. Really. I just . . . Do you ever get scared living all by yourself?"

"No. It doesn't bother me." Kallene wasn't sure she was being com-pletely honest. She remembered her reaction to a piece of blowing trash earlier, but until Linda's disappearance, she really hadn't given being alone in her house much thought. "Are you nervous with Jeff away? If you are, there's no reason you shouldn't stay here tonight. My guest room is made up, and I'd love to have a roommate for the night."

Brittany eagerly accepted Kallene's invitation. After clearing up the kitchen, Kallene popped a bag of popcorn in the microwave while Brittany checked the cabinet filled with DVDs in the family room.

"Do you have a favorite?" Brittany asked.

"Not really. To be honest, I don't often watch movies. I only have a large collection because my friends and family never know what to give me for birthdays or Christmas and usually settle for a DVD."

Brittany giggled. "I love movies. Going to a theater isn't as much fun since I got pregnant, so Jeff and I rent a couple movies every weekend." She hesitated. "If you don't want to watch a movie, that's okay; we could play games or something."

"Just because I don't watch many DVDs doesn't mean I don't like movies. It's just not the same watching a movie alone and watching one with someone you enjoy sharing it with. Go ahead, pick one."

"Okay. Here's one I haven't seen, and since the seal isn't broken, it will be new to both of us." She ripped off the clear wrapping, pulled out the disc, and put it in the DVD player.

Kallene pressed the remote to turn on the TV, pausing a moment before changing the channel to the video auxiliary. She'd caught the end of a sports broadcast and recognized raven-haired Julie Grayson being interviewed by a well-known sportscaster.

"Oh, look. It's Julie Grayson," Brittany said, coming to stand beside her. "She's beautiful. I can't believe I live on the same street as someone famous."

"I think that's the fourth different hair color she's had in as many months, although I haven't seen her for a while around here. She must be on a prolonged trip. Maybe she and Ted are having troubles. It wouldn't be a stretch to imagine that—with how seldom they seem to be together." Kallene regretted the catty remark as soon as it left her mouth. Brittany didn't seem to notice.

"I wish I looked like that." Brittany sighed. "Sometimes I think I'm going to be a fat lump forever."

"You're not fat! You're just very prego."

Both girls laughed, then Brittany added, "Even before I got pregnant, though, I wasn't thin and buff like Julie or you. I used to dream of having that kind of shape, but somewhere along the way I discovered I prefer ice cream to being skinny." She settled in one corner of the sofa with the bowl of popcorn, and Kallene pushed the PLAY button on the remote.

They paused the movie twice—once when Jeff called to check on Brittany and once when Jon called to change his date with Kallene from an early-morning run to dinner the next evening. "You're not planning to run in the morning, are you—with all this snow?" he asked.

"No, I haven't gotten around to signing up for an indoor track yet. I'd better put that on my to-do list for tomorrow."

"I'll go with you," Jon volunteered. "I need to sign up, too." He made arrangements to pick her up in the early afternoon so they could investigate gyms together before dinner.

Comments about the movie shifted to talk about themselves and their interests as Brittany and Kallene talked through the evening. It was close to midnight and both were almost asleep when they finished talking and made their way upstairs.

"Thanks." Brittany yawned before entering the guest room. "I enjoyed this evening, and thanks for letting me spend the night. I know I shouldn't be so silly about being afraid while Jeff is gone."

"I enjoyed our evening, too, and I'm glad you wanted to hang around. I've missed having a friend to talk about girl stuff with."

"Oh, Kallene." Brittany stepped back to her side and put her arms around her. "I can't imagine how hard losing Linda has been for you."

"You're a good friend." Kallene hugged Brittany in return and swallowed hard to dislodge the lump in her throat. Brittany couldn't possibly know that Kallene needed a friend probably more than Brittany needed her. She and Jon and Scott had grown closer, and she valued their friendships and love, but sometimes a woman just needed the friendship of another woman.

The storm blew itself out before morning. Kallene woke feeling happier than she'd been for some time. She hadn't been awakened once by strange sounds or worries. Just knowing another adult was in the house must have been more reassuring than she'd expected. She sang while she showered and dug out a pair of cords to wear for her date with Jon a little later.

Making her way toward the kitchen, she paused out of habit to open the blinds that hid the sliding doors to the deck. It took a moment to register what she was seeing: Rupert Meyer's big dog lay curled in a ball against the door, partially sheltered by a canvas-covered lounge chair. He raised his head and seemed to grin at her.

The dog stretched and yawned. Without a backward glance, he trotted down the stairs to disappear from her view. Should she call animal control? Maybe she should call the police. She recalled the way the dog had gone after Mr. Haney and shuddered. It seemed quite clear Rupert Meyer didn't keep his dog confined to his own property nearly as well as he'd promised he would.

"Is something wrong? You look worried." She jumped. Brittany's arrival beside the sliding doors had gone unnoticed while her attention was focused on the dog. Not wishing to alarm her visitor, she said, "It was just a stray dog in my yard, but he's gone now." She linked her arm through Brittany's. "Come on. Let's find some breakfast."

"I really should go home."

"Not without breakfast." Kallene was adamant, and the two were soon sharing toast and scrambled eggs.

"Are you going anywhere for Christmas?" Brittany asked.

"My dad is an Air Force officer. He was recently transferred to Andrews Air Force Base near Washington DC. My parents want me to join them there for Christmas, but I haven't made up my mind yet. Neither of my brothers will be with them for Christmas, so I feel a little guilty to be considering staying here."

"If I were you, I'd go. I'd love it if Jeff and I could spend Christmas with either set of our parents. If the baby gets here before Christmas, we just might have both sets of parents here with us for the holiday."

Kallene walked Brittany the short distance to Brittany's house after they finished eating, taking care not to let Brittany become aware that she was keeping a watch out for Rupert's dog. She didn't like the idea of the dog running loose. Mr. Meyer had assured her the dog wouldn't hurt her, but Rupert Meyer wasn't a man she found easy to trust. After Brittany went inside, Kallene shoveled her walk—while

Brittany protested on the front porch. When she finished, she hurried back to her own house to shovel her driveway.

If that dog shows up, I'll drop my shovel and run for the house.

When Jon arrived, she told him about the dog visiting her yard. "It looked like he might have spent the night sleeping on my deck," she said.

Jon didn't seem concerned. "I think that dog likes you. At least with that big mutt guarding your back door, you don't need to worry about a burglar breaking in."

But what about the dog's owner?

CHAPTER SIXTEEN

SEEING THE SEAT BELT SIGN turn on, Kallene closed her laptop and tucked it under her seat. Her journey was almost over. She was looking forward to seeing her parents again, but the flight across the country had been one of the longest and most annoying she'd ever experienced. She'd booked late and had to take what she could get, which meant delays in Denver and St. Louis.

In Denver it had been questionable whether the plane would even be allowed to take off, due to snow, and when she finally was able to board, she'd been stuck in the center seat. Two little boys in the row behind her fought and screamed all the way from St. Louis to Reagan International in Washington DC while their mother read a book and ignored them. She'd planned to work on the long flight but found using her laptop or concentrating impossible. Knowing that Jon was also flying east for Christmas and would land in Baltimore at almost the same time she would arrive in Washington DC compounded her annoyance with the flight. They'd tried to book the same flight, but they'd been unable to.

At last the seat belt sign went off, and she gathered her few belongings and waited until her seatmates struggled into the aisle and the family behind her exited before attempting to retrieve her bag from the overhead bin and make her way into the aisle. Dragging the small case behind her and clasping her computer case, which was doubling as a handbag for this trip, she hurried down the concourse and into her parents' welcoming arms.

"Welcome home, honey!" Her father's hug nearly smothered her, and she couldn't help smiling at the irony of her father's greeting.

Washington DC wasn't her home; she barely remembered a couple of visits there with her family when she was a child. Dad had never been stationed near the capital before, though they'd lived in many different places. She returned the hug and felt a moment's pride that her father was still trim and solid, looking more like forty than fifty-two in his precisely tailored uniform. She took a moment to rub her knuckles across the new star that graced his coat.

"Congratulations, Dad." He grinned and hugged her again.

"My turn, Frank." Her mother held Kallene in a big hug, and she realized how much she'd missed her mom since moving west on her own, especially during the past few months. With her father's many deployments and the moves that had carried them to diverse places, she and her mother had grown particularly close.

"Now don't get all weepy, Carol," Frank admonished. He looked back at Kallene. "Do you have luggage to pick up?" he asked.

"This is it." She lifted her carry-on a few inches off the floor. Her father took it from her and led the way to his parked car.

Home turned out to be a redbrick, two-story house on a quiet, tree-lined street situated on Andrews Air Force Base just over the state line from Washington DC in Maryland. The house was unfamiliar, but the furnishings brought back memories, especially the bedroom set that had been hers since she was thirteen and had moved along with her family to ever nicer quarters as her dad's rank had increased over the years. The familiar aroma of her mother's double-fudge cake lingered in the air and completed her sense of homecoming.

It didn't take long to unpack the few clothes she'd brought. She only planned to visit her parents for a few days over Christmas. She almost hadn't come, but when she'd learned the Piersons were planning a memorial service for Linda two days before Christmas, she'd decided to make the effort, even though Ben McCallister had fussed and objected to her taking the time off. He'd insisted she had to be available during the holiday week since so many others would be off, and she hadn't requested the time far enough in advance. She couldn't see why he cared, since she spent little time at the office, anyway.

"Dinner's ready," her mother called. Kallene hurried down the stairs to join her parents at the table. She was glad her mother had insisted on cooking the meal instead of allowing her father to take them to the officers' club. It was good to relax and just be together. She enjoyed the life she'd chosen for herself, but a part of her would always relish gathering around her parents' table and basking in their love and approval.

While they ate, her parents filled her in on her brothers' activities. Dallin and his wife were stationed in Germany and were enjoying the experience, though they hoped to be back in the States well before their second child's birth. Chris was serving a mission in Brazil and had just been transferred to a remote mountain village and had an "awesome" new native companion.

Leaning back in her chair, she doubted she could ever swallow another mouthful. Kallene was so full she didn't think she could eat a bite of dessert. But then her mom slid a generous slice of chocolate cake in front of her. She eyed it for a moment before lifting a forkful of the deep double-fudge to her mouth. She closed her eyes and sighed. It just wasn't possible to lack room for her mom's cake.

"Dear, we were sorry to hear about your friend," her mom began in a tentative voice. "We've been concerned and wonder if it's safe for you to be living alone. And don't you think it's a little silly and dangerous for a grown woman to be out running around on roads and trails where someone might take advantage of her?"

"I thought Salt Lake was supposed to be one of the safest cities in the country," her dad added. "I read in the paper about that young woman's murder, and I'm not sure your neighborhood is all that safe."

"I'm perfectly safe," she attempted to reassure them. "I even had my alarm system upgraded. Anyway, the police and Linda's family are pretty certain her husband killed her and that there's no real threat to anyone else. Domestic violence can happen anywhere."

"I don't know. There was a jogger killed last year on a trail that runs near the Capital Beltway, and I heard a story on the news not long ago about another female runner being found dead in a wooded area in Wisconsin."

"Mom! There's no way those two deaths are connected to each other or to Linda. They're more than a thousand miles apart. Besides, Jon has been running with me ever since Linda was killed, and now that there's snow on the ground, I run at an indoor track." The mention of Jon was enough to divert her mother's attention.

"You've mentioned Jon several times. Are the two of you getting serious?"

"We're friends, and we enjoy a lot of the same things." Kallene spoke in an even voice. She'd avoided speculating about where her friendship with Jon might be headed. She liked him a lot and felt more comfortable with him than with anyone else she'd ever dated, even more so than with the man she'd been briefly engaged to while attending BYU. Still, there was Scott. Her dates with him had been less frequent, but she couldn't deny the attraction she felt toward him. She didn't know how much longer she could develop such strong relationships with two men without something giving way.

"I'd worry much less about you if you had a husband."

"I hate to break it to you, Mom, but there are a lot of women who are in far more danger *with* a husband than they'd be without one. It's not a get-out-of-trouble-free card. Good marriages take work."

"I'm sorry, honey. That was a thoughtless thing to say. I guess it's just a mom thing to want to see a daughter happily married. All my years as a military wife have certainly taught me there are a lot of unhappy—even abusive—marriages, and I don't want that for you or any other woman. But I don't want you to miss out on a relationship like your father and I have."

"I want that, too, Mom, but there aren't many men out there like Dad." She winked at her Dad and he grinned.

"When do I get to meet this Jon of yours?" he asked.

She groaned in the dramatic way she'd perfected as a teenager then laughed. "He'll pick me up tomorrow morning to take me to the memorial service for his sister, but I don't think he'll be as easily intimidated as my high-school dates you used to scare off."

* * *

Kallene's parents drove her to the air base's front gate to meet Jon the next morning and arranged for a visitor's pass for him for the next few days. Greetings were cordial, and Jon and Kallene were soon on their way.

"How was your flight yesterday?" Jon asked as he pulled onto the beltway.

"Don't ask," Kallene said with a laugh. "I hope yours was better than mine."

"I slept all the way."

"No fair!" Kallene leaned back against the seat of the car Jon had borrowed from his mother, enjoying the luxurious feel of real leather. Being with Jon felt right and comfortable. It was hard to believe it had only been a little more than twenty-four hours since they'd said good-bye at the Salt Lake airport and boarded their separate flights. Her parents' probing of her relationship with Jon came to mind as she glanced over at him. He was focused on the heavy traffic. He was a good-looking man with a sharp mind, a sense of humor, and he was dedicated to the Church and his family. He was everything she'd always thought she was looking for in a man. And there was that breathless feeling that came each time they were apart then reunited or at odd moments when she was with him. Was she falling in love with him? She thought she might be, but why did she still find Scott attractive if she was in love with Jon?

"You seem deep in thought."

She couldn't exactly share her thoughts. "I'm not sure I'm even thinking. In a way, I seem to only be feeling. It's a dark, overcast day, yet I'm enjoying the scenery. There's something that feels right about trees and grass coming right to the edge of the highway. I haven't lived with my parents since I left to enroll in college, yet it's comforting being a daughter again, sleeping in my old bed, and being surrounded by the security of being on a military base." She paused before adding, "It feels right to be with you today, too."

"I'm glad you're with me today. I'm not sure I could face this alone." He took one hand from the wheel to cover hers for just a moment.

"I don't think either of us will ever stop missing Linda. You knew her a lot longer than I did, yet when we were together, it was like we'd been friends forever."

Jon drove in silence for several minutes then said, "The lab in Utah sent Dad a copy of the autopsy report. He showed it to me, and I can't get it out of my mind."

"I've never heard the exact cause of death." She spoke in a tentative voice, uncertain whether she really wanted to know how her friend died.

Jon's face hardened. "She was struck repeatedly by a heavy, blunt object about the face and side of her head. The coroner believes she then fell backward, hitting her head against a hard surface, which fractured her skull. The blow to the back of her head is consistent with a fall and wasn't inflicted by the same object that caused fractures to the side of her skull. There's also evidence she may have been strangled, though the marks about her throat might have been inflicted after her death. It appears she was moved to the place where she was found but was killed somewhere else."

Kallene blinked and held her hand to her mouth to hold back tears and the churning in her stomach. "Then it might have been an accident if she fell against something."

"Because of the strangulation marks and the deterioration of the body, the lab couldn't definitively say whether or not she was already dead when her head made contact with something hard." He pounded a fist against the steering wheel. "I don't understand why the police haven't arrested Carson. In a battle that violent—even though he's bigger than Linda was—there should have been enough marks on him to raise suspicion. Linda wouldn't have docilely allowed anyone to knock her around like that."

"He'd just taken a shower when I arrived at their house that morning. The only marks I saw on him were splatters of oatmeal Macie had thrown instead of eating." Kallene tried to remember details of that morning. "There were pieces of tissue paper on his neck where I assumed he'd cut himself shaving, and when I bathed Macie, his wet towel was on the floor in the main floor bathroom. There were a few blood spots on it."

"Did you tell Scott about that?"

"I can't remember if I included it in my statement or not, but I'll make sure he knows when I get back."

"We're almost to the church." Jon took the next exit and followed a road that wound through tree-lined streets.

The scent of flowers was almost overpowering when they walked into the room where Jon's parents were greeting those who had come to offer condolences. She greeted Jon's parents with sympathetic hugs, and Jon insisted she stay beside him in the Relief Society room for the family prayer. Tears welled in her eyes when she looked toward the closed casket. There would be no last farewell to her friend. She would be haunted for the rest of her life by her last glimpse of Linda embodied in that hand lying like a piece of refuse among half-rotten leaves and debris.

The service was short, lasting little more than an hour. Kallene discovered her spirit was lightened, and she'd found more closure than she'd expected as one speaker spoke of the Atonement and another spoke of all of the good Linda had accomplished in her short life. Carson wasn't present, but a large spray of flowers near the casket had WIFE and MOTHER spelled out in glitter on trailing ribbons. At first Adam and Jon objected to the tribute being placed near the casket, but Janet's more charitable view prevailed as she insisted that someday Macie might want to know that she was represented in some small way at the service for her mother.

Kallene's heels sank into the grass as they made their way across the cemetery to an open grave beside the one where Linda's sister lay. Carson had finally given permission to the Piersons to let them bury Linda with family, but Jon had told Kallene that he gave it somewhat grudgingly, as though consenting only because he wanted to get the Piersons off his case. Janet Pierson buried her head in Adam's shoulder and cried quietly into a crumpled lace handkerchief she held in one hand. Adam and Jon each placed an arm around her.

The skies grew darker, and a chill wind swept across the cemetery. Kallene pulled her coat closer. A rumble of thunder sounded nearby, and she bowed her head. More accustomed to military funerals than civilian, she found the sound a fitting salute, like a heavenly trumpet had played a requiem for her friend.

When the service concluded, Jon and his parents were surrounded by family, friends, and ward members who wished to pay their personal condolences. As one person after another embraced Jon or drew him into conversation, Kallene found herself separated from him. Not knowing any of the people, Kallene drifted a short distance away. A pretty woman in an extremely short skirt and wearing heavy makeup tugged on Jon's sleeve. Her coat was unbuttoned, revealing advanced pregnancy. He appeared startled to see her but bent to listen as she took what seemed a long time to speak with him. Her familiar gestures as she clung to his arm, stroked his jacket lapel, then leaned against his shoulder stirred jealous feelings in Kallene.

She turned away, not wishing to watch any longer. A few minutes later Jon appeared at her side. "I think we should return to the church. The Relief Society sisters have prepared a luncheon."

Adam and Janet chose not to attend the luncheon, but Jon and Kallene stopped in for a short time before beginning the drive back to Andrews Air Force Base. It was late afternoon, and the congested traffic moved at a snail's pace. Jon was quiet, and Kallene wasn't sure if it was because of the need to concentrate on traffic or because he was emotionally drained.

When he did speak, his words startled her. "I hadn't expected to see my ex-wife at the funeral."

"She was there?"

"Yes. At the cemetery. I don't think she attended the service at the church."

Kallene remembered the woman who had clung to Jon's arm. She knew at once she was the woman who had once been his wife. There was no mistaking the coil of jealousy that wormed its way into her heart.

"Jessa liked Linda, so I suppose I shouldn't have been surprised she came," he went on. "She isn't with the guy she left me for anymore, and she dropped a couple of hints that she'd like for us to get back together." Kallene's heart sank. Was Jon telling her he wanted to get back with his ex-wife? The swift bite of jealousy stung, requiring a deep breath and a reminder to be an adult. There had been no promises made between her and Jon.

"I thought she lived in California." It was an inane comment, but she couldn't think of anything that wouldn't betray her own sense of loss. Her heart would take a long time to heal if Jon were no longer in her life. She wasn't certain it ever would heal.

"She does, or at least that's where she met the man she thought she couldn't live without two years ago. Now they're separated, and she's not sure she wants to raise a baby alone." A short laugh hinted at some residual pain that lingered from his divorce. His face was grim as he clarified. "We were married four years. I wanted to start a family right away, but she wasn't sure she was ready. Anyway, it never happened, and she had just agreed to see a fertility specialist when she met Mr. Wonderful. Since she obviously had no trouble getting pregnant with him, it looks like I'm the one with a fertility problem."

"I'm sorry." Kallene didn't know why she was apologizing. It just seemed the thing to say, but her heart kept saying she really was sorry—sorry for herself. She'd finally met a man she could consider marrying, and his ex-wife was offering him not only reconciliation, but the chance to fulfill his desire to become a father.

"It's funny," Jon went on. "I felt nothing. The bitterness is gone, but so are the feelings I once had for her. I don't hate her, but neither do I feel even any mild interest in her."

Kallene didn't know what to say or if she should say anything. Was it possible he really wasn't interested in what Jessa was offering, or would he change his mind as time further healed the wounds he'd suffered?

The familiar ring of her cell phone saved her from having to say anything. She fumbled in her purse to retrieve it. Without checking the caller ID, she said, "Hello."

"Kallene? I'm glad I was able to reach you. This is Scott."

CHAPTER SEVENTEEN

"Hi! I didn't expect to hear from you until I got back home."

Scott chuckled. There was something odd in the sound, almost as though he hadn't expected to hear her voice. "That's one of the hazards of cell phones. Friends can catch up to you anywhere. Anyway, I found myself thinking about you." He paused, and his voice turned serious.

"Look, I know you're busy, and you said you might go to visit your parents back east, but something has come up I feel you shouldn't learn about from some distorted newscast, and I promised I'd let you know if anything connected to your friend turned up. You told me you were attending a memorial for her while you were near Baltimore, and since I've been unable to reach the Piersons, I hoped you'd be in contact with them and could share the information. Some of the early news programs have already made assumptions that aren't warranted by the facts."

"Uh-oh." Her heart started to pound. She couldn't help wondering if the police had arrested Carson. She gripped her phone so tightly that her knuckles turned white. Scott got right to the point.

"Some bicyclists found a woman's body a short distance from one of the trails through the Legacy Parkway. The Davis County Sheriff's office contacted us because of similarities to the Longdale case. Both bodies showed signs of severe beating around the head, and jogging clothes were found near both bodies. Today's victim was also covered with a thin layer of dirt and rotted plant material."

"Who . . . I mean . . ." She didn't know what she meant. Her thoughts were a jumble.

"The body hasn't been identified yet, and queries have gone out to surrounding law enforcement groups concerning women with light-brown hair, a little taller than average, probably a regular runner, reported missing during the past few months. The description made me a little uneasy."

"Why? I don't understand."

"Uh, no reason. That description fits a lot of women."

Including me. Was that the reason Scott called—to make certain I'm in Washington DC, where I said I would probably be?

"I don't think her death occurred more than a week ago and probably sometime during the past few days," Scott continued. "It's been cold here, but you'd expect more decomposition if she'd been there longer. You're probably wondering if this removes Carson Longdale from suspicion concerning his wife's death, but it changes little. He's not a formal suspect, but he hasn't been cleared. Before the media begins playing with this information, you need to know there are enough differences in these cases to cast doubt on the possibility that they might be linked."

"What differences?"

"I can't talk about that now."

"What can you tell me?"

"Not much concerning the investigation, but more is going to come out than should, since both of the bicyclists were seen talking to news people."

"I'll tell Jon and let him warn his parents."

"Okay. I've got to go now. I shouldn't have said anything to you since it's an ongoing investigation, but I felt you should know enough to set your mind at rest. Take care . . . and Merry Christmas. I'll see you when you get back."

"Merry Christmas," she whispered back. She closed her phone.

"What was that about? You seem upset."

"If you see a place to pull over, take it. You need to know what Scott told me."

"That was Detective Alexander?" Was it her imagination or was there a bristling tone to Jon's voice.

"Yes."

In minutes they were parked along an unpaved road that angled away from the freeway. Gray light filtered through a backdrop of skeletal trees, leaving Kallene with an odd sense that she'd stepped out of reality. Cars rushed by mere feet from their position, but she paid them no attention.

Jon turned off the engine and turned to face her. Not knowing where to begin, she just started talking about everything Scott had told her. "A woman's beaten body was found in Davis County this morning." She filled in the details. "Though her death is similar to Linda's, he doesn't think the murders are connected because of differences he couldn't tell me about," she concluded.

"They sound similar. Like Linda, the victim was a runner, both received head wounds, and little effort was made to hide the body other than leaving it in a remote location and giving it a superficial covering of vegetation. I'd really like to know what differences the detective is talking about."

"I can think of some differences." Kallene began ticking them off on her fingers. "That woman was jogging in a remote area; Linda disappeared from a suburban neighborhood. A greater effort was made to hide Linda's body than it appears was made to hide that woman. Linda had red hair, and this victim had light brown hair."

"It could be a copycat murder," Jon said. "I'm pretty certain Carson killed Linda."

"Scott hinted that he thinks so, too."

"But you don't?"

"I just don't know. Sometimes I think it's the only logical conclusion to make. Then I remember how much he adores Macie and how kind and helpful he's been to people in our ward, and I just can't see him as a murderer. I can't imagine him leaving Macie alone so he could dispose of Linda's body, and there's no way he could have dragged his daughter along on such a sick undertaking, even if the rough terrain wouldn't have made the task difficult."

"The only time I question his guilt is when I wonder how someone who's no smarter than he is managed to cover his tracks so well."

"Linda told me once that he considered her family intellectual snobs who looked down their noses at him."

"Point taken." Jon winced. "Perhaps we did make him feel that way. We certainly tried hard enough to convince him and Louise to finish school. I'm not sure I looked down on him for not finishing college or thought any less of him for preferring blue-collar employment over finishing his degree and finding a better-paying job. I just felt frustrated for Linda's sake that he lacked the ambition to stay with a job, forcing his family to live under worse circumstances than was necessary. If anyone was a snob, it was him. When I got a divorce, he decided I wasn't good enough to continue my relationship with my own sister and niece. Snubbing me was one thing, but he extended his disapproval to my parents. He went so far as to return all of the pretty clothes my mother bought for her first and only granddaughter."

"Yeah, he's pretty fanatic. But I still have difficulty seeing him as the murderer." Kallene stared sightlessly through the window, only noting absently that a fine drizzle of rain had begun, lending to the otherworldly feeling she had experienced since getting the call from Scott.

Jon hunched his shoulders and reached for the ignition. "I'd better get you back to the base. My parents, especially Mom, are struggling with losing both daughters just three years apart, and I need to pass on the information Scott shared."

"Are you all right?" Kallene noticed his hunched shoulders and his ashen face that made his eyes appear sunken. "This day has been a strain for you, even without this added news."

"It hasn't been an easy day, but having you beside me helped a great deal." He turned to her without starting the car. His hands cupped her face. "My timing is way off, I'm sure, but I want you to know that I can't imagine how I would have survived these past months without you. Today as I stood listening to Jessa, I was struck with considerable force by the certainty that you have become a more important part of my life in three months than she was during the four years of being my wife." He seemed to study her face for several long seconds before touching his lips to hers.

There was an aching sweetness in his kiss that drew an emotional response from deep within her. She felt her lips tremble and the sting of moisture in her eyes as he ended the kiss. She attempted to smile and his returning smile appeared as wobbly as her own. He placed a quick kiss on her forehead and turned away to start the car.

"We'd better go." His words were a husky whisper, telling her he'd been as shaken as she was by that potent kiss.

* * *

Kallene spent the following day touring some of the historic sites in the city with her parents and finishing some last-minute Christmas shopping. She and Jon had agreed to spend Christmas Eve and Christmas morning with their respective families and not see each other again until it was time to return to Utah. They'd been able to book the same return flight leaving Baltimore late Christmas afternoon.

Christmas music wafted through the house as Kallene and her parents sat down to a simple dinner of clam chowder in bread bowls and a tossed salad. It seemed strange to celebrate Christmas without her brothers. The previous year they'd all been together in Texas. Midway through the meal, a call came through from Dallin in Germany. Kallene's mom turned on the speakerphone, and they took turns speaking to him and to his wife, Corrianne.

"Dad," Dallin said through the speaker, "I'm being deployed to Afghanistan the first of February." Other than a gasp from Kallene's mother, the room remained quiet as they each strained to hear.

"I don't want to leave Corrianne and Justin here in Germany while I'm away, and she'd rather have the baby in the States than here. It would relieve my mind if they could stay with you during my deployment."

"Of course they can stay, but what about her parents? Won't they want her to stay with them?" Carol asked.

"Ordinarily, yes, but they've been called to serve a mission and will be leaving in three weeks. I've got a furlough coming before I leave, and we thought we'd leave here the tenth of January so we'll have plenty of time to travel before the baby comes and so Corrianne can see her parents for a few days before they leave." The conversation continued for several minutes with questions and answers about travel plans and Corrianne's parents' mission.

As soon as the call ended, Carol began planning which rooms to give their son and daughter-in-law's little family. Kallene smiled, knowing her mother couldn't have been given a better Christmas gift than the expectation of having her only grandchild and his mother come for an extended visit. Her mother would have far less time to worry about Dallin being deployed to a war zone with Corrianne and Justin living in her house. Her mind flashed back to the kiss she and

Jon had shared. Her mother would have less time to worry about her only daughter's marital prospects, too.

Christmas morning flew by in record time. Gifts were opened, and Kallene spoke with her brother Chris for a few minutes when his much-anticipated call came through from the mission field. Dinner was the sumptuous feast her mother always prepared on Christmas day, and soon it was time to begin the drive to the Baltimore airport.

The usually hectic airport was quiet since most holiday travelers chose not to fly on Christmas day. They had no trouble finding Jon and his parents. She felt almost shy meeting Jon after their last encounter, and she suspected her mother noticed and would have something to say about the blush she felt creep up her neck when he casually placed an arm around her waist.

"Mom, Dad, this is Adam and Janet Pierson," she managed to keep her voice steady.

"Call us Frank and Carol." Her mother stepped forward to take Janet's hand, and the men gave each other a firm handshake. They conversed for a short time before Jon and Kallene said their farewells in a flurry of hugs and kisses before making their way to the security checkpoint.

Jon took her bag from her and stowed it beside his in an overhead storage bin while she slid into the nearest row of seats. Jon sat beside her, and they both fastened their seat belts without waiting for the stewardess to instruct them, leaned back, and took a long breath. Kallene turned to face Jon and found him watching her. He smiled, and his hand reached for hers.

She was pleased no one claimed the seat beside them, guaranteeing more room and relative privacy. It was growing dark, and some passengers turned on their overhead reading lights, while others welcomed the darkness with obvious plans to sleep until they reached their destination. Jon touched the tiny lights over their heads, creating an island of brightness. They talked about their separate Christmas celebrations as the plane took off. After the plane leveled off, Jon handed Kallene a small, rectangular box wrapped in gold foil paper. "Merry Christmas," he said.

"I have something for you, too," she told him, "but you'll have to wait until we reach my house." She thought of the portrait of Linda she'd painted from memory. She'd decided it was too bulky to haul to Baltimore then back to Utah again.

She slid the ribbon off the small package and picked at the tape until the wrapping fell free. She swallowed when she saw the Cartier logo on the box. Lifting the lid, she stared at a gold charm bracelet with a single charm, a tiny artist's palette with each color represented by a different color stone. She swallowed hard before she could speak. "I'm not sure I should accept something this expensive."

"Do you like it?"

"Yes! It's beautiful."

"That's all that matters. It's my hope that I'll have the opportunity to add more charms to it in the future." He lifted the bracelet from the box and fastened it around her wrist. Watching her eyes, he lifted her wrist to place a kiss on it.

Kallene grew sleepy as the plane flew westward, and Jon turned off the overhead lights. With her head resting on his shoulder, she drifted toward sleep. Just before sleep claimed her, she sat up with an abruptness that startled Jon, who had also been nearly asleep.

"What if there's a serial killer?"

"What?" Jon was struggling to become fully awake.

"Scott said he didn't think that woman found along the Legacy Parkway and Linda were killed by the same person, but Mom mentioned a woman who was beaten and killed near the beltway in Washington DC last summer and a similar case a year ago in Wisconsin. What if they were all murdered by the same person?"

CHAPTER EIGHTEEN

"Two in Utah, one in DC, and one in Wisconsin? That's a pretty long stretch."

"But what if there are others?"

"If the police even suspect a case is connected to a serial killer, they check national databases and exchange information."

"That makes sense," Kallene said. "But what if they don't know about the other victims? Women runners are always being warned against running alone. If one becomes the victim of an attack, the police aren't too surprised and certainly aren't likely to link the death to another such incident thousands of miles away."

"Then why do you think there may be a connection between these four murders?" Jon said.

"I'm not sure, but it's a possibility I think should be checked."

"Okay. Ask Detective Alexander about it when we get back." He yawned and drew her head back against his shoulder.

She'd let it go for now. She was tired, too, but the first opportunity she found, she would see if she could find any other similar cases on the Internet.

* * *

Kallene didn't see Jon at the gym where they both had memberships the following morning, and she went straight to the office after her workout. Though she hadn't been gone long, she felt like she'd been away a month, judging by the amount of work waiting for her after her visit to her parents.

"Good morning," Lori Cassidy chirped in her ever-cheerful way. Kallene was surprised to see her at the receptionist's desk. Lori usually worked in the business office, but with so many people taking time off during the holidays, she supposed some of the office staff were doing double duty.

"Good. You're here." Ben McCallister greeted her as she walked down the hall toward her office. He was standing next to her door holding a thick project folder in his hands. She suspected his effusive greeting didn't bode well for her being able to finish her current projects before the end of the week. He followed her into her office and set the bulging folder on her work table.

"We've landed a large contract for a national campaign for the Western Dairy Association. It's an important deal and means good money for the firm. It involves multimedia, and the deadline is tight, but if anyone can do it, it would be you." She suspected he was really saying she was the only graphic artist on the staff who hadn't taken the whole week between Christmas and New Year's off, and since she didn't have a husband or kids, she couldn't possibly have anything else to do, so by default the job was hers. It was hard to be certain, but it seemed her project assignments were far more numerous than those of the other artists. She suspected Ben was shifting his workload to her but still taking credit for his share.

After he left her office, she opened the folder and discovered paperwork in the file that should have been given to the business office to file. Her temper flared when she saw the contract for the project had been signed over a month ago and a few clumsy attempts had been made to outline the project. Most upsetting was the discovery that Ben's name was listed as the project leader, and the company's best writer had already submitted slogans and text. She slammed the folder shut in exasperation. It wasn't the first time Ben had started a project that was beyond his ability then dumped it in her lap at the last minute. Finding models and arranging studio time on short notice, especially during the holidays, would be difficult.

Why couldn't Ben accept that he was a better salesman than artist? She'd seen some of his early work, which had appeared mostly in local newspapers and which had done well, but his ability hadn't kept pace with the more sophisticated clients the company now represented—the very clients he was so good at attracting for the company. While he'd been building the clientele side of the company, advertising had exploded into multimedia campaigns requiring different technical and artistic skills than those he possessed.

A suspicion grew in her mind. Ben had held her back several times from personally presenting a couple of her best campaigns to the board and to clients—projects for which she suspected he'd taken credit. She'd deserved credit for all of the work she'd put into the Davidson project a few months ago, but she hadn't received one word of recognition for it. It had earned a prestigious award, which had been presented to Ben at a gala in New York. She'd let that side of her career slide while she was engrossed in the search for Linda.

Not this time, she vowed. At first she'd appreciated his generosity in encouraging her to do most of her work at home. She'd been merely annoyed when she wasn't notified of staff meetings. It had struck her as odd that he'd balked at her taking time off at Christmas when he usually urged her to work at home. Was it because almost no one else would be around, and he'd planned all along to turn the new account over to her and didn't want anyone else to know? Now she wondered if Ben had an ulterior motive for keeping her isolated from other members of the staff.

She sat for several minutes tapping the eraser of her pencil against her bottom lip while considering her options for dealing with her suspicions. She was too angry to think about the new project. Besides, she was almost finished with the layout for the new shopping center ads. Once it was completed, she would take the Dairy Association portfolio home with her, clear her mind, and cool off enough to begin the campaign. But this time she would take steps to make certain Ben couldn't take advantage of her.

Three hours passed before she heard a light tap on her door. She looked up to see Lori poke her head around the doorframe.

"Sorry to bother you," the young woman said. "Everyone else has gone home, and I was just wondering how much longer you'll be. Don't you usually work from home?"

"Are you waiting for me so you can leave?" She felt embarrassed to be keeping the secretary from leaving early along with the rest of the staff. She really had meant to leave a long time ago.

"Well, kind of." Lori looked embarrassed.

An idea began to form in Kallene's mind. If, as she suspected, Ben had claimed her work because she did most of her work at home and she didn't interact enough with her coworkers for them to know which projects she worked on, then she needed to make certain plenty of people knew about the Dairy Association ad campaign. She needed to make certain the business office had corrected forms concerning the account.

"I only have a few details to finish on the shopping center layout for the Sunday newspapers, then I'll be taking work home with me. I could be ready to leave sooner if you'd help me with a few questions I have on the Dairy Association project Ben assigned to me."

Lori's eyes nearly popped out. "Mr. McCallister is letting you work on his precious Dairy Association ad campaign? He's talked about little else for weeks and how it's going to be the most exciting achievement of his career."

"Not work on it," Kallene corrected. "He hasn't even started it, though he signed as project leader. He turned it over to me completely. I just need you to see if you have a home telephone number for Greg Malcolm. There are some changes that need to be made in the text he submitted. Oh—could you find a new project form, too?"

"You're going to ask Greg to make changes?" Now Lori was practically stammering. "I'll be right back with his number and a project form."

* * *

Kallene was almost home when she remembered she hadn't called Brittany. She'd meant to call from work, but her encounter with Ben had distracted her so much she'd forgotten. "Darn!" she said aloud. "What kind of friend am I? She could have had the baby while I was gone and be back home by now."

She drove into her garage and made certain the door closed before stepping out of her car. She hadn't seen Darnell Gines for several weeks, but she wasn't taking any chances he might be hanging around. Only taking time to unload the items she'd brought from her office, she picked up the phone and dialed Brittany's number. She let it ring ten times before giving up. Promising to try again in half an hour, she opened the new project folder and began to read the client's requirements and suggestions. When she finished, she set up a fresh set of boards on her drawing table and began making rough sketches. Later she'd photograph the sketches and begin the more serious work using the computer.

With preliminary sketches before her, she began checking photo services for cows and modeling agencies to see which models were available on short notice. She was preparing to call the marketing manager for the Dairy Association to set up an appointment when she heard her doorbell ring.

She thought of Jon, but when she peeked through the security window, it was Jeff she saw standing on her porch. She pulled the door open.

"Brittany . . . ?" she began.

"It's a boy!" he interrupted. "Brittany's doing great, and she made me promise to stop on my way home to tell you in person."

"That's wonderful news. Congratulations! Come on in and give me all the details. What time was he born? How much does he weigh? How soon may I go see them?"

"For just a minute." He stepped through the door. "He's big; eight pounds, two ounces. He was born early this morning, just before five. Brittany's pretty tired, and the nurse said she needed to rest. Brittany insisted I go home and sleep for a few hours, too."

"I'll let her rest tonight and go see her in the morning," Kallene told him.

"That'll be fine. I know she's anxious to see you and show you our baby." Jeff backed toward the door. Opening it, he stepped onto the porch to be greeted by a low, ominous growl.

Kallene sighed in exasperation. Something had to be done about that dog. Rupert Meyer was doing a poor job of keeping the animal confined. "Maybe you should come back inside," she whispered to Jeff.

"Stay back," Jeff warned Kallene. He stood perfectly still and slowly extended his hand toward the dog. The dog seemed to be studying him, but after some hesitation it took a step closer.

Kallene forgot to breathe as the dog crept closer to Jeff. When he got close enough to sniff the extended hand, he gave it a thorough examination with his nose. When the dog seemed satisfied, Jeff reached forward to pat the animal. Kallene remembered to breathe.

"There you are!" Rupert came striding up her sidewalk. He bent to snap a leash to his dog's collar.

"Your dog seems to be loose an awful lot." Kallene stepped onto the porch to confront her neighbor.

"I'm sorry." Rupert spoke in an abrupt voice. "Raider's not used to being in a kennel, and he's an awfully smart dog." He stroked the big dog, and Kallene could see how much the animal meant to him.

Jeff didn't appear put out by the encounter. "He seems to be a good dog. What breed is he?"

"He is a good dog, better than most people might suspect. He's a mixture of breeds. His mother was a German shepherd, but the vet says he has a healthy amount of Lab and mastiff in him, too, and possibly a little Rottweiler." He snapped his fingers, and the dog obediently followed him back across the street. Kallene watched them go, feeling a little stunned that he'd actually carried on an almost civil conversation with Jeff.

"Well, I'd better go." Jeff looked back at Kallene. "Brittany will be expecting me in a couple of hours."

Jeff's step was almost a bounce as he hurried toward his front gate.

CHAPTER NINETEEN

THE WEEK BETWEEN CHRISTMAS AND New Year's passed in a flurry of appointments as Kallene threw herself into the Dairy Association ad campaign. The campaign would include television and radio spots, magazine spreads, billboards, a nutrition unit for use in schools, an Internet fun-and-information site for kids, and guest appearances by key people on talk shows. Reaching the marketing manager at the association took a persistent effort, and when she finally did get through to him, she found him reluctant to talk to her or discuss the campaign.

"Why doesn't Ben McCallister call me himself? He guaranteed me when we signed with your company that this campaign would receive his personal attention."

Kallene didn't want to make Ben look bad, but she was determined no one would be in doubt over who designed and pulled together the many areas of the campaign.

"I am his personal choice to handle your account," she assured him then launched at once into the concept she had in mind. Little by little his attitude changed from impatient to acceptance, bordering on enthusiasm. When the call ended, she pumped her fist in the air and mouthed a silent *yes*! She felt confident she'd won the man over. He'd been pleased when she informed him she planned to contact him each day while working on his account to keep him abreast of the campaign's progress and to discuss with him any changes either of them wished to make. She also made arrangements to present the final product to his manager and board of directors before revealing it to the public to kick off June Dairy Month.

Approaching Greg Malcolm about changes in the script worried her more. He had a reputation for exploding and going straight to the senior partner, Mr. Benson, if someone found fault with his work. To her surprise, he was cordial and invited her to send concept sheets to him via e-mail. He even expressed enthusiasm for expanding the ideas they discussed for programs aimed at children. He didn't seem surprised that she had taken over the account, only that she was approaching him directly instead of going through Ben. It was becoming more and more apparent that she was the last to become suspicious of her supervisor's glowing reputation. The realization left her feeling like a fool and wondering if Ben's father and Mr. Benson were aware of Ben claiming her work as his own. She debated confronting them directly but then decided making it clear to one and all that she was handling one of the biggest contracts in the firm's history would say all that needed to be said.

She finished her calls and hurried to dress for her lunch date with Scott. A cryptic message from the detective had arrived on her computer earlier that morning. *I need to talk to you. Meet me for lunch?* She'd quickly e-mailed him back setting a time and place. Even with all she'd needed to accomplish that morning, she hadn't been able to stop wondering if Scott had new information concerning Carson or Parker.

When she walked into the restaurant, Scott was already there. He appeared composed, and he laughed and joked as usual, yet Kallene got the distinct impression something was troubling him and that he had reservations about sharing whatever it was. They exchanged casual conversation until their lunch was delivered and she'd taken the first two bites of her sandwich.

"Our Jane Doe has been identified," he told her. "She recently moved to North Salt Lake from Tennessee and was living alone. She was to begin a new job next Monday, so her family didn't expect her home for Christmas, and she hadn't had time to make friends in her new community. Consequently, no one reported her missing." He took a large bite of his sandwich before continuing.

"I requested the coroner's report from Seattle for the woman Meyer was convicted of killing and had our state forensic expert compare the marks on the body to those of the woman killed on the Legacy Parkway and to Linda Longdale." He paused.

"And . . ." Kallene prompted. She gripped her sandwich until her fingers left deep impressions in the bun and mayonnaise dripped to the table.

"It's likely the Seattle woman and the Legacy woman were killed by the same person. The marks on both appear to have been made by the same instrument. However, the marks don't match those found on your friend. The husband is still our only suspect in that case."

"It just doesn't seem possible that he would hurt Linda." Even though no other explanation seemed possible, she still had trouble seeing Carson as a murderer. "Why does the use of a different weapon rule out Linda being murdered by the same person who killed the other two women?"

"The two murders were committed nearly three years apart with a single object; it's unlikely a murderer would use a different weapon for the one in between. I couldn't tell you earlier, but it is significant that Linda Longdale's body was moved from the place where her death occurred. The other two women died within a few feet of where they were found. Also, a piece of evidence was removed by Parker Grayson from that ledge where Linda's body was hidden. It was retrieved and contains blood smears that match Carson Longdale's blood."

"The towel! Parker told me there had been a towel with brown stains on it near where he found the rope and that he threw it away. Which reminds me of something Jon said I should be sure to tell you. The morning Linda disappeared, I took the baby into the bathroom to bathe her and found a wet towel on the floor. I picked it up and noticed it had a few spots of blood on it, which I assumed were from some shaving nicks. He had bits of tissue paper stuck to his neck when he answered the door."

"Hmm. It could be the same towel, but that's not likely. Why would he leave it on the floor then take it back up the mountain later? I'll ask him about it."

"What about Rupert Meyer? Is he being questioned for the Legacy Parkway murder?"

"Yes, the Davis County Sheriff's Department considers him a person of interest, but several witnesses swear they saw him around Pine Shadows at the time the coroner says the murder occurred."

"It doesn't take long to drive from here to the Legacy Parkway."

"No, it doesn't. There are other time factors involved. The department handling the investigation believes the meeting between the murderer and victim was a chance encounter and that it occurred within a few feet of where the body was found, which is a considerable distance from the road. Even if the murderer rode a bike along the trail, it is estimated that a minimum of two hours would be required for someone to travel from your neighborhood, find the victim, attack and kill her, and return again. Your neighbor, Delbert Haney, swears that the only time Meyer wasn't in his yard working on that kennel he's building the day in question was between five and five forty-five that morning. He said Meyer left the neighborhood with the dog on a leash and that he was dressed in running clothes at that time. He also spent about an hour in his house around noon."

"I'm not sure how reliable Mr. Haney is as a witness." Kallene leaned forward and spoke in a quiet voice. "He spends a lot of time looking out his windows, but he's old and may have fallen asleep or been mistaken." Kallene struggled with the news Scott delivered. *I'm living across the street from a murderer. No—nothing has been proven.* She discovered it was much easier to accept the "until proven guilty" concept in theory than when faced with the possibility her own life might be at risk.

"Has he been arrested?"

Scott shook his head. "There isn't enough evidence against him yet to make the charge stick. Nothing from his previous trial can be used. Both of the dead women were early-morning runners . . . same height, coloring, and build. Your friend matched that description as well, except for the bright red hair. You, however, match perfectly. Please promise me you won't run alone." She was touched by his concern and wondered if he was breaking some police procedure rule by sharing information with her.

"I don't suppose it means anything." She twirled a French fry between two fingers. "It seems a little silly to even mention it." She took a breath. "Rupert Meyer's dog isn't confined as well as he promised when he had that altercation with Mr. Haney. Most nights I find him sleeping on my deck, and a few days ago he threatened Jeff Adams, who lives two doors down, when he stopped by to tell me his wife had given birth to a little boy."

Scott frowned. "Did the dog bite your neighbor?"

"No. Jeff stayed calm and spoke quietly to the dog. He even let it sniff him. Then Rupert Meyer arrived with a leash and took the dog back to his house."

"It's probably nothing to be concerned about, but I'll have an animal control officer speak to Meyer about it."

Two uniformed female officers entered the restaurant, and Kallene noticed the way the pretty smaller one's eyes lit up when she noticed Scott, then her evident disappointment when she noticed Kallene sitting across from him. After a short whispered conversation between the two women, they settled in a booth nearby. Kallene felt a sliver of amusement seeing how often the young officer's eyes sought out the booth where she sat with Scott. *She has a crush on Scott!* She ducked her head to hide a smile.

For just a moment, she wondered why she found humor in the situation. A long-ago memory came to mind. She recalled going to a movie with her brother Dallin when they were in high school and getting the giggles watching two girls, who didn't know she was his sister, attempt to flirt with him behind her back and glare at her when they thought she wasn't looking. With a tingle of shock, she realized she wouldn't find the situation nearly as humorous if the woman was flirting with Jon. The thought was unsettling.

"I have an appointment in a few minutes. Thank you for lunch and for the warning." She reached for her handbag.

He put out a hand to clasp her arm before she could stand. "I'm serious. Don't take chances. I know running is important to you, but don't run alone."

"I have a membership now at an indoor gym with a track. Jon often runs with me. I don't plan to run in the canyon again until the snow is gone. It means a lot to know you worry about me, and I appreciate your sharing information with me." She stood then leaned toward him to kiss his cheek. "Don't stand. Finish your lunch."

She took rapid steps toward the door, fighting an urge to cry. She had the strangest feeling she'd just said good-bye to one of her dearest friends. Scott was fun and the most handsome man she'd ever dated, but she wasn't in love with him. She knew that now. As she passed the policewoman who was trying not to watch her, she silently wished her luck.

* * *

Tramping through muddy fields photographing cows on a late January afternoon wasn't Kallene's idea of a good time. Clearly the activity didn't appeal a great deal to the model she'd hired either, but the young woman was a good sport—or she needed a paycheck badly. The photographer went out of his way to capture excellent shots, including one of the dairy farmer's three-year-old son holding a sippy cup up to a cow's nose. Kallene was enchanted with the little boy, who seemed to be making a personal request for a refill. Seeing the shot's potential, she convinced the farmer to sign a release with a promise of remuneration if the shot was used in the ad campaign.

By the time she returned to the city and made her way home, Kallene was exhausted. She wanted nothing more than something hot to eat and to crawl into bed. It wasn't to be. Darnell Gines's truck was parked in her driveway.

CHAPTER TWENTY

MAYBE IF SHE DROVE AROUND the block, he'd give up and leave. She couldn't just pull into the garage and close the door behind her, because Darnell's truck was blocking access. Slamming on the brakes to avoid rear-ending him, she glared at the offending vehicle. He didn't appear to be in it. She seethed, thinking Darnell had a lot of nerve parking in her driveway. With her luck, there would be a big oil stain on her driveway from the rusty old heap.

She honked the horn and drummed her fingers against the steering wheel. She wanted dinner and to go to bed. When Darnell didn't appear, she began to grow nervous. She wasn't about to get out of her car and go looking for him. Even though she hadn't found his name on the sex offenders list, she didn't trust him. It would be just like him to be hiding, waiting for her to leave her locked car to make a run for the house. She pushed her car horn again.

She was just getting ready to call Jeff Adams to see if he would see her safely to her house when a figure stepped from the shadows beside her house. He walked past the truck blocking her driveway and moved directly toward her car. As he got closer, she could see it was Darnell. He was almost to her car when she noticed he was carrying something in one hand. At first she thought it was a gun, and her heart began to pound. It soon became clear it wasn't a gun but a hammer. She wasn't certain it was any less threatening.

Scott's words ran through her head. Linda had been killed by some unidentified small tool.

She jumped when Darnell rapped on her closed window. He said something, but she couldn't make out his words. Carefully, she eased the window down about an inch.

"Come with me. I want to show you something," he said.

"Just move your truck so I can park in my garage."

"You need to see what I found," he argued.

"What are you doing here?"

"I thought I saw someone in your backyard and decided to check."

She didn't know how to make it clear to him that she wasn't going anywhere with him. She was tired and smelled like the barn she'd recently left. All the way home she'd dreamed of a hot shower and a good night's rest. She vacillated between wondering if she was being childishly paranoid or if she should call the police. Perhaps she should throw the car in reverse and drive away. But it was her house, and Darnell was the one who should go away.

A pair of headlights came down her street, and a car parked at the curb in front of her house, saving her from a situation she was unsure how to handle. Jon stepped out of the car and hurried toward her.

"What's going on? Are you all right, Kallene?" he asked as he reached the car and noticed her window was only open a crack. Darnell was obviously upset.

Darnell turned to Jon with his hands turned palms up and gave a helpless shrug. "I don't know what her problem is. I was driving by and saw someone run behind her house, so I pulled in and went after him. When I got to her backyard, there was no sign of an intruder. I looked around until I found footprints in the snow that hasn't melted by her back fence."

With Jon's arrival, Kallene felt safe enough to open her window further to hear better.

Darnell went on. "I poked around and found the boards back in that corner swing aside, forming an opening big enough for a grown person to walk through."

"What?" She practically screamed as she opened her door to stand beside the two men. "Are you saying someone has access to my yard anytime he wants?"

Darnell glanced at her and nodded. "Looks that way."

"What's on the other side of that improvised gate?" Jon asked.

"Near as I could tell, it just goes to that open slope between this subdivision and another one farther down. Planning and Zoning won't allow any building there. They said it's too steep and the weight of houses on the slope might cause a slide."

"Let's go take a look at it," Jon suggested.

Darnell gave her a pointed look, which she ignored. She ducked her head and reached for Jon's hand. He gave it a slight squeeze. Together they followed Darnell to Kallene's backyard and followed the fence to the far corner.

Darnell reached down and swept a pair of boards aside.

"You're sure it isn't just a loose nail?" She knew it was a stupid question before Darnell answered. A board might swing on a single nail if other nails weren't there to hold it in place, but in this case, the other nails had been flattened so that they only appeared to be holding the boards in place. "Are there any more gates like this in other back fences?" Jon asked.

"I only had time to check a few fences before I heard Kallene honk her car horn," Darnell told him. "There aren't many wood fences around here; most are vinyl. This is the only wood fence I found that had been tampered with, but I only searched as far as the vacant lot a few doors down. I did notice that a couple of slats in Mr. Haney's fence look newer than the rest of the fence, and the fence was never finished behind the empty house near the end of the street."

"I don't understand." Kallene drew her coat closer about her. "Why would someone want to come into my yard?"

"Someone as smart as you should be able to figure that one out." The appraising look Darnell gave her left no room for misunderstanding. Jon put his arm around her, and she snuggled into his embrace. She and Jon watched as Darnell pried the nails loose with the claw end of the hammer then drew several long nails from his pocket and proceeded to pound them into the fence, effectively eliminating the gate.

When he finished, all three made their way back to the front of the house. "Well, I guess I'll be leaving," Darnell said as he reached for the door of his truck. He looked at Kallene, and it may have been her imagination, but he seemed regretful as he added, "It looks like you've got all of the protection you need."

Kallene backed her car out of Darnell's way and then parked it in the garage once Darnell disappeared down the road. Even though

Darnell seemed to be putting on his Good Samaritan act, she always felt like she needed a shower after being near that man. What a creep!

Jon followed her into the house. Seeing the liberal amount of mud her shoes had collected, she slipped them off, leaving them beside the door. Jon looked down and followed her example.

"Are you hungry?" Kallene asked as she moved toward the kitchen.

"Not really. I ate earlier, but you go ahead."

"I'm too tired to cook." She opened the freezer and pulled out a frozen dinner. While it heated, she poured two glasses of milk and set them both on the table. Jon took a seat next to her.

"Did I forget we had a date tonight?" she asked while stifling a yawn.

"No, and if that's your way of asking why I'm here, I'll be honest. I wanted to see you, so I came."

"I'm glad you did." She bit her lip and attempted to control her weariness. "I don't trust Darnell Gines. There's something about him that gives me the creeps."

Jon picked up her hand from where it lay on the table and smiled.

She smiled, too, but her smile was a little weak. "Do you think he made that gate himself to gain my trust and make himself look like some kind of hero?"

"I suppose it's possible," Jon said, but there was a lack of conviction in his voice. "I think his anger was real."

"What other reason could there be? You don't think it was the work of a burglar, do you?"

"I don't know. That's a lot of trouble for a burglar to go to."

"Someone took the jacket I left on the deck a few weeks ago."

"I doubt someone went to the trouble of creating a doorway to your yard to swipe a jacket." He hesitated as though reluctant to voice another theory.

"What are you thinking?"

"There might be a more innocent reason for the gate, though you should have been consulted about it. You said Rupert Meyer's dog often sleeps on your deck at night even though you keep the gate to the backyard locked. What if Rupert made that gate so that when you're at your office, he can use it as a shortcut to that big open slope to let the dog run? The dog might be so used to taking a shortcut through your yard that he considers it an extension of his own, and that's why he feels comfortable sleeping here."

"Are you serious?" She stared at Jon, trying to understand why he considered someone making a shortcut through her yard even remotely innocent. "Unless there's another improvised gate in my fence Darnell didn't find, that swinging plank only provided a way in or out of my backyard—not a way to cut through it. Besides, Rupert takes that dog with him every morning when he runs. I doubt he'd go to such lengths to give him a second run. With that man's record, if he built that gate, I'm sure it has nothing to do with exercising his dog."

"You're right. I'm worried about you, and I guess I'm grasping at straws, trying to convince myself I'm worrying for nothing. How does Rupert's dog get in your yard anyway?"

"Have you taken a good look at that dog? I swear he's part horse. If he can jump over a six-foot kennel fence to run loose, he can jump over my gate to come sleep on my deck."

Jon smiled and conceded she had a point then became serious again. "I really believe Carson killed Linda, but there's just a sliver of doubt, especially since that other woman was killed not far from here. It's very possible there's a second killer loose in this area, and I couldn't bear it if something happened to you, too."

The buzzer on the microwave sounded. Jon released her hand, and she hurried to retrieve her dinner. When she was seated again, she picked up her fork then carefully laid it back down. "Scott says that the Legacy Parkway woman and the one Rupert Meyer was charged with killing in Washington State were killed with the same small, heavy instrument. He also said whatever was used to hit Linda on the sides of her head was not the same tool and that it was lighter in weight and more blunt. He also said that she died more quickly than those other two women because of the severe trauma to the back of her head. The injury to the back of her head might have been caused by falling backward against a hard surface, although they haven't ruled out the murderer possibly inflicting the damage."

"I know all that, but it doesn't ease my concern for you," Jon said. "Whether Linda was killed by Carson or not, someone killed that other woman. Meyer is the most likely suspect, and you live across the street from him. I should have found an apartment closer to you."

"Your apartment is perfect for you, especially until you can finish the renovations for your new business office and studio."

"Perfect, except it's too far from you."

She briefly wondered if she should call Scott then decided to wait until later. "I'm all right. I had the new alarm system installed. I look before I open the door, and I only run at the gym now, where there are a lot of other people."

"I've been thinking about something you said when we were flying back here after Christmas. At first I thought the idea of a serial killer a little far-fetched, but knowing now that there is a link between two runners who were murdered, I can't help wondering if there are more. Did you do the search for other victims you said you were thinking of doing?"

"No, I got involved with a big project I'm doing for the agency and never gave it any more thought."

"Eat your dinner, then if you're not too tired, let's see what we can find." He gestured toward her untouched plate. The microwaved casserole had lost its appeal, or her appetite had deserted her. She took a couple of bites, washed them down with what remained of her glass of milk, then dumped the rest of the dinner in the trash.

They began their search for similar murders. Two hours later, Kallene looked up from the list they had compiled, feeling a little sick. The horror of the stories she'd read were all that was still keeping her awake. Even after eliminating victims who had died of causes other than blunt-force trauma, there were thirty-one women's names on their list. A stack of paper consisting of newspaper reports of those deaths sat beside the printer.

"You need some rest." Jon reached out to touch her cheek. "I shouldn't have kept you up so late."

"Once we started, I couldn't leave it any more than you could."

"Look, I'll take the papers with me. I can go through them looking for patterns over the next few days. Until I get the office set up and a staff hired, I'll have some free time. Let's check your doors and windows, then I'll be on my way."

Long after Jon kissed her and told her good night, she lay awake staring at the shifting shadows on her bedroom ceiling. She wasn't sure whether it was a good or bad sign to not find Rupert Meyer's dog on her deck when they checked the sliding doors. It wasn't the absence of the dog that kept her awake, but one simple pattern she'd observed in more than half of the runners named in news stories she and Jon had unearthed. The victims' descriptions, and in many cases their pictures, bore an uncanny likeness to herself. Sometimes the only difference was the color of the victim's hair.

CHAPTER TWENTY-ONE

NOT LONG AFTER SHE FELL asleep, Kallene was awakened by the wind howling with extra ferocity around the house, and when morning came she discovered half a foot of snow on the ground and snow continuing to fall at a rapid rate. It was a day to work from home, she decided. Anyway, it was time to work on the various concepts she'd outlined and put them together for a presentation to her client and the executive committee of the agency. Never again would she leave presentations to Ben.

She spent time perfecting stylized sketches of an old-fashioned milkmaid on a three-legged stool milking a spotted cow. When the video and still pictures from the previous day's photo shoot appeared in her inbox, she smiled in satisfaction as she printed them. In minutes she had the modern milkmaid photos lined up to contrast with the sketches and captions.

She held the photo of the farmer's son for several minutes then began a drawing of a similar little boy dressed in knickers.

The next step was to arrange for the conversion of her sketches to video and to set up a presentation time. She hummed in satisfaction. Everything was coming together well.

Jon called and she leaned back in her chair to take the call. His voice was filled with excitement. "I met with a builder this morning who just received approval for a planned community along the Oquirrh foothills. He asked me to submit drawings for several home designs. If he accepts my bid, I'm considering working out an arrangement with him to build a house for me on one of those lots."

Kallene congratulated him, and they talked for several minutes before he said, "I haven't had much time to look over those newspaper articles we copied last night, but I'll keep checking them and making lists. I might even show them to Scott."

"Good idea." She'd considered making a copy for Scott but had decided it might be best to distance herself some from the handsome detective. She wanted to remain on friendly terms with him, but since she felt certain a romantic relationship with him wasn't meant to be, it seemed wise not to date him or spend time on the phone with him.

* * *

The morning of her presentation, she drove to the airport to meet her client and the aide Mr. Martindale said was accompanying him. She paced the baggage area, holding a sign with BENSON & MCCALLISTER written on it in big letters. When a distinguished man with silver streaks in his sideburns approached her, trailed by a younger man with a friendly smile, she held out her hand to welcome them.

"Miss Ashton, you're younger than I expected."

"So are you," she replied and hoped he wouldn't think she was being impertinent. He chuckled and introduced his aide as Preston Wells. The younger man smiled warmly and held her hand a moment longer than necessary as he acknowledged the introduction.

They drove directly to the agency offices. When they walked into the boardroom, she was careful to avoid Ben's puzzled face. He'd been to her office several times in the past few weeks, asking about the project and offering to preview it. He'd gone so far as to inform her he needed to present it to the Dairy Association's Denver office by mid-April and demanded that it be completed by the first of April. She'd put him off each time with assurances that she was working on it and promises that he would know when it was ready. She was sure he'd seen the agenda by now and had noticed that the project was on the schedule two weeks ahead of the date he'd given her for a deadline.

Following introductions and a warm welcome from the senior partners, Robert McCallister looked hesitantly at Kallene then at his son. Ben waved with a negligent air toward her, and she stepped toward the head of the table, doing her best to hide her nervousness and her awareness that Ben was seething with anger. She picked up the remote control Lori had placed on the table beside a stack of copies of the proposed magazine and billboard layouts.

"Before beginning the television spot, I want to tell you how great Mr. Martindale and his staff have been to work with and acknowledge their input in devising a campaign meant to appeal to adults, children, and, well, everyone who uses dairy products. Greg Malcolm is responsible for the text and even provided the musical background. You'll see the video first then copies of the ads for print distribution. I'll follow up with a program for suggested use in schools and daycare centers." She pressed the button.

When the presentation ended, she hesitated to look around the room. Reminding herself of her vow to appear strong and poised, she raised her eyes just as Mr. Martindale began a round of applause, which was quickly taken up by the partners and other staff members present. Only Ben's applause appeared lackluster.

Mr. Martindale rose to his feet, and the room quieted. "When I first learned Ben had turned the association's account over to Miss Ashton, I was annoyed and considered withdrawing. In five minutes Miss Ashton convinced me to listen to her ideas, and though still nursing some skepticism, I began looking forward to her calls and electronic submissions. I came here today expecting the best ad campaign ever launched, and I'm not disappointed. I'd like to suggest a second round of applause for Ben McCallister for his astute assessment of the association's needs and his wise selection of the talented Miss Ashton and Mr. Malcolm to put together this incredible campaign." He started the applause, and Kallene was the first to join in.

This time the celebration luncheon included Kallene and Greg. Greg gave her hand a quick squeeze beneath the table, which she took as a sign of his approval. She wasn't sure if it was the campaign presentation or her success in getting recognition both for him and for her that appeared to be opening a new level of cooperation between the two of them.

On the drive home, she couldn't stop going over in her mind all of the positive remarks that had been heaped on her for a job well done. She could hardly wait to get home and call Jon.

Just as she pulled onto her street, she remembered that the Cub Scouts were to meet the following afternoon, and it had been several months since Parker had attended a den meeting. Parker was a difficult child, but she felt she'd been making progress with him before he discovered Linda's body. She couldn't help worrying about him now. He didn't play with the other children and spent too much time alone. His parents seemed almost indifferent to him, and in her opinion, although he was now nine, he was still too young to be on his own after school. She couldn't dismiss a niggling suspicion that he was sometimes left alone overnight.

It was almost five o'clock. He should be home, and with a little luck, one of his parents would be home, too. She parked on the street, making certain she wouldn't be blocking the garage.

As she hurried up the walk, she pulled the sides of her coat tighter as protection from the wind that seemed sharper and colder than it had felt downtown. She'd learned that the weather wasn't always the same all over this mountain valley, and the homes perched higher up the sides of the mountain suffered from more extreme weather than those in the lower valley. There were advantages, though: her neighborhood rarely suffered from the weather inversions and smog that were the scourge of the neighborhoods lower in elevation.

She pressed the doorbell and waited. When there was no response, she knocked as hard as she could then stood shifting from one foot to the other and feeling her toes growing numb from the cold. After a few minutes, she turned her collar up to protect her ears from the wind and pressed the doorbell again. Finally admitting defeat, she returned to her car to write a note, which she left in the door. She'd have to hope for the best—that Parker would make an appearance at Cub Scouts, proving that he was doing okay.

* * *

As soon as she walked in the door of her house, she called Jon. There was something satisfying in sharing her professional triumph with him. She'd downplayed her concerns about the risk she was taking by thwarting Ben, but now she found a sense of freedom in knowing she'd undertaken two major challenges and had come out on top. It was a new experience to have someone in her life who understood the subtle feelings she experienced in meeting her goals both in her career field and in dealing with an uncomfortable and unfair professional relationship. Jon congratulated her and invited her out to celebrate the following evening.

* * *

Parker didn't come to den meeting the next afternoon, and as the boys were finishing up their projects and preparing to leave, she asked, "Have any of you seen Parker lately? I haven't been able to contact him."

"He doesn't go to our school anymore," one of the boys volunteered.

"When school first started, he said his dad wanted to send him to a private school. Maybe he's going there," another boy added.

"I'm glad he's gone. He's a bully, and my mom said I didn't have to play with mean kids. He was in my class at school, and he used to come here. It seemed like I couldn't ever get away from him."

Kallene felt a twinge of sadness. It seemed she was the only one who missed Parker. After the boys left, she barely had time to straighten the house and change her clothes before Jon arrived carrying a large bouquet of red roses. She'd been looking forward to their date all day, and the moment she answered the door and saw him standing before her, her pulse began to pound. Holding the roses in one hand, he pulled her close with the other and kissed her until electric vibrations sizzled all the way to her toes.

When he released her, it took a moment for her senses to clear. She noticed Jon was dressed formally in a dark suit, making her glad she'd worn a long, black skirt with a ruffled, cinnamon-red blouse. He smiled as he handed her the roses, and she felt her heart give a double beat.

The recent snowfall hadn't remained on the ground long, and the roads were clear and dry as they drove across the valley. She guessed their destination was Log Haven when Jon turned up the Millcreek Canyon Road. She'd never been there, but she'd heard it was a premiere place to dine.

The parking lot was full, and snow was still plentiful. It was piled in mounds around the popular restaurant where the walkways had been cleared. When they stepped inside, she admired the rustic decor and was pleased when the waiter escorted them to a table near one of the windows looking out over the scenic landscape.

They held hands and talked of inconsequential matters. Kallene found a welcome sense of peace just being with Jon and sharing such a beautiful setting. Jon congratulated her again on her successful ad campaign. It was like a romantic fantasy come true.

"I owe a lot to Mr. Martindale. His smooth salute to Ben flattered his ego and saved me from repercussions that would have come my way otherwise."

"I admire your generosity. Many people wouldn't have been so generous in sharing honors, especially after the way he's selfishly taken credit for your work before."

"Trent Sawyer was the writer I worked with on the Davidson account. Like me, he had only been with the company a few years, and I'd worked with him on other projects. He quit right after Ben received that award for the Davidson account. There was no mention of Trent's work on the text or mine for doing the artwork. I'm sure now that Ben's glory-hogging was the reason he left. I wish I'd put two and two together sooner. When I interned for the company, I never questioned why there were so many positions open to new graduates each year."

"Do you think there will be a continued problem?"

"No. I think it will be harder for Ben to get away with something like that in the future, and I intend to stay more alert. I really like the company and respect the people who have been there for a long time. If I'm wrong, I'll move on to another agency, but I don't think it will come to that." She patted her lips with her napkin and changed the subject. "Now what about you? Did you get the contract for the planned development?"

"Yes, we're ready to sign the papers. Everything is going well with the new office, too. All of the renovations I asked for have been completed. I'll have to fly to San Diego to get the contract signed and make final preparations for transferring my accounts to my partners or arranging for clients to transfer to this office."

"When will you be leaving?"

Jon reached across the table to place his hand over hers. "Not until next weekend. That will give me time to set up staff interviews and arrange for the delivery of the furniture. I'm hoping to accomplish everything I need to do in San Diego in a week and get back here as soon as possible to get started on that development."

"I'll miss you." In the past few months they'd grown closer, and she looked forward to sharing each day's events with him, running with him most mornings, and sharing time with him. With each passing day, she was becoming more convinced that she wanted Jon to be a permanent part of her life.

"I'll call you every day." He seemed to read her thoughts and share them.

Jon paid the check, but instead of walking toward his car, he suggested they take a walk along one of the cleared paths. As they walked, he laced her fingers through his and tucked both of their hands inside his coat pocket. The stars overhead looked like tiny chips of ice in the night sky, and the air smelled fresh and piney. Large trees, bare of leaves, formed a network of lacy patterns overhead, and dark pine added a touch of shadow to the path down which they wandered.

"Kallene," Jon drew her to a stop beside a lofty pine tree that blocked their view of the restaurant. "My marriage to Jessa was over almost before it started. It wasn't a happy time for either of us, and when we divorced, I couldn't imagine ever wanting to marry again. These past months with you have changed my perspective on many things. I realize now that she and I would never have married if we'd taken the time to get to know each other better. We were never friends, our values were not the same and neither were our goals in life. With you, I've caught a glimpse of what marriage should be and of a life I want to share with you. I love you and hope you'll say yes to being my wife."

Tears filled Kallene's eyes, and she blinked them away. "Oh, yes," she whispered as her heart filled with warmth and joy. She'd known for some time that becoming Jon's wife was her greatest desire. His arms came around her, and his lips touched hers, gently but with undercurrents of passion. After a few moments, he pulled back, and they exchanged smiles.

"Will you be free one day this week to shop for a ring before I leave for California? I'd like you to pick one you'll actually enjoy wearing."

CHAPTER TWENTY-TWO

THERE WERE SO MANY THINGS to think about and plans to make. Her thoughts turned to dreams as she admired the emerald-cut diamond on her left hand. A small smile crept across her face; her mother couldn't stand it that they were so far apart when a wedding was being planned. Her only consolation was having a new baby in the house. Corrianne had given birth to a little boy three weeks earlier. It had taken all of Kallene's powers of persuasion to convince her mother to wait until she and Jon picked a wedding date before rushing to Salt Lake to help her choose her dress and set in motion plans for a reception. Only the reminder that her help was needed with her two small grandsons kept Carol from boarding the first plane traveling west.

Kallene shook her head as though that would chase away the daydreams and enable her to get back to work. She really wanted to have her current project completed before the weekend, when Jon would return and they could be together again. True to his word, he called her every day, but it just wasn't the same as running together, sitting across the dinner table from each other, or snuggling as they pretended to watch a movie.

Once again she pulled her project back up on her screen and began the careful detail work needed to complete the layout. She jumped when the phone rang, interrupting the concentration she'd finally achieved.

"Hello," she said in a distracted voice.

"Kallene, this is Scott." She pulled her thoughts abruptly away from the highlights she'd been adding to the photo on the screen. It had been almost two months since she'd last heard from the handsome detective.

"I understand congratulations are in order." There was no animosity or hint of wounded pride in his voice. She relaxed and felt herself sliding into the casual friendship they'd formed ever since she'd made the missing person call in the fall.

"Thank you. I'm surprised word has already gotten around about Jon's and my engagement."

"Hey, I'm a cop, and cops know things." He laughed and she joined in. "Actually, I just talked to Jon's parents. They told me he is in California, finalizing arrangements for the opening of an office here in Salt Lake. I was letting them know about current developments in the case and decided you should know, too. I'll be flying to California tomorrow to pick up Carson. We finally have a warrant for his arrest."

"Oh!" The announcement came like a blow. All along she couldn't believe he did it. "What about Macie?"

"For now, she'll remain with her grandfather. However, the Piersons plan to file for custody."

"I'm not surprised. Janet and Adam love their granddaughter and can provide her with a much better home than a crusty old hermit living on a boat can. Are you able to tell me what changed or what evidence you've found to bring charges against Carson?"

"I can't discuss that." She hoped the police had something more than the towel Parker had thrown in a Dumpster. She couldn't help believing that it was the same towel she'd found on the floor at Carson and Linda's home. But it just didn't make sense for Carson to take that towel up the mountain after he'd already hidden her body. It might have been another towel just like it. But unless Linda had more than one set of those towels, she'd seen its mate in the dirty clothes hamper when she tossed Macie's pajamas into it on that fateful morning.

"One other thing," Scott continued. "I gave the information you and Jon turned over to me concerning a string of female jogger murders to a newly formed Unified Police unsolved crimes analyst team. They're quite certain there is a connection between at least some of those murders. You made a good call there. We're being careful not to let anything out to the media yet, but you should be careful. There's strong evidence that Meyer was in some of the areas where the murders occurred, and he has been named a person of interest by several police forces."

"Why hasn't he been arrested?" Kallene couldn't resist moving aside the curtains a few inches to peer across the street. "Oh!"

"What's the matter?" Scott sounded concerned.

"He's right in front of my house with that dog of his. He's talking to my neighbor, Brittany Adams. With the weather becoming nicer, she has begun taking her baby for a ride in the stroller every day."

"I'm sure she's all right just talking to him. The attacks on women have all occurred in isolated areas, and the victims were all runners."

"I'm going to go invite her to come in for a rest, anyway."

"All right, but don't scare her. Meyer is a person of interest, but so far there's no hard evidence against him, and therefore he's presumably innocent."

"I know. Thanks for calling, and please continue to keep me informed concerning Carson."

"Will do." The phone clicked in her ear, and she hurriedly set it down and rushed to the door. Forcing herself to adopt a casual walk, she approached Brittany and Rupert. Brittany looked a little flustered.

"Hi! I was wondering when I'd get the chance to see that darling baby again." Kallene bent over to peek at the sleeping infant.

"We were out for a walk and nearly got run over when Ted Grayson's car came flying down his driveway. I've seen him back out before and should have been watching better. He always drives like a madman, but he looked particularly angry today. Mr. Meyer stopped to ask if I was okay. We'd never formally met before, even though I know he's met Jeff. I was just telling him about that night I stayed at your house and when we got up the next morning, his dog was asleep on your deck." Brittany laughed and gave the big dog's head a pat. She might be afraid of being alone, but it was evident that dogs didn't worry her.

"He sleeps there most nights." She couldn't resist giving Meyer a pointed look. He appeared a little uncomfortable but didn't apologize or promise to keep the dog confined better at night.

"Jeff Jr. will be waking up soon, and when he does he'll be hungry, so I better be on my way," Brittany said as she bent to adjust the quilt covering the sleeping baby.

"I was hoping you were coming for a visit."

"I'll try to stop by tomorrow." Brittany waved and began pushing the stroller at a rapid pace the short distance to her house.

Kallene turned slowly back toward Rupert and was surprised to see him just disappearing inside his house. She couldn't help feeling relieved that he was already gone.

* * *

Kallene woke to a beautiful early spring morning and slowly dressed for her trip to the gym. It was difficult forcing herself to run on the indoor track with signs of spring beginning to show everywhere. That was one more reason to wish the week would pass quickly and Jon would be back to run with her. She stepped onto her deck and took a deep breath. Delbert Haney's yard was a mass of flowering crocuses, tulips, and daffodils. From her deck, she paid particular attention to the flowerbed where Parker had replanted the daffodil bulbs and took a measure of satisfaction in the brilliant splash of yellow she glimpsed there.

"Miss Ashton!"

Now what? she thought as she saw Delbert Haney striding toward the fence dividing their yards.

"I've been thinking . . ." At least he didn't sound angry. "Doesn't that boy's father sell tools? You know . . . the one who dug up my daffodils?"

"I heard he's a sales representative for a tool company, yes." She wasn't sure why the old man was bringing up Parker's misdeed again now.

"Do you think he'd sell me a trowel like that one the boy used? I need to replace mine since the police won't give mine back to me."

"I guess it wouldn't hurt to ask."

"I haven't seen the boy for a while, and I see most everything along this street."

"One of the other boys said his parents sent him away to a private boarding school, but perhaps you could ask his father yourself. When he isn't away on a business trip, he runs right past your house each morning."

"I don't know why those fools think they have to go running up a mountain before decent folks are even out of bed." He continued to grumble as he turned back toward his house, leaving Kallene with a touch of melancholy. Scott and Jon had both assured her she had no reason to feel guilty, but she couldn't help thinking she'd let Parker down. Somehow she should have stayed with him that night or made a greater effort to see him before he was whisked away to a boarding school. She'd had nightmares since seeing Linda's hand, and she was an adult. How much worse it must have been for a child. Slowly she turned back to the house.

A few minutes later she stepped outside again to pick up her newspaper, which had only made it as far as the middle of her front walk, she was surprised by a familiar voice calling her name.

"Kallene, drag your pretty tush over here and join me for a run at the high school." Darnell Gines leaned out of his truck window at the edge of her lawn.

"No, thanks." She turned back toward her open door.

"Aw, c'mon. Your boyfriend's out of town, and I know this spring weather is getting to you. Besides, those long legs of yours are being wasted in a stuffy old gym."

She schooled herself not to react too abruptly. "Jon's my fiancé. The gym is close to my office, and I have to be to work early this morning."

Scott had assured her Darnell didn't have a record and had never been arrested. Running on the high-school track was a temptation. There were always plenty of people around, and it was outdoors. Darnell was obnoxious and much too personal, but he wasn't dangerous. She just had to let his remarks fly right over her head, though, because she *wasn't* going to run with him. She reached her door and stepped inside her house, closing the door with a none-too-gentle push.

Gathering up her gym bag, portfolio, and smart drive, which she dropped in her handbag, she started toward the garage. Just as she unlocked the door leading from the garage to the mudroom just off her kitchen, her phone began to ring. She hesitated. She didn't have time for a phone conversation, but it might be Jon. They'd talked until late the previous evening, but if he was calling at six in the morning, five his time, then it must be important.

She leaned the portfolio against the side of a cupboard and dropped her gym bag and purse onto the counter.

"Hello!"

"Kallene?" A whispery voice she couldn't identify was barely audible. *Oops, I should have checked the caller ID.*

"Who is this?" She debated just hanging up.

"Kallene, this is Carson." His voice was clearer now. "I need your help. The police came to arrest me last night, but I escaped over the side of Dad's boat with Macie, and we've been hiding out all night. I didn't kill Linda, and I'm not worried about being found guilty, even though I'm pretty sure the police have already made up their mind that I am. I want to give myself up, but I need someone to take care of Macie. Dad isn't well, and I don't want her going into foster care. Will you take her?"

"Of course I will. Jon Pierson is in San Diego. If you'll tell me where to find you, I'll send him to get Macie." She was appalled at the suggestion Macie might be placed into foster care in another state when both she and the Piersons loved the child and would do almost anything to ensure she had the care and protection she needed.

"No. I have a friend who will fly me to Utah. Just meet me at the little airport on the west side of Jordan Landing at noon. I'll turn Macie over to you, then maybe you can give me a ride to the police station. Please don't say anything to anyone until you have Macie and I've turned myself in."

"Okay. I'll be there."

Kallene hung up the phone with trembling fingers. She considered calling Scott. Or Jon. Perhaps she should call Janet Pierson. No, she'd given her word. She'd do as Carson asked and hope she wasn't being a fool or abetting a wanted fugitive.

CHAPTER TWENTY-THREE

KALLENE STOOD BY THE FENCE watching as small aircraft took off and landed. At frequent intervals she checked her watch, bit her lip, and turned her attention back to the sky. The smaller airport was nothing like the big international airport west of Salt Lake City. It was not only more informal, but she wasn't sure where she should wait for Carson's arrival. She hadn't noticed a waiting room or even knew if one existed. She'd noticed a couple of men in business suits leave a small plane and hurry directly to a waiting car while their pilot taxied a short distance to a hangar. Two men she concluded were student and teacher practiced takeoffs and landings.

She checked her watch again. It was 12:30. Would Carson really show up? Had something gone wrong? She couldn't bear it if anything bad had happened to Macie.

A small plane came in fast and low. It touched down then taxied beyond where the other planes had come to a stop. It sat unmoving for what seemed a long time but was probably only a minute or so. A door in the side of the blue-and-silver plane opened, and a figure jumped out. She knew at once it was Carson. He reached back toward the door to lift out Macie. There was no luggage, and as soon as Carson stepped away from the plane, its engines revved, and it began taxiing back toward the runway. In moments it was airborne.

"Macie! Carson!" She began to run toward the pair. Carson scooped Macie up in his arms and began sprinting to meet her.

"Where's your car?" He didn't pause to greet her, and his voice betrayed his nervousness. She pointed, and he continued running. When he reached her car, he pulled open the back door and slipped inside with Macie. By the time Kallene reached the vehicle, he was already buckled in with the toddler strapped in next to him.

Carson pulled a roll of bills from his pocket and handed it to her. Seeing her startled expression, he added, "Dad insisted I give the money he's been squirreling away for years to you to get whatever you'll need for Macie until this mess is cleared up."

"You might need that." She attempted to refuse the money. "I can afford to get whatever Macie might need. I was thinking of checking the Deseret Industries for a youth bed, and it will be fun to take her shopping for clothes."

"They'll lock me up until the trial, so I won't need much cash." His voice was dry with a touch of bitterness. "Besides, Dad and I agreed—it's our responsibility to support Macie. There's a paper with that money, too. I signed it and had it notarized, giving you custody of my daughter until I'm free again."

"What about bail?"

"I ran, so no judge will set bail. Can we go now? I figure the cops will be watching airports, and it's important for me to turn myself in."

"Okay." She backed out of the parking spot and headed for the street. Several times she glanced back at Macie, curling against Carson, who kept a protective arm around her. Her head drooped, and she appeared to be asleep. The little girl had grown a great deal in the months since Kallene had last seen her. Her face and hands were dirty, and the coveralls she wore were too small. Her red curls had been clipped short and were matted and in need of shampooing.

"I just want to get this over with," Carson suddenly said, "and I can't risk anyone recognizing me and calling the police before I can turn myself in."

Kallene thought she understood what he meant. Now that he knew Macie was going to be safe and sound, he felt an unwavering determination to face the law.

"I should have asked earlier . . . are you hungry?" She handed him a package of cookies she'd stored in her glove box. He seemed uncertain then ripped off the end of the package and shoved one into his mouth.

"What about your attorney?"

"I can't afford one. I'll have to settle for a public defender."

"What about Linda's family? They need to know Macie is safe."

She thought he might not respond, but after a few minutes, he said, "Let them know she's with you. They can visit her, but she stays with you."

Kallene had avoided speaking of Linda and the charges against Carson, but now she asked, "Carson, how did a towel with your blood on it end up on the mountain in the exact place where Linda's body was found?" She wasn't certain he would respond to her question.

"The police asked that question, too. I just don't know."

"There was a towel with spots of blood on it in your bathroom the morning she disappeared."

"There was?" He didn't seem to remember.

"You had tissue paper stuck to your neck, and I thought you might have cut yourself shaving."

"I don't remember, but I was upset enough that I'm surprised I didn't cut my throat shaving that morning." He thought a few minutes then said, "I remember when I came home that night I tried to keep busy. The next day was garbage pickup, so I emptied the trash and took it to the curb. I washed a load of laundry, too, and hung it out because the dryer wasn't working right. I suppose I threw the towel in the washer without noticing it had blood on it or took it out with the trash. I thought the whole thing—her going missing—was a trick Linda had planned to prove I couldn't care for Macie properly so she would get custody of her and keep me from having her."

They drove in silence. Kallene found that she didn't have a lot to say to Carson. Most of what he'd said confirmed in her mind that he couldn't possibly be the killer, but would a sociopath be able to pretend well enough to convince her?

A block from the police station, Carson said, "Pull over." Kallene wondered if he'd changed his mind. She pulled to the curb and turned to look at Carson in time to see him press a soft kiss to his sleeping daughter's cheek. He turned his head and stared straight ahead until he could speak.

"Do you have your cell phone with you?"

She nodded.

"Call this number, please." He gave her a number he had memorized. "Tell the detective who answers that I'm giving myself up and to meet me in front of the station in five minutes." She recognized Scott's number. Slowly she pressed the numbers.

"Scott Alexander." His voice was sharp and impatient.

"This is Kallene."

Before she could go on, he said, "I'm sorry. I didn't mean to snap at you. This hasn't been a good day. When officers went to arrest Carson last night, he took off with his little girl. I cancelled my flight and have been waiting for word that he's been located. I just got off the phone with the police department down there and was told they still haven't found a trace of him."

"It's okay, Scott. He's right here."

"What do you mean, 'right here'? Is he holding you hostage?"

"No, he's a short distance from the police station and is planning to turn himself in. He just wanted to make certain Macie would be with me and not in the California foster-care system. He wants you to meet him in five minutes in front of the station."

After they'd parked, Kallene watched with a lump in her throat as Carson walked away. He never looked back, and after only a few seconds' hesitation, she drove away with tears in her eyes.

She was halfway to the store—where she meant to purchase a car seat and a few changes of clothing for Macie—when she glanced in her rearview mirror and saw that Macie was awake. The little girl didn't cry but stared at her with round, bewildered eyes.

"It's okay, Macie. Your daddy wants you to go to my house with me. We're going to drop by the store to pick up a few things so that we can have a good time while you're having a sleepover at my house." She kept up a soft monologue, hoping to soothe the child before they got to the store.

They purchased the essentials for Macie, during which time Macie was perfectly calm, if a little morose, almost as if she were suffering from mild shock after the escape from the boat, the plane ride, and now seeing a familiar face that she hadn't seen for months. After paying for her cartload, Kallene drove them home.

Inside the garage, with the door closed, Kallene picked Macie up from the car seat she'd just purchased and gathered up several bags to carry into the house. As soon as they entered the kitchen, Macie squirmed, wanting to be let down. Kallene watched the child wander from room to room. She was much steadier on her feet than she'd been the last time she'd been in Kallene's house. Sometimes she paused with a puzzled expression on her little face, as though she might almost recognize something once familiar.

"Are you hungry?"

Macie hadn't spoken yet, and Kallene wasn't certain how much she understood. The toddler put her head to one side and appeared to be thinking about her question. Finally she nodded her head.

"Let's wash your face and hands first." She gestured toward the bathroom, and Macie made no objections, so Kallene lifted her to the sink, where she scrubbed off an accumulation of dirt and stains. When she set her back on her feet, Macie scowled and smacked her hand against the seat of her pants. Taking that as a request for a clean diaper, Kallene took care of that matter and was appalled to see how red Macie's skin was. It had been much too long since the last diaper change. She applied a small amount of a soothing ointment she found in her medicine cabinet to the reddened area and was rewarded with the first smile she'd seen on the child's face that day.

Moments later, Macie chewed on a cracker while Kallene prepared mac and cheese for both of them. She was surprised to discover the little girl could drink from a small cup on her own and no longer needed a sippy cup. When her small guest held out her hands toward a bowl of fruit sitting on the kitchen counter, Kallene peeled an orange and sectioned it for her.

When they finished eating, Kallene set Macie on the floor while she cleared the table and put their few dishes in the dishwasher. To her delight, Macie went straight to the drawer that held plastic storage containers and began to play with them, building towers and giggling as she knocked them down.

After running a couple of inches of water in the bathtub, Kallene was surprised to see Macie pulling at her clothes and smiling in anticipation of a bath. The moment Kallene freed the child from her clothing, the toddler climbed over the side of the tub and into the water before Kallene could assist her. She scooted from one end of the tub to the other, splashing and kicking. Kallene couldn't believe one small child could splash so much water all over a bathroom. Clearly Carson had given his daughter frequent baths or had taken her swimming often, and the girl loved water.

Getting Macie out of the tub was much harder than getting her into it, but eventually she was dry, wearing fresh clothes, and the tangles were combed out of her hair. She didn't object when Kallene carried her to the comfortable rocking chair in the front room. At first the little girl was curious about her surroundings and wished to play, but in a short while she snuggled down in Kallene's arms.

She seemed almost asleep when her head lifted, and she asked, "Daddy?"

"He had to go away for a while. I'll take care of you until he comes back." The child seemed satisfied and was soon asleep. Kallene waited until she felt certain Macie wouldn't wake up by being carried upstairs to her makeshift bed.

After placing the little girl on a clean sheet covering the love seat and pulling a light blanket over her, Kallene stood watching Macie sleep for several minutes, feeling a deep sadness for the little girl who would grow up without her parents. Linda had loved her daughter so much. It didn't seem fair that she wouldn't be there to guide her in the years ahead.

Linda. You have my promise I will always love her and help her every way I can.

Leaving the bedroom door open, Kallene stood in the hall a few minutes, contemplating the changes that would have to be made in her household. There were three bedrooms and a sitting room on the second floor. The sitting room opened onto the deck. She slept in the master bedroom, used one bedroom for a guest room, and the room next to hers was nearly empty. She used the closet as storage space for seasonal clothing. Beginning tomorrow, she'd turn that room into a bedroom for Macie. For now, she'd better throw the few pieces of clothing Macie had arrived in into the washer and make some telephone calls. Spotting Macie's grimy rag doll lying on the floor, she gathered it up with the load of laundry.

She approached calling Adam and Janet with mixed feelings. They would be thrilled to learn Macie was with her, but she suspected they would expect to fly right to Salt Lake to take charge of their grandchild. It wouldn't be easy for them to accept that Macie wouldn't be returning to Baltimore with them.

CHAPTER TWENTY-FOUR

THOUGH THEY PUT A GOOD face on it, Kallene could tell that Adam and Janet weren't pleased to learn Carson had taken steps to ensure that his daughter would remain in Utah until his guilt or innocence could be established and that Kallene had been given custody of their granddaughter. They grumbled, but in the end they assured her they wouldn't attempt to circumvent Carson's wishes.

"It could be years," Adam complained.

"At least you'll soon be family, so she'll grow up surrounded by family, and we'll be able to see her often," Janet consoled herself.

"We won't interfere, but we'll be on the first flight out there."

"Don't book a hotel room. I have a guest room, you know."

"Thank you." There was a catch in Janet's voice. "We'll look forward to spending time getting to know both you and our granddaughter better."

"Adam," she said hesitantly, "would you think about making certain Carson has a good attorney? No matter what happens, someday Macie will need to know her father was treated fairly."

"You're still sticking up for him?"

"I was with him and Macie a few hours ago. He's done his best to care for her. There were many reasons why he and Linda shouldn't have married, but . . . no, I still don't think he killed her. He'd have to be an Oscar-winning actor to be as genuine as he's seemed. Besides, why would he turn himself in if he was guilty?"

The grunt Adam made conveyed clearly that he didn't agree with her.

After she ended the call to the Piersons, she settled in one corner of the sofa and pressed the speed dial number for Jon. He answered on the first ring.

After she told him about Carson and Macie, he seemed upset. "You took an awful chance. He might have hurt you."

"But he didn't, and now Macie is here with me."

"I'm glad you have Macie. Carson couldn't have chosen a better guardian for her. How do you feel about this becoming a permanent arrangement?"

"I love Macie and would be happy to raise her, but I'm not going to plan on it. When Carson is free, she'll have to be returned to him."

"I don't think Carson will ever be free again," Jon said. "The police feel confident that the towel they found with his blood on it is proof he killed Linda."

"That towel doesn't prove anything. It was in the bathroom of their house the day after Linda disappeared," Kallene argued.

"It couldn't have been the same towel," Jon said.

"I think it is. I don't know how it got there unless the killer stole it from the clothesline where Carson left it to make him look guilty."

"I guess we'll have to wait for a jury to decide that."

She didn't like arguing with Jon, but she couldn't help thinking both he and his father were unreasonable in their insistence that Carson had killed Linda. Yet she couldn't explain why she was equally certain he hadn't.

They talked about other matters, and Kallene filled him in on everything she'd observed about Macie.

"And you're sure it won't bother you if Macie becomes a long-term part of our household?" She suspected there was an underlying question he was asking.

"Not at all. Will it bother you?"

"I would love to raise her. Linda sent me pictures, but I only have what you and Linda have told me to go from. Then there's my concern that I might not be able to father a child. She might be my only chance to be a father."

"Jon, Macie isn't your only chance for fatherhood. We both want children, and if we can't have our own biological children, we'll adopt. There are children in this world who need parents as much as people like us need to be parents."

"You're not going to feel cheated if I can't give you children?" His voice revealed his deep concern.

"I'll be honest. I want to have babies, but if it doesn't happen the usual way, I believe God will help us become parents another way. Whatever happens, I won't feel cheated—a little disappointed, perhaps, but grateful to have you beside me."

* * *

Kallene awoke with her mind already filled with plans for the day. She stretched and was shocked to discover a warm lump against her side. Looking down, she found Macie curled close to her, her red curls in wild disarray and her eyes scrunched tightly closed.

"Hey, sweetie, are you awake?" she whispered.

Macie's eyes popped open. She seemed to be studying Kallene, then a wide smile spread across her face. She scrambled to her feet and gave a little jump. She giggled and jumped harder. Laughing, Kallene scooped her up in her arms to carry her to the bathroom. After removing her pajamas and diaper, Kallene reached for a dry diaper. Macie wiggled away and escaped down the hallway, giggling, to the sitting room. Kallene chased after her, reaching her as she attempted to hide behind the blinds that covered the deck doors.

"Doggie!" Macie shouted. She patted the glass and crooned to the big dog that stared back at her.

"Go away!" Kallene made a shooing motion toward the dog before swooping up the little runaway. No matter how many times she chased the dog away or made certain her back gate was locked, the darn dog still slept on her deck almost every night. If this kept up, she'd have no choice other than to call Animal Control to pick the dog up.

"Doggie! Play wif doggie," Macie pleaded.

"No way. The doggie is supposed to go home." She marched back to the bathroom to finish dressing Macie then carried her down the stairs to the kitchen, where she discovered the little girl's breakfast preferences hadn't changed.

After Macie gorged on French toast, Kallene dressed her in one of the pant sets she'd purchased the previous day and informed the little girl they were going shopping for a big-girl bed just for her.

"Look!" She handed the clean doll to Macie, who let out a little squeal and hugged it with fierce enthusiasm.

"Baby! Baby!"

Shopping with a two-year-old proved to be more challenging than she'd anticipated, but Kallene found the experience strangely rewarding. When she didn't find what she wanted at DI, she went to a furniture store and arranged to have both a junior bed and a matching chest of drawers delivered, paying extra for same-day delivery. She ordered a high chair, too. After almost losing the child twice in the big store, she added a stroller to her purchases.

After a couple of hours, Kallene could tell that Macie was getting exhausted with all the shopping. When the child stuck out her bottom lip and appeared about to cry, Kallene promised only one more stop, then they'd go get lunch. As she wheeled the newly purchased stroller into the toy department, Macie clapped her hands and squealed. Soon she was straining at the seat belt, trying to free herself. Kallene had almost as much fun as Macie exploring the various wonders and adding treasures to the growing pile of new toys for the toddler.

Half an hour later, with the back of the stroller heaped with bags, they made their way back to the car. After a quick stop for lunch, they were ready to start home. Macie fell asleep with her rag doll clasped in her arms almost as soon as the car pulled out of the parking lot.

Kallene spent as much time opening the new toys and removing the packaging as Macie did playing with her new toys. When the new toys were all opened, and she'd found a plastic bin to use as a toy box, she sat down at her desk to work on a sketch with Macie playing nearby. Not much was accomplished before she was interrupted by the arrival of the delivery truck.

While directing the delivery men where to place her purchases, she noticed a police car stop across the street. A few minutes later, she watched as an officer escorted Rupert Meyer to the police car and drove away with him. She wondered if he was, at last, being arrested and what would become of his dog. Then Adam called to say they'd arrived at the airport and were renting a car. Her thoughts returned to the little girl who had been her constant companion since the previous morning. She looked toward the toys scattered across her office but didn't see Macie. She stood to begin checking on her.

A giggle came from upstairs. Taking the stairs two at a time, she hurried to see what the little girl was doing. She stopped and stared in chagrin. Rupert Meyer's dog had his nose pressed against the glass, and Macie was smearing the glass with pats and kisses. She debated what she should do. She didn't know whether Meyer had been arrested or just taken in for questioning. It seemed kind of mean to call Animal Control to pick up the dog if he was coming back.

Deciding the best course of action would be to ignore the dog for the present, she attempted to lure Macie away from her newfound playmate. "I guess it's time to fix dinner," she said. "Grandpa and Grandma will be here pretty soon."

"Gampy?" Macie's face lit with excitement. She pointed to the dog. "Gampy see."

An idea came to her. She'd looked up Carson's father's phone number months ago when she'd first learned where Carson and his daughter were living. She'd been surprised to discover his boat had a phone, but Jon had explained that the houseboat probably wasn't even seaworthy and was permanently docked. She pulled her cell phone from her pocket. It took only a few moments to find and dial his number. She should have called him sooner to let him know his son and granddaughter had arrived in Utah.

When a weak voice answered, she said, "Mr. Longdale, this is Kallene Ashton. There's a little girl here beside me who would like to talk to you." She switched on the speaker phone.

"Say hello to Grandpa Longdale," she instructed.

"Gampy?" Macie looked puzzled.

"You okay, Red?" Macie looked around, unsure where her grandfather's voice was coming from. After a moment, she nodded her head and held up one of her new toys, which was still clutched in her hand.

"She's fine, Mr. Longdale. I took her shopping today for a bed and a few toys. She's trying to show you her boat. I don't think she understands that you can't see it."

A soft chuckle came from the speaker. "Red, that's a mighty fine boat. Now you be a good girl and do what Miss Ashton tells you. I love you, kiddo."

"Wuv too, Gampy." She hunched her shoulders and continued to look around.

"She really is all right, and as soon as I get any word about Carson, I'll call you."

"Thank you." His voice was little more than a wheeze. "Means the world to me." His words ended in a bout of coughing.

"Are you all right? Can I call someone to help you?"

"I'll be all right, thanks. Better hang up now. Bye."

Before she could add a farewell, Macie spoke up. "Bye-bye, Gampy."

From the corner of her eye, Kallene spotted something moving in her backyard as she returned the phone to her pocket. She stared with an open mouth as she saw the dog that had been on her deck moments earlier nose aside the boards Darnell had hammered back in place, slip through the opening that appeared, and disappear from sight.

Someone had fixed the board to open again.

As Kallene hurried to prepare dinner, she tried to explain to Macie that she had another grandpa and a grandma, too, but clearly the explanation went over the child's head. She'd just have to hope for the best when they arrived. Her mind kept returning to the dog, and she couldn't help wondering why his owner had made a secret doggie door to give his dog a free run of her backyard. She felt certain now that the big dog really couldn't jump a six-foot fence, which meant Meyer had been turning the dog loose at night. It was no accident the animal found its way to her deck night after night.

The doorbell sounded, and Macie, who had been playing with a mixture of toys and the plastic containers near Kallene's feet, leaped up, clapping her hands.

"Daddy!" she squealed as she ran toward the front door.

"No, sweetie, Daddy can't come yet." She tried to soften the child's disappointment before opening the door to Janet and Adam. Still, Macie's disappointment was evident when she saw two strangers standing in the doorway. Her lip turned down and tears sparkled in her eyes. Kallene picked Macie up, and the little girl buried her face against her shoulder. No amount of coaxing would persuade her to acknowledge her grandparents.

Midway through dinner, Macie struggled to get down from her chair. Kallene released the safety restraints and set her on her feet beside the chair. Once free, she ran from the room and returned moments later, carrying her rag doll. With slow, hesitant steps she approached Janet and held out the doll to her. With an uncertain look on her face, Janet accepted it. She held it in her hand for a few seconds then raised it to her shoulder to give the doll's back an awkward pat. Macie's round face remained solemn for almost a minute, then a smile broke through like the sun rising in the morning.

"Baby!" Macie reached for the doll, and her grandmother handed it over. Little arms squeezed the doll, then with the doll held in the firm grasp of one hand, Macie climbed back into her chair. She set the doll beside her plate and began eating her dinner.

Janet and Kallene exchanged a smile.

The evening went well, and Macie warmed up to both of her grandparents. She didn't even object when Janet bathed her and got her ready for bed. Once her pajamas were fastened, she hurried down the hall to the sitting room again. This time she went straight to the blinds and swept the vertical slats aside to peer outside.

"Doggie!" Macie called. Kallene was glad to see her neighbor's large dog was not on the deck, even if his absence disappointed her small guest.

"No doggie. He went home." She picked up Macie to carry her to her new bed. She wondered if arrangements had been made for someone to take the dog to the animal shelter or someplace where he'd receive care. She hoped so. It would be cruel to just abandon the dog.

She'd set up the bed in her own bedroom since she hadn't had time to prepare the spare room. With Adam and Janet's help tomorrow, she hoped to get the room cleaned out and turned into a bedroom a little girl might love. She was certain Janet would love helping her pick out a bedspread and curtains.

Janet and Adam watched from the doorway as Kallene pulled back the top quilt and set Macie on the bed.

"No!" Macie shook her curls, making them bounce. She slid from the bed to her knees beside it. Kallene wasn't certain what she should do. Macie barely talked—surely she was too young to say a bedtime prayer. Kallene sank down beside her, and without prompting, Macie said, "Fader, bess Daddy. Bess Mama in Hebbin. Bess Gampy. Be good girl. Jesus. Amen."

Macie accepted good-night kisses from all three adults before Kallene tucked her in and admonished her to go to sleep. She stayed close by until she was certain the child had fallen asleep.

Returning to the front room, she found Janet and Adam waiting for her. "We've been talking," Adam said. "It's clear Carson has been caring for Macie and that prayer is a familiar part of her life. You may be right about him. Macie's father should be represented well in court. I'll take care of that tomorrow."

CHAPTER TWENTY-FIVE

KALLENE AWOKE EARLY AND GLANCED toward the junior bed a short distance away. Macie was sleeping soundly. She probably wouldn't awaken for several hours since she didn't have a long nap the previous day, and she was still adjusting to the time change. She slipped out of bed and dressed in a sweat suit. The days were warmer now, but early mornings were still cold. She picked up her running shoes and stepped out of the room.

It had been two days since her last run, and she was anxious to get in a good run while Janet and Adam were available to listen for Macie. Once they left, it might be difficult to run on a regular basis. She might have to invest in one of those strollers with big wheels she'd seen young mothers jog behind on numerous occasions.

She tiptoed down the stairs and took time for a few stretch exercises. She'd mentioned her intention to run to Janet the previous evening, so she could slip quietly from the house without waking anyone. She let the door close behind her, zipped up her jacket, and began a rapid walk down the street. The high school was only a few blocks away.

She looked up at the mountains. The sun was just peaking through a low saddle between two higher peaks, promising a brilliant spring morning. Delbert Haney's yard was a profusion of tulips, daffodils, hyacinths, and forsythia. The air smelled bright and clean. It was hard to believe that just a week earlier there had been two inches of snow on the ground.

She looked longingly toward the nearby canyon. It was too beautiful a morning to run circles on the high-school track, especially if Darnell Gines was there. Besides, it was beginning to grow light now, and the nearby canyon seemed to be calling her name. It had been months since she and Jon had run there, and she longed for the mountain beauty she'd come to love and the challenge of the mountain trail. She wished Jon were there to run with her, but he wasn't scheduled to return until late that evening. Just knowing he'd be arriving that night gave her step an added spring.

A twinge of guilt hit her as she approached the south arm of the trail and acknowledged that she was seriously considering taking the trail instead of going on to the track. Jon wouldn't approve. Since that woman's body had been found along the Legacy Parkway, he'd become paranoid about her running alone, but she had no intention of allowing fear to rule her life. Linda's death supposedly had no connection to those other women across the country who had been found dead. The porch light wasn't on at Rupert's house as it usually was at this time, and she hadn't seen him return since the police took him away, so he wasn't a threat either.

If her future runs were going to include a baby stroller, there would be few opportunities to run on the canyon trail. Her steps turned toward the dirt path.

The trail was dry at the lower end, and it felt good to breathe the cool mountain air and feel her shoes pounding against the soft dirt surface. A faint haze of green floated about the treetops, promising foliage would soon appear. The chatter of birds welcomed her back. She felt her lungs expand and contract as the trail wound upward. Even the pull of her calf muscles made her feel more alive.

She'd confined her workouts to tracks for so long that the climb required more exertion than she was accustomed to, and it took longer to reach the bridge and the picnic area than it should have. Pausing on the wooden bridge, she took several long breaths and looked around. It was worth the extra push to reach this spot. Patches of snow dotted the ground in the shadier places, and water rushing under the bridge had lost its melodic chatter and now roared, sending a fine spray skyward. The little glen where the two trails merged was cooler than the more open trail farther down had been. She shivered and knew it was time to start moving again.

Stepping off the bridge, she was dismayed to discover that the path crossing the picnic area was a sea of thick mud. Eyeing several clumps of last year's dried grass, she began picking her way across to the path that would lead her back down to her neighborhood. She'd taken only a few steps when she noticed some kind of animal tracks in the mud. They looked like large paw prints. Cougars and wildcats had been known to come down from the mountain from time to time, but to Kallene the stories had seemed more urban legend than anything to seriously worry about.

Looking around with a sense of unease, she stepped to the next small hillock. There were more prints near it. They were more like those made by a dog. She'd never heard of wolves in the area, but she wasn't sure about coyotes.

A dark shadow seemed to dull the bright spring day. Her stride lengthened. Some instinct in the back of her mind urged her to go faster. The trees blurred as she sped down the path. Years of running knowledge kicked in, warning her to slow down. She was more apt to fall in a downward rush than on flat ground or an upward slope. Still, her feet seemed to fly, and a sense of urgency consumed her.

She became aware of sounds she hadn't noticed earlier, or rather the lack of sound. No bird songs rang in the cool mountain air. Off to the right, there was a crash as if something large was moving through the brush. A twig snapped nearby. Was it her imagination, or were footsteps pounding behind her? Every story she and Jon had researched about women runners killed by a predator sprang to mind. Her legs moved faster.

It's just my imagination. There's no way I can hear other sounds over the roar of the water running down the center of the gully . . . over the pounding of my own feet.

Her toe hit a root poking through the ungroomed path, and she could feel herself falling. Instinct took over, and she reached out her arms to stop her fall. Her hands struck the path, and she rolled out of control. The voice of fear cautioned against screaming, and she stifled the cry that rose in her throat. The dirt seemed to rise up to meet her again and again.

She hit hard and lay stunned, unable to catch her breath for several seconds. A voice whispered in her head, "Get up! Run!" Even in her panic, she questioned whether the voice was a spiritual warning or hysteria. She struggled to regain her feet, but with her breath knocked out of her, she could only gasp. It took an immense effort to move a hand toward her chest, as though begging her lungs to pull in another gulp of air. The movement sent sharp daggers of pain through her wrist, and bright lights danced before her eyes, which slowly faded to dull gray.

She couldn't pass out! She had to get back on her feet and run. Shaking but using greater care, she lowered her other hand to the ground and applied small amounts of pressure. It held. She drew her legs beneath her and pulled herself forward until she was kneeling. The trees seemed to sway.

"Need a hand?"

She almost fell back to the ground. Fearing to look but knowing she had to, she lifted her eyes and almost cried with relief. Ted Grayson stood over her, a hand extended to help her to her feet. Steadying herself on her knees, she lifted her good hand toward him.

Testing each movement to be certain she hadn't injured more than her wrist, she let him pull her upright.

"Thank you." Her words came out mumbled as she realized her mouth was filled with mud and debris from the trail. She spit it out the best she could then wiped her face with the back of her hand.

Ted chuckled. "I don't think you'd want to see yourself in a mirror right now." He pulled a tissue from his pocket and dripped water from his camel pack onto it. Instead of handing it to her, he placed one hand under her chin, and lifting her face, he gently dabbed at the smear.

At last he leaned back to examine her face. "Much better." He grinned, and she wondered why she'd never noticed before that he was quite good looking. *Perhaps because he's a married man,* she reminded herself, then she stifled an almost hysterical giggle. *And I'm almost married, too, so I better continue to not notice.*

"It looks like you took quite a fall," Ted commiserated with her. "Are you able to keep running?"

"I don't think I have much choice, though I may be walking more than running." She tried to sound cheerful, but her wrist hurt so badly that she feared she wouldn't make it to the end of the trail without experiencing terrible pain the whole way.

"Here, I'll help you. You can lean on me." He fit one arm around her waist and drew her good arm around his. She tucked her injured hand into the pocket of her sweat jacket to partially immobilize it.

"But you won't be able to finish your run," she protested. "Julie will worry when you're late." She took a tentative step, attempting to prove she could go on without help.

"Don't worry. Julie is in Minnesota visiting her parents. She took Parker with her."

"How long have they been gone? Parker hasn't been to Cub Scouts for a long time, and I've wondered about him."

"Julie was concerned about him after he found that body. He didn't bounce back like we thought he should, so we decided it might be best that he go somewhere else to heal and get counseling. Julie's parents have a large home and are close to a good hospital." They were moving at a far smoother pace than Kallene had expected, and the path beneath their feet was becoming drier as the trail sloped downward.

"I think I can walk a little faster now." She pulled away, intending to walk on her own, since she was no longer feeling dizzy.

"You mustn't take chances." He tugged her back against his side. "That was a nasty fall, and jarring that injured wrist isn't going to do it any good."

"I'm no longer dizzy, and I really can move faster. The sooner I get down this trail, the sooner I can see a doctor and have it checked." Again she tried to put a little space between them. It didn't feel right to her to be held so tightly by a married man, and something in his teasing voice and insistence in keeping her practically glued to his side made her suspect that with his wife out of town, Ted Grayson was coming on to her.

"Great," she muttered under her breath.

"What was that?" He bent his head, brushing her hair back with a gentle stroke of his fingers.

"Nothing. I just wondered when Julie and Parker would be coming back. I miss seeing Parker around." It certainly wouldn't hurt to remind Ted of his family.

"They won't be coming back. Julie and I have decided to separate. She plans to stay in Minnesota for a while then get an apartment in New York. I haven't decided where I'll go, but I've already listed the house with a real estate agent."

"I'm sorry." She supposed the divorce explained his sudden friendliness.

"Don't be. Our marriage has been a sham for some time, and we've only stayed together for Parker's sake. But there's little point now, and Julie has made it clear she prefers playing around on her business trips to being tied down to me. Parker's doctor believes it's best that he be institutionalized."

"Oh no!"

"You've been around him enough to know he's not a normal child. He had problems before finding Linda Longdale's body. That discovery seems to have pushed him over the edge."

Kallene didn't say so, but she felt Parker's problems had more to do with parental neglect than with psychological problems. She remembered his vacant, staring eyes and clumsy movements the last time she'd seen him. Were those symptoms of some kind of psychosis, or had he been overmedicated, as she had supposed at the time? Had she been wrong?

A horrible thought popped into her mind. Was she wrong in some of her other assumptions, too? Parker was larger and stronger than most children his age. Could he have killed Linda and dropped her over the cliff himself to hide the body? He'd admitted he'd been in Mr. Haney's yard yanking out rosebushes the night before the murder. That certainly wasn't the action of a normal eight-year-old. He could have easily taken the rope and shovel then, too. But why would a child kill someone he barely knew?

"I'm not sure you realize it, but Parker is terribly possessive of you. We caught him throwing rocks one afternoon at Mr. Pierson's car when he parked in your driveway and he heard the two of you laughing on your deck."

For a moment she thought she might have spoken her terrible thoughts aloud.

Was he suggesting his child might have killed Linda because of her closeness to me? He couldn't possibly be suggesting his son had a motive for killing my friend. No father would do that. No.

She was reading too much into Ted's words.

She stumbled and, looking down, realized they'd left the path and were now walking among the trees a short distance from the trail. She must be dizzier than she thought.

"Oops!" She twisted to return to the path, but Ted's arm about her waist kept her angling deeper into the trees.

"What are you doing?" Kallene struggled to keep annoyance out of her voice. "I need to get back to my house and have my wrist looked at by a doctor. I have guests who will wonder where I am."

"You need to rest a few minutes, and I know just the place."

"I don't need to rest . . . I need to go home!" She tried to twist away from Ted's hold. His grip tightened, and she felt a sick weight of fear.

"Ted! Stop this! Let me return to the trail." He was steadily moving her farther from the trail and deeper into the trees. His arm about her waist was no longer gentle assistance but an imprisoning grip.

"You're hurting me!" Digging in her heels, she attempted to halt their forward momentum. Ted only paused long enough to throw her over one shoulder and continue walking with her injured arm painfully crushed between them. Stunned, it took a couple of seconds to react. She attempted to scream, but Ted's hand cut off the sound, and he pressed something into her mouth before she could gather her breath to try again. The walk changed to a trot, and she thought they were moving uphill. This couldn't be happening! She wondered if she'd knocked herself out when she fell. The agonizing pain in her wrist that came with each jolting step he took was proof she wasn't imagining anything.

CHAPTER TWENTY-SIX

SHE'D NEVER BEFORE EXPERIENCED SUCH awful pain as that shooting through her injured wrist as it was crushed between her abductor's shoulder and her own body. Fighting waves of blackness, she became aware of the small, hard lump in the pocket where she'd stuffed her injured wrist for support. If she could find the right buttons! Blackness rippled in waves from Ted's pounding lope as she tried to visualize the tiny keypad. She prayed her fingers touched the right keys. While pressing keys with the fingers of her injured hand, dizzying waves of pain hit her, and she knew she'd failed. Gritting her teeth against the pain and nausea, she made a second attempt then pressed what she hoped was SEND.

She was so near losing consciousness that she couldn't guess how much time passed between when Ted threw her over his shoulder and when he finally stopped. Fear roused her enough to continue her struggle to free herself. Trying to remember everything she knew about vulnerable body areas did no good, and she kicked wildly at any spot where she could make contact. Using her uninjured hand, she clawed in a wild frenzy with little success. He groped for something in his backpack, and an agonizing blow to the side of her head caused a reflexive contraction of her throat, expelling the gag Ted had placed there. Another blow struck the other side of her face, and she felt herself falling. Thoughts of Linda appeared in her mind, along with jumbled bits and pieces of the puzzle surrounding her death. Answers began to fall into place as she struggled to stay conscious.

The homicidal rapist traveled extensively to cities with major airports. As a sales representative for a major tool corporation, Ted traveled a great deal, and he had access to prototype tools law enforcement might not readily identify. All of the bodies were found along isolated stretches of jogging trails. He lived between Linda's house and her own. He could have intercepted Linda that morning. Why had she never suspected him of murdering her friend? A strangled, weak scream left her throat.

She hit the ground hard. Before she could gather her breath to attempt another scream, Ted's foot struck her ribs. Instinctively she attempted to roll away, but his heavy foot landed in her midsection, pinning her to the hard rock on which she lay. Glimpses of blue, green, and stark gray blurred around her.

"Scream all you want. No one is going to hear you," Ted snarled. He ground his foot harder against her abdomen. "I want you awake and screaming. That stupid friend of yours died too easily." He bent forward and slapped her hard across her face before his full weight settled on top of her. A small voice, almost drowned out by the pain, warned her not to cry. She'd bitten her lip with such intensity that she tasted blood.

"You killed Linda."

"I saw you weren't on your step waiting for her, so I intercepted her. The fool believed every word I said when I told her you didn't feel well and had asked me to run with her that morning. I even said you promised to call her later." His voice was smug.

A hand touched her sweat pants, and her panic level escalated. Something brushed against her mouth, and she bit down hard. Ted drew back enough to grasp his bleeding ear then raised his fist that held a small steel shovel—one that looked like the one Parker had used to replant the daffodil bulbs. Parker was afraid of his father and had probably guessed that because he had taken the little shovel from his father's backpack, it was his father who'd stolen Delbert Haney's shovel. He probably feared punishment if his father discovered that Parker sometimes secretly borrowed his father's tools. Mr. Haney's shovel had been used to kill Linda, which was why her wounds were different from those of the other women.

"Poke! Stab! Don't slap and don't be squeamish!" Her father's words from a long-ago lesson on self-defense rose over the roar in her head. Dad had considered self-defense techniques an essential part of her and her brothers' preparation for life. Her index finger followed thought with action, and her stomach threatened to revolt as she sank her finger into Ted's eye. His reflexive recoil gave her the opening she needed to roll to the side. She struggled to her feet as he reached for her in blind fury.

Kallene bolted from the rocky clearing. With her own vision blurred and waves of nausea threatening every step, she had no idea which way to go or how far she was from the path where she might find help. Each breath she took brought agonizing pain to her chest, and she feared Ted had broken at least one of her ribs.

"Fight through the pain! Survive!" She didn't know if Dad ever said those words or if it was her own survival instincts pushing her forward as she lurched toward a thick cluster of trees. She was moving downward; surely that was good.

Reaching the shelter of the trees, she wrapped her good arm around her aching chest and tried to think. Ted would know she'd seek some kind of shelter and head straight for the copse of trees. She had to keep moving.

The sound of pounding footfalls reached her ears, warning her Ted was running toward the trees where she hid. Trying not to make any revealing sound, she threaded her way through the trees. The grove ended in a profusion of wild rosebushes. Using the bushes as cover, she crouched low to make a dash for the next cluster of trees. Brambles tore at her hair and clothes, but she pushed on, never daring to look back for fear she'd see Ted racing after her.

Kallene stumbled into the shelter of a sentry pine, knowing her hiding place was too obvious, but most of the trees were aspen or scrub oak, which offered little concealment. She couldn't go on. She couldn't breathe without blackness swirling around her and the pain in her wrist and her ribs muddling her thinking. She sank to the thick carpet of pine needles beneath the tree.

Her phone! How could she forget her cell phone! Her fingers searched for it without success. No amount of self control could keep the tears from sliding down her cheeks. It must have fallen out of her pocket during her struggle with Ted.

She couldn't go on. Neither could she meekly wait for Ted to capture her again. Frantically she searched for something—anything—with which she could defend herself. Seeing one of the many rose thickets that dotted the canyon, she half crawled toward the brambles. Ignoring the deep scrapes to her face and arms, she slid on her belly as deeply into the tangle as she could go. Feeling a sharp jab to the palm of her good hand, she clawed at the partially buried rock until she could grasp it firmly.

She heard Ted's roar of anger and the curses he hurled at her only seconds before his hand grasped her ankle and she felt herself yanked backward.

Ted's face distorted with rage as he shouted, "I gave you everything, Julie! You never cared that I saved you from your father's fists by claiming your brat as my own. I knew you were a tramp, but I loved you. What you refused me, you gave all the others. I was a fool to think you'd love me." Over and over he sobbed as he yelled obscene threats while calling her Julie and beating her with the shovel. Grasping every bit of her waning strength, she fought back, slamming the rock she still held against his head. When he appeared dazed, she struck him again. Although almost blinded by pain and the roar in her head, she kept trying to free herself from Ted's weight that held her pinned to the ground. A horrible sound overrode all else, and a black blur blocked her narrow vision. Instinct forced her eyes closed in anticipation of the blow. She felt nothing but heard a piercing scream. The scream ceased with unnatural abruptness. The weight pressing against her pushed the air from her lungs and she lost the ability to breathe. She made a desperate attempt to shove the weight from her chest and struggled to open her eyes.

Her eyes were open, but she could see nothing. The weight moved away, and she gasped for breath. A strange sensation of something soft dancing across her face, then hands pulling at her shoulders, added to her confusion. Once again she attempted to see.

"It's all right, Kallene. You're safe now." The voice seemed to come from a distant place, but it was almost familiar. Arms held her in a comforting, nonthreatening embrace.

It took a moment for her vision to clear. Less than ten feet away, a familiar, massive dog stood atop a man's chest. She knew the man was Ted, but his face was unrecognizable, and his body lay perfectly still. The dog growled and gave the limp body another shake. She shuddered and let her eyes drift closed.

"That's enough, Raider! Get back here." A voice rumbled against her back before the arms holding her shifted her to the ground and pushed something soft beneath her head, raising it enough that when she opened her eyes, she could see the dog obediently trotting toward the man who was just out of her range of sight. Instead of continuing on toward him, the dog stopped beside her. She twisted her head aside as gorge rose in her throat and she vomited all over her rescuer's bloody coat. He licked her face and didn't seem to mind. She stretched her good arm toward the animal and grasped his coat with her fingers. Raider settled beside her, and she rested her throbbing head against his.

"The cops will be here soon. I called that detective friend of yours." This time she was able to focus on the man who knelt a few feet away. "Try to stay awake. You might have a concussion, and it won't cause as much trouble if you don't lose consciousness."

"I'm sorry my dog scared you all those times you found him in your yard. He's a good dog and is trained to protect anyone he's been ordered to watch over. I assigned him to look after you as soon as I noticed your resemblance to other victims, including your friend Linda. I've studied Grayson a long time and suspected he was the one killing runners. I knew you were in danger when he didn't move on after the second murder. I've been following him ever since I was accused of what I suspected was another in his chain of murders. I wasn't sure whether he killed Linda or not and thought the husband might have done it. Now I figure he hid her body better because the killing was practically in his backyard—and because he still meant to go after you."

"Thank you," she whispered. Her throat was raw, and the sound came out so faint and distorted that she wasn't certain Rupert had heard her.

"Don't try to talk. Raider will stay here with you while I go back to the trail to show the cops the way."

From where she lay, she could just see the soles of Ted Grayson's Nikes. Panic welled inside her, and she wanted to beg Rupert to stay. Accurately reading the tremor that shook her body, he attempted to reassure her. "Grayson's dead. He isn't going to hurt another woman. Ever.

"Raider, look after her." The dog moved closer, offering both comfort and warmth. Her hand clung to the dog's thick hair, and she found herself praying.

Kallene felt a comforting peace come over her. If she lay without moving, the pain in her wrist and ribs subsided to a bearable level. Darkness swirled around her, bringing a floating sensation. Raider's rough tongue bathing her face reminded her she mustn't give into the inviting darkness.

She turned her head a slight degree and saw something shiny lying in the grass. She wrinkled her brow as she tried to concentrate. Where had she seen that object before? It had been in Ted's hand, and he had smashed it into her temple. She was lucky to be alive. She felt certain it was also the tool Parker had used that day in Mr. Haney's garden. An awful unease settled over her. Parker hadn't been seen for months. Was the boy in Minnesota, or had Ted learned his son was on to him or was at least making mistakes that would lead police to him? Ted may have sent his son away because he feared the boy might tell the police he'd taken then later returned the small, heavy tool. Or something worse may have happened in order to keep the boy silent.

Raider gave her face another lick with his rough tongue. Rupert Meyer must have suspected Ted Grayson of committing the murder for which he'd been sent to prison. Had he bought the house across the street so he could watch Grayson, then? Had he sent Raider to watch over her all those nights because he feared for her safety, or was he waiting for an opportunity to take revenge? She might never know.

She released her grip on Raider's fur and slowly stroked his head with her good hand. Raider barked once and rose to his feet. A chill set her teeth chattering, and she struggled in vain to sit up. She'd never felt so vulnerable before in her life. She could barely lift her head on her own and could offer no defense against a wild animal or a man like Ted Grayson. She looked at the dog standing over her and knew Raider would defend her with his life; she closed her eyes and prayed he wouldn't have to.

A shout came from the woods, and men began to pour into the clearing. Scott was at the forefront. He glanced briefly at Ted then hurried to her side. He stopped when Raider bared his teeth and emitted a low growl.

"It's okay. He'll help her." She heard Rupert speak to Raider then move close enough to grasp the dog's collar.

Dropping to one knee, Scott reached for her injured wrist.

"No. Broken," she whimpered, holding the arm close.

"Medic! Over here!" He turned to shout over his shoulder.

Then Jon and a man with EMT embroidered on his shirt were beside her. She reached for Jon's hand, and he gripped her scratched and blood-smeared hand in both of his.

"Jon, it was Ted . . ."

"Shh, you're safe now. Don't try to talk."

The medic interrupted Jon. "She needs to be in a hospital. She has a concussion and some ugly head wounds, possible broken ribs, and her wrist is broken. I'm giving her something for the pain. My partner is coming with a stretcher." Kallene felt a small prick in her arm.

"Ted killed Linda—and those other women, too. Carson—Rupert—didn't . . ." In spite of the dizzying waves of blackness, Kallene felt an urgency to remove suspicion from two innocent men.

"It's all right. You can talk later." Jon attempted to soothe her. "I'll stay right beside you."

"Find Parker and Julie," she begged as darkness closed around her. She wanted to tell Jon of her fear that Ted may have killed them, too, but she couldn't seem to form the words.

CHAPTER TWENTY-SEVEN

LYING MOTIONLESS, KALLENE TOOK IN as much of her surroundings as she could without opening her eyes. She wasn't alone. Nearby she could hear steady, even breathing. There was a faint odor of medicine and roses. Roses! She opened her eyes, and she saw a huge bouquet of red roses resting on a wide window ledge. She turned her head and met the source of the quiet breathing. Jon sat on a chair pulled up close beside her bed.

"Hello, beautiful." He smiled, but the smile didn't disguise the fatigue and worry in his eyes.

"Hello, yourself." Her voice came out in a soft whisper that scratched her throat, and she remembered Ted's fingers pressing against her windpipe, choking off her screams. She became aware of an IV feeding into one arm and a heavy cast on the other. "I'm supposed to be watching Macie!"

"She's fine. She and Mom are the best of friends now, but Mom said she's been asking about you."

"I'm glad your mom is there to look after her."

"I think I better let a nurse know you're awake." Jon pressed a button on the side of her bed and spoke to the voice that answered his call. A moment later, a nurse entered the room. She was cheerful and pleasant as she checked Kallene's vitals and assured her the doctor would be in to see her in a little while. "Rest as much as you can. You can have visitors, but send them away if you feel tired. And if your head is still bothering you, press the CALL button, and I'll bring you more pain medication."

After the nurse left the room, Kallene picked up where she'd left off. "I feel like I let Macie and Carson down."

"Really, Macie's happy with my parents. It's you I'm concerned about. I don't understand why you decided to run alone yesterday morning."

"Yesterday? I've been here overnight?"

"Yes. You suffered some severe blows to the head and are lucky to be alive. The doctor said you have a concussion, your wrist is broken, and several ribs are bruised. When I think of what that man did to you, I'm glad Meyer's dog got to him before I did." He leaned forward and lightly brushed her mouth with his. She shuddered, remembering her gruesome glimpse of what used to be Ted Grayson.

"Was my kiss that bad?" Jon gave her a wry smile. "Remind me to pack my toothbrush the next time I go rushing off to rescue my sweetheart."

She couldn't help smiling. "The kiss was fine, more than fine, in fact. You might say it's the best thing that has happened to me since you left for San Diego. I know Rupert called the police, but how did you get there so fast?"

"After talking to you two nights ago and learning Carson had turned himself in and that you had Macie, I called one of my partners and asked him to finish up for me. I rushed to the airport and caught the first plane I could secure a seat on. I caught a red-eye and landed here around four the next morning. Thinking you wouldn't be running because of Macie, I slept until almost seven then called your house. Imagine my surprise when Dad answered. He said you'd gone for a run, and I got chills. I felt you needed me. I knew I was speeding, but when half a dozen police cars passed me instead of pulling me over, I followed them to the trailhead and started running."

"I know it was stupid of me to run alone, but I really thought the danger was over. I saw the police take Rupert away the day before, and any other suspect wasn't available to cause me any trouble. It never crossed my mind to fear anyone else. I'm just grateful the police didn't keep Rupert and that he took his dog for a run yesterday morning." She shifted, trying to find a comfortable spot. She ached in more places than she'd ever imagined possible. She rubbed her temples and found touching them caused more pain than it eased.

"Scott and Rupert were both here last night." Jon held her hand and spoke with care. He seemed to understand her need to know the facts concerning the terrible events that had transpired the previous day, but he was reluctant to upset her.

"Rupert admits he's been following Grayson. While in prison he did some meticulous Internet research and discovered one company held trade shows in each city near where a woman runner was found assaulted and murdered. From there, he found Grayson had been involved in each of those trade shows, so as soon as his lawyer got him out, he set out to find Grayson and to keep an eye on him. He wasn't sure Grayson had killed Linda, but when the Legacy Parkway murder occurred, he was convinced he was right about Grayson. Unfortunately, he was unable to convince the police Grayson was the guilty party or even a person of interest, since there was nothing linking him. They figured he was grasping at straws in trying to exonerate himself."

"That's understandable. Ted always seemed a bit snobbish but respectable, even admirable, in many ways." Kallene stared into the distance for several minutes. "I never once worried about Ted; it was Rupert Meyer, Darnell, and maybe even Carson who made me nervous."

"Raider was just a half-grown pup when Rupert stumbled on that woman's body near Seattle. They were on a training run. Rupert searched long and hard for his dog when he got out of prison until he found him, but after finding Raider he had a difficult time proving his claim was greater than that of the police force that had claimed the animal and trained it as a service dog. They only recently returned Raider to him."

There was a tap on the door, and without waiting for a response, Scott pushed it open and walked in. He was carrying a bouquet of mixed spring flowers. "You're looking a little more chipper this morning." He walked across the room and set his flowers beside the roses before pulling up a chair opposite Jon.

She did her best to smile at him. He grinned, looked pointedly at their linked hands, and said, "I heard you were engaged, and then I caught a glimpse of a big, shining rock on your hand yesterday." He turned to Jon. "Congratulations. You're a lucky man."

"My ring!" The ring wasn't on her hand! She should have noticed the empty space sooner.

"It's in my pocket," Jon assured her before she could reach full panic mode. "The emergency room staff removed it and your watch. They gave them to me to keep for you until you're discharged."

"I tried to call you." She turned to Scott. "But Ted was carrying me, and my phone was in my pocket. I couldn't see which numbers to push."

"You did fine. My phone rang, and the caller ID displayed your number, but when you didn't say anything before the line went dead, I got worried. Especially since the Davis County police officer who interviewed Meyer mentioned that he told them of his suspicions concerning Grayson, which they dismissed as an attempt to deflect suspicion from himself. I tried to call you back. When you didn't answer, I called your home phone. Mr. Pierson informed me he and his wife were your houseguests and that you'd gone for a run. I was just getting into my car to go looking for you when dispatch sent Meyer's 911 call through to me."

Kallene tried to sit up, and Jon pushed a pillow behind her back. The slight movement elevated her headache and reminded her of dozens of aching places all over her body. "Scott, did you check on Parker and Julie? I hate to think Ted would kill his own son before risking what the boy might tell the police, but when he was attacking me, he called me Julie, and I think he'd gone insane."

"We tried to reach Mrs. Grayson. Her boss said she's on vacation and is spending time with her parents in Minnesota. He promised to have someone call back with their contact information." He leaned forward, looking apologetic. "Our people are doing everything they can to notify her of her husband's death and the circumstances surrounding it before the press learns the whole story and starts releasing names and details."

"I need to call my parents!" Her hoarse croak was as close to a shout as she could manage.

"I already spoke with your father," Jon said. "He and your mom are flying out. I'll meet them at the airport this evening and bring them here."

"Thank you. Your parents are in the guest room. Mine can have my room until I'm released from this place." She gave the drip line running into her arm a disapproving look.

A commotion at the door caught her attention, and she turned to see Jon's parents, Carson, and Macie bearing a huge woven basket of tropical flowers.

"Kallee!" Macie escaped her grandmother's handclasp and evaded Carson's lunge to catch her. She tore across the room, intent on reaching Kallene. Jon swooped her up, holding her wiggling and kicking over the bed.

"Take it easy, Macie. Kallene has a big owie. We have to be careful not to bump her." He set the wiggling toddler on the floor beside the bed but kept a hand on the back of her shirt.

"Big owie?" Macie gave Kallene's cast a gentle pat then leaned forward to kiss it. "Better now?"

"Oh, sweetie, I feel better just seeing you again."

Carson edged closer to gather up Macie. His awkward stance as he looked down at Kallene betrayed his lack of ease with the position he found himself in and his determination to square himself with her. "Thank you," he said in a subdued voice. "You and my dad are the only ones who never gave up on me. If you hadn't helped me with Macie, I might have lost her."

"I loved spending time with Macie."

"And the Piersons took care of me, too, thanks to you. Adam hired an attorney for me before the charges were dropped." He looked down, and Kallene knew it had been difficult for him to accept Adam's help or to acknowledge his in-laws' kindness.

"What are you going to do now?" Kallene asked him.

"I reckon I'll head back to California. Dad's not got long, and I need to be with him. After that I don't know, but I don't think I'll come back here. The bank repossessed the house, and well, the publicity . . ."

"I understand, but I'll miss Macie."

"I won't try to stop you or Linda's family from seeing her."

Scott's phone rang, and while he left to take the call, Darnell Gines walked in with a fistful of Mr. Haney's prize tulips. "The old man said I should give these to you." For once Darnell sounded unsure of himself.

She started to stammer her thanks just as Scott came back into the room. "I've got to go. Julie Grayson's parents have been dead for five years. Grayson lied about her being with them in Minnesota."

Darnell dropped the flowers he held. They scattered across the bed, a few rolling onto the floor. "Something funny has been going on at the Graysons' house. Sometimes when I shoveled their walks the last few months, I heard strange sounds when they should have both been at work and the kid at school. Today when I stopped to see if Ted wanted me to spray his lawn with a broadleaf grass killer along with fertilizing it, I heard it again."

"You better come with me." Scott motioned for Darnell to follow him. "We'll talk on the way."

"Okay." Darnell paused before he left. "See you later, gorgeous." He and Scott disappeared into the hall and closed the door behind them.

* * *

Kallene pushed a button to elevate the back of her bed. She looked at the meal on a tray in front of her and bit into a toasted ham and cheese sandwich. The toasted wheat bread had sat too long under a cover, making it soggy, and she'd never liked processed cheese. She took a few bites then put the sandwich down. Rubbery Jell-O didn't appeal to her, so she took a sip of soup. It wasn't too bad. She hadn't eaten a meal for a day and a half. Under the circumstances, she thought she could eat anything, but she was wrong. She wanted to leave the hospital as soon as possible and find some real food.

She picked up a carton of milk and drank it slowly, savoring the coolness of it. This was the first time she'd been alone since waking a few hours earlier. The doctor had come in and cleared her room of guests while he examined her. Jon had kissed her and promised to go back to his apartment to sleep for a few hours before picking up her parents.

Dr. Michaels had assured her that her bruises would fade and her wrist would heal in a few weeks, but because of the concussion, she would need to remain in the hospital another night. He also pre-scribed a painkiller for the pain in her head, which helped her sleep for a couple hours.

"You're a fortunate young lady," he'd told her. "Another blow to your right temple could have caused brain injury or even death."

Her mind strayed to Parker. *Was it possible Ted had killed the boy to keep him from talking? No. Surely not even a monster like Ted would destroy his own child.* But there was a possibility Ted wasn't Parker's father; she remembered Ted's reference to the boy as Julie's brat.

Pushing her tray away, she leaned back against her pillow and waited for the pain medication to take effect. She was almost asleep when her door opened again and Scott walked in. He looked around. He took a chair, and his expression was grim.

"We located Julie," he began without preamble. "It seems she flew to Paris with a friend several months ago and has no intention of returning anytime soon. Her reaction to Ted's death was, 'That'll save me the time and expense of a divorce.' She spoke candidly of her marriage, claiming she and Ted hadn't lived together as husband and wife from the beginning. Her parents forced her to marry him at sixteen when they discovered she was pregnant, and he was the only one of the boys in their small town who would claim responsibility. She said he idolized her, but she didn't even like him."

"Lovely marriage." She couldn't avoid the sarcasm that crept into her voice. "But what about Parker? Did you find him?"

"She said she signed a document and left it with her attorney, relinquishing all rights to her child. She also verified what Ted told you. The boy was committed to an institution for disturbed children in Minnesota."

"Something tells me that's a lie. Did you check the house?"

"After we made contact with Mrs. Grayson, the judge turned down our request for a warrant to search the house, saying since the FBI had already been issued a warrant and planned to search on Monday for evidence that may link Grayson to other similar murders across the country, he can't let us go in ahead of them." His words didn't bring her assurance but increased the sense of urgency she'd been feeling concerning Parker.

"Did you find out which institution he's in and if he's really in one? If he's not there, he could be alone in the house or dead. What if Monday is too late?"

"Take it easy. Tomorrow is Sunday, so it won't be much longer. I'll do some more checking, and if I don't discover which children's hospital he's in, I'll go back to the judge." Scott rose to his feet. He appeared exhausted.

Leaning toward her, he placed a kiss on her cheek. "You're quite a woman. I just may regret for the rest of my life that I let you get away." He turned and walked out the door.

CHAPTER TWENTY-EIGHT

DINNER WASN'T ANY BETTER THAN lunch. She was still trying to swallow it down when Brittany tiptoed into her room. She was carrying her son's diaper bag, though she appeared to be alone. She looked around then pulled a box from the bag and set it beside the dinner Kallene was trying to eat. Before Brittany removed the lid, Kallene caught a whiff of pepperoni.

"You sneaked in a pizza?" She eyed the box, wondering if she was hallucinating. She hoped it was real.

"It hasn't been that long since I spent a few days here. I don't know about you, but when I'm sick, the last thing I want is Mexican casserole or whole-wheat pasta." Both women giggled, and Kallene reached for a slice of the fully loaded pizza.

When Brittany left, she took all evidence of the pizza with her except for a lingering whiff of pepperoni and spice.

Jon and her parents arrived shortly after. Her mom shed a few tears then launched into catching her up on the family news, including every detail about her newest nephew. Her head began to ache again, and a nurse brought her medication. The last thing she remembered was Jon kissing her good night and promising to get her parents settled at her house.

* * *

Kallene awoke feeling a restless urgency. After the doctor made rounds, a nurse removed the IV from her arm and encouraged her to walk a little bit. He also gave approval for her to go home later that morning. Moving around made her aware of more aches and pains, but her head felt much better, and she waited anxiously for Jon to bring her fresh clothes and to drive her home. Catching sight of herself in the bathroom mirror, she wanted to cry. Huge bruises covered both sides of her face; cuts and scrapes were everywhere; a white bandage covered most of one ear where it had been sliced by the sharp edge of the shovel that had struck her; and stitches decorated both temples. Her hair stuck out in every direction.

Knowing how terrible she looked, she felt self-conscious when Jon arrived, but he quickly assured her she was beautiful to him.

She found her mind drifting to Parker as Jon drove, and her fingers drummed nervously on the armrest. She wanted him to go faster. She couldn't get home fast enough to suit her. *Why hasn't Scott called? It was Sunday, but if there was a chance Parker was alone in the Grayson house, shouldn't Scott be doing more to search it?*

Walking into her house brought a feeling of peace. Now her life could get back to normal. She shuddered, remembering how close she came to never returning. As her eyes scanned the familiar room, she noticed the carpet was freshly vacuumed and there wasn't a speck of dust on any surface. Her mom and Janet both rushed to envelop her in gentle hugs. Her mother led her to the first-floor room Kallene had made her office. The daybed she used as a sofa was now made up as a bed.

"You should rest." Her mother turned down the sheet, encouraging Kallene to lie down. "Since your father and I are using your room, this seemed the best place for you, which works out well since it will save you going up and down the stairs."

"There's nothing wrong with my legs. It's my wrist that's broken, and I'm tired of lying in bed," she protested. "But I am hungry. I'll just fix myself a sandwich, then I'll . . ."

"No," her mother insisted. "You need to rest. I'll bring you a sandwich."

Kallene sighed in resignation. Arguing with her mother would be useless. She sat down on the edge of the bed, feeling too restless to actually lie down. After eating lunch, Kallene moved from the daybed to her office chair. She looked at the partially completed project on her desk but didn't feel motivated to work on it. What she really needed was to go outside; a walk would do her more good than a nap. Maybe if she put a paper bag over her head . . .

She swiveled her chair back and forth until an object caught her eye. Either her mother or future mother-in-law had found Parker's backpack when she pulled the vacuum cleaner from the hall closet and decided it belonged in her office. It had sat in her closet so long that Kallene had almost forgotten about it.

Picking it up by the straps, she carried it to the daybed and sat holding it, thinking of the day the boy had left it at her house. Tears trickled from her eyes, and she brushed them away with a burst of anger. She had no idea how many women had died at Ted's hands, but she knew her closest friend had, and she nearly had. What about Parker? He didn't deserve to be another of Ted's victims.

She unzipped the small canvas pack that had always seemed to be a part of the boy. School papers covered with red marks were the first items she removed. A handful of dried, shriveled carrots came next and brought a lump to her throat. Her fingers touched something hard, and she knew what it was even before she pulled it out. She held a small, flat key in her hand. A dirty, tangled string dangled from one end of it.

Her fist closed around the key, and she knew what she was going to do. Scott might need to wait for a warrant, but she didn't intend to. Peeking around her office door, it appeared the coast was clear. She was almost to the door leading to the garage when Jon appeared beside her.

"Running away?" he asked teasingly. "If so, take me with you."

Kallene paused then nodded. She reached for the door, and Jon shook his head. Taking her hand, he led her to the front door. Once outside, he explained, "Our parents are visiting in the upstairs sitting room, where they have a perfect view of the backyard. If they saw us exiting from the garage or heard the garage door go up, we'd both be in hot water."

She laughed. "This is ridiculous letting our parents call the shots at our age."

"Yeah, but at our age we let them get away with it because we know they're motivated by love, and we no longer need to prove our independence by defying them. Now where are we going?"

She held up the key. "I have a key to Grayson's house."

"Hmm, I don't think we should . . ."

"I know and you're right, but I have to do this. If I get caught, I can claim I have a key and therefore permission. It's not breaking and entering in that case. If Parker is in there, he probably needs help, and I couldn't live with myself for not giving him that help if I give up this chance."

"All right. I'm with you, but I hope my dad kept that attorney he hired for Carson on retainer."

They debated whether to boldly march up to the front door or make their way around to the back. The back won. After checking the street for possible witnesses, they ducked through the gate leading to the backyard. The key turned in the lock. Although Julie was in Europe and Ted was dead, they entered the house with caution.

"Parker?" Kallene called in a voice little over a whisper. There was no response, and Jon took her hand as they began to explore the ranch-style house. The living and dining rooms appeared to be richly furnished but unused for some time. The kitchen held a small amount of clutter. They didn't linger to examine it thoroughly but hurried down a hall where they found doors leading to two complete master suites. One was bare of personal items other than a few almost-empty bottles in the shower caddy. The furnishings shouted money and lavish taste. The other suite was Ted's room, they concluded from the masculine articles filling the closet and attached bathroom.

"Parker's room must be at the end of the hall," Kallene whispered. She tiptoed to the closed door and pushed it open a crack. It was a boy's room but looked nothing like she remembered her brothers' rooms. The bed was made, toys were precisely placed on shelves, and not a speck marred the carpet. It looked more like a magazine layout than a real boy's room. She wondered if Parker had ever set foot in it. "I think we better check downstairs."

They returned to the living area where they'd noticed stairs earlier. There was little light as they moved down the stairs, and Kallene felt a creeping uneasiness, making her wonder if she was being as foolish as the girls in old mystery dramas, who against all common sense made their way down rickety steps to dark cellars, where the audience already knew danger lurked.

Jon touched a light switch when they reached the bottom of the stairs, and they found themselves standing on the bare concrete floor of an unfinished basement.

"Parker!" she called, louder this time.

"I thought I heard something." Now Jon was whispering. "This way." He started toward a door that led to a partitioned-off area. When he reached the door, he found it locked.

"Parker, are you in there?" Kallene called.

"Parker!" Jon shouted. He leaned his ear against the door and listened. "Someone or something is in this room!" He put his shoulder to the door and pushed without success. When he paused in his efforts, Kallene also leaned against the door.

"Someone *is* in there! It must be Parker." They couldn't force the door for as much as they tried.

"What about the window. I noticed window wells before we came in," Jon suggested.

Kallene shook her head. "All of the basement windows in this subdivision have bars that can only be lifted from inside."

"There has to be a way!" Jon gave the door another useless shove. "Perhaps we should call the police."

"The walls don't look as sturdy as the door. I think they're a single layer of Sheetrock." Kallene kicked as hard as she could at the Sheetrock in front of her. It didn't break, but she left an impressive dent in it.

"Okay. Step back." Jon gave the Sheetrock a firm kick against the spot where her shoe had left a mark. His foot went through the chalky board, and he fell backward, landing hard, his foot caught in the hole he'd made. He winced as he wiggled his foot free and struggled to stand.

"Are you all right?" Kallene tried to help him to his feet.

"I'm fine." He leaned against a wall stud, catching his breath. "Can you see anything through that hole?"

She knelt, and it took a few minutes for her eyes to adjust to the darker interior of the room. Her range of vision was narrow. A terrible stench caused her eyes to water, and for a moment she struggled to keep from retching. All she could make out was a disheveled heap of what appeared to be clothing or blankets and various kinds of debris on one side of the room. A wave of disappointment swept over her. She'd had such a strong impression that she should look for Parker in the Grayson house.

A moan came from the pile of junk, and it was all she could do to keep from screaming. She turned back to Jon, and her voice shook. "We have to get inside. I think he's hurt."

Jon's response was to begin tearing at the Sheetrock with both hands. He paused several times to slam his foot against it to crack it more. Kallene watched the hole widen, and she longed to help. But with her broken wrist, she'd only be in the way if she tried to pull at the wallboard. At last Jon paused.

"I think if I help you, so you don't strike that cast against anything, you might be able to crawl through," he said.

She stepped closer, and he held on to her for balance, as she slid her feet through the hole, ignoring the blinding pain in her ribs. Her body followed, and she soon found herself in a tiny cubbyhole of a room, scrambling to her feet. The horrible odor hit her with greater force, and she fought nausea again. Once she felt steady, she rushed to what she could now see was a mattress on the floor with a noxious-smelling bucket beside it. A motionless figure lay tangled in a blanket amid boxes, cans, empty water bottles, paper, and other trash. Parker was so thin she could hardly recognize him. He appeared to be wearing only shorts, and she could see welts and bruises across his back and arms. His hair was long and unkempt, his lips cracked and covered in blood.

Fear clutched at her heart as she knelt beside the boy. She reached out her hand. His bare shoulder felt warm. "Parker? Oh, Parker, it's Kallene Ashton. Can you speak to me?" There was a barely audible moan, but she found it encouraging.

A loud crash sounded behind her. Startled, she turned to see Jon push his way through the flimsy wall. He held his phone in his hand.

"I called for an ambulance and left word with dispatch to get Scott over here." He looked down at the nearly unconscious boy then at her, and they shared an indescribable moment of shared pain. It was unthinkable that anyone could treat a child in such a monstrous way.

"Water," she whispered. "He probably hasn't had food or water since the night before Ted followed me up the canyon. If you'll bring some down here, I could give him a small amount and wash his face while we wait for the ambulance." Jon rushed upstairs to find water, and she continued to stroke the boy's face and whisper encouraging words to him.

Jon returned with a bowl he'd filled with water, a cup, and a towel. She wet a corner of the towel in the bowl and used it to squeeze a few drops of water into Parker's mouth. He moved his lips as though searching for more, so she dribbled a tiny bit more into his mouth. She waited a few seconds before wetting the other end of the towel and using it to wipe away the accumulated grime on his face.

Parker's eyes opened, and his lips moved. Jon lifted him high enough for Kallene to place the cup to his mouth. He took a small sip then collapsed back onto the grimy mattress. In the distance, sirens sounded. Parker's small hand struggled toward her, and she took it in hers.

"It's okay," she told him. "An ambulance is coming to take you to the hospital. Soon you'll be strong again."

"Dad said . . . you went away and . . . you'd never come back." Parker struggled to talk, but the exertion was too much, and he slipped once more into unconsciousness. Jon dashed back upstairs to usher in the EMTs and police officers.

It took only a few minutes for the officers to widen the hole Jon had made and the emergency team a few minutes more to move Parker to a stretcher and attach an IV to his arm. Two of the officers stayed behind while the others followed the EMTs carrying the stretcher back up the stairs to the ambulance. Scott arrived just as Kallene was arguing with Jon over whether or not she was accompanying the boy to the hospital.

"You're not going anywhere," Scott ordered. "I need to talk to the both of you and the uniformed officers who are downstairs, then I'll drive you to the hospital myself."

She agreed with a great deal of reluctance then spoke to Jon. "You'd better call your dad. If our mothers discover we're missing, they'll be frantic."

"Too late. They heard the sirens and are standing right over there trying to get your attention." He pointed. With a sigh she walked toward them.

"Mom, Dad," she began, "I had to come here."

"You did right, and I'm proud of you." Her father's voice was gruff. "Tell me where your car keys are, and I'll come pick you and Jon up when you're ready to come back. Just give me a call."

CHAPTER TWENTY-NINE

AN OFFICER MET THEM AS they entered the emergency room. "He's conscious but confused. The doctor said he'll let you know as soon as he's stable."

"Miss Ashton?" A nurse approached them. "Dr. Grange asked that I take you to him. He's with the little boy who was just brought in. The child is upset and is calling for you."

Kallene saw Parker thrashing about and calling her name while an orderly held his arm to keep him from pulling the IV out.

"I'm here, Parker." She set her hand on his forehead and stroked it gently as she had back at the house. He calmed down immediately. "Dr. Grange is going to help you, and I'll stay with you as long as you like."

"Dad said I had to stay in my room because I stole his shovel. He hit me because I tried to crawl out the window. He said if I talked to anyone, he'd kill me." The pleading look in his eyes awoke every maternal instinct in her.

"It's okay to talk to me. I won't let anyone hurt you. And your father will never hurt you again." She pressed a kiss to his flushed cheek.

"He said my mother went away because I was a bad son. She's not ever coming back. He said you were going away forever, too."

"Parker, listen to me." She pressed a finger to his lips. "Your father is the one who won't ever come back. My friend, Detective Alexander, talked to your mother. She's far away and didn't know what happened to you. She's not well and is afraid to come home. I don't know if she'll come back someday or not."

A look of panic entered Parker's eyes. "Where will I live?" There were no tears for his absent parents, and he showed no regret over their absence. Perhaps that would come later. His immediate future would doubtless involve hours of therapy. Parker searched for her hand, and she felt a tug at her heart as his fingers closed around hers.

"Until you're well, you'll sleep here at the hospital, and the nurses will bring you food. I'll visit you every day and will bring whatever you need. When you're well, you can live with me."

She knew she was promising more than she might be able to deliver. She'd have to petition the court for custody, and she should have discussed the matter with Jon before making promises.

The tenseness left the boy's face, and he drifted asleep without releasing her hand. She lifted her eyes in time to see Dr. Grange brush a sleeve across his eyes before meeting hers.

"Parker is severely malnourished and dehydrated. I doubt he's had a bath in a very long time, and it appears he's been heavily sedated for long periods of time as well. We'll get him cleaned up and will pump fluids and nourishment into him. Unless we discover any complications, you should be able to take him home by the end of the month." She let the doctor assume she would be the one taking Parker home. She hoped she could make his assumption come true.

She bit her lip to control its trembling. This time it wasn't fear but anger that made her tremble. How could Ted do such awful things to a child? And how could Julie be indifferent to her son's needs?

Dr. Grange left the examining cubicle, and she could hear the low rumble of men's voices just beyond the curtain. An orderly entered the small space carrying a small tub which the nurse put beside Parker. Dipping her hand into the soapy solution, she withdrew a cloth and began to wipe Parker's arms and hands. Kallene was reluctant to lose physical contact for even a few moments and was glad when the nurse put Parker's hand back in hers.

"An orderly will move him to a room in a few minutes." The nurse gave Kallene a sympathetic smile. "The doctor has ordered light, clear liquids for tonight. By tomorrow he'll be able to take a shower and eat whatever he likes and can tolerate."

She felt an arm circle her waist and was glad Jon had been permitted to join her at Parker's bedside. She leaned her head back against his shoulder and drew from his strength. They stood together for several minutes as the nurse continued to scrub Parker's emaciated body. When she finished, she left the cubicle, giving Kallene and Jon some time beside the gurney.

"Scott and I heard all you and Parker said." Jon's voice was soft, little more than a tickle against her ear. "Scott feels there's no longer a need to rush speaking with the boy, and he'll talk to Family and Child Services about granting you temporary custody and getting him set up with a counselor. I told him we'd be applying together for permanent custody, and in time, if it's what Parker wants, we can start adoption proceedings."

"I love you," she whispered back. "Because you understand, and for a million reasons more."

"Only a million?"

"Something tells me I'll discover more reasons in the next jillion years."

"You'll never find half as many reasons as I'll have for loving you." He held her close and brushed his lips against her hair.

ABOUT THE AUTHOR

JENNIE HANSEN graduated from Ricks College in Idaho, then from Westminster College in Utah. She has been a freelance magazine writer, newspaper reporter, editor, and librarian.

Her published novels fall in several genre categories, including romantic suspense, historical, and westerns.

She was born in Idaho Falls, Idaho, and has lived in Idaho, Montana, and Utah. She has received numerous first- and second-place writing awards from the Utah and National Federation of Press Women and was the 1997 third-place winner of the URWA Heart of the West Writers Contest. She was awarded the 2007 Whitney's Lifetime Achievement Award.

Jennie has been active in community affairs and currently serves in the Jordan River Temple. In addition to ward and stake responsibilities in the LDS Church, she served a term on the Kearns Town Council, two terms on the Salt Palace Advisory Board, and was a delegate to the White House Conference on Libraries and Information Services.

Jennie and her husband, Boyd, live in Salt Lake County. Their five children are all married and have provided them with eleven grandchildren. When she's not reading or writing, she enjoys spending time with her grandchildren, gardening, and camping.

Jennie Hansen loves to hear from her readers. She can be contacted through her blog: www.notesfromjenniesdesk.blogspot.com.